D. W. BRADBRIDGE

# The Combermere Legacy

www.dwbradbridge.com

First edition

Published by Valebridge Publications Ltd,
PO Box 320, Crewe, Cheshire CW2 6WY

Cover design by Electric Reads
Cover image (soldiers) used with thanks to Cliff Astles

Typeset for print by Electric Reads
www.electricreads.com

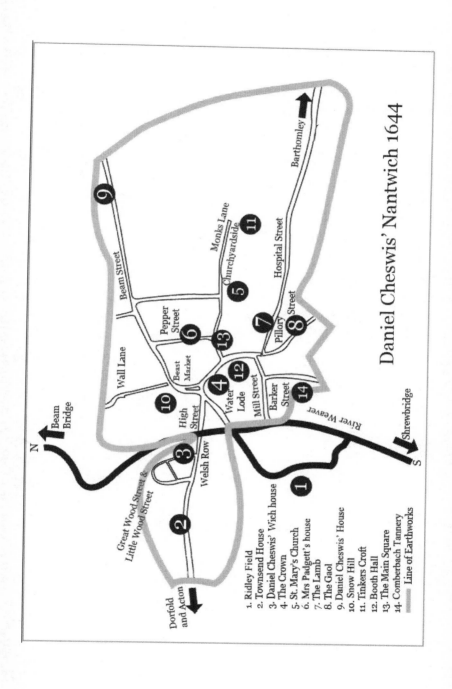

Daniel Cheswis' Nantwich 1644

N

Beam Bridge

Beam Street

Wall Lane

Pepper Street

Monks Lane

Churchyardside

Hospital Street

Barthomley

Great Wood Street & Little Wood Street

Welsh Row

High Street

Beast Market

Water Lode

Mill Street

Barker Street

Pillory Street

Dorfold and Acton

River Weaver

Shrewbridge

S

1. Ridley Field
2. Townsend House
3. Daniel Cheswis' Wich house
4. The Crown
5. St. Mary's Church
6. Mrs Padgett's house
7. The Lamb
8. The Gaol
9. Daniel Cheswis' House
10. Snow Hill
11. Tinkers Croft
12. The Main Square
13. Booth Hall
14. Comberbach Tannery
— Line of Earthworks

# Key Characters

| | |
|---|---|
| **Simon Cheswis** | Daniel's younger brother |
| **Rose Bailey** | Simon's ex-sweetheart |
| **Edmund Wright** | Tanner's apprentice, Rose's new sweetheart |
| **Roger Comberbach** | Owner of Nantwich's largest tannery, Edmund's employer |
| **Arthur Sawyer** | Constable |
| **Eldrid Cripps** | Constable |
| **Andrew Hopwood** | Bailiff |
| **Ezekiel Green** | Nantwich's court clerk |
| **Colonel Thomas Croxton** | Deputy Lieutenant responsible for the payment of Sir William Brereton's army |
| **Colonel George Booth** | Nantwich garrison commander |

| | |
|---|---|
| **Thomas Maisterson** | Gentleman – from one of Nantwich's leading families |
| **Roger Wilbraham** | Gentleman – from another of Nantwich's leading families |
| **Gilbert Kinshaw** | Merchant |
| **Marc Folineux** | Sequestrator |
| **Joshua Welch** | Minister of St Mary's Church |
| **Henry Hassall** | Wich house owner |
| **Jacob Fletcher** | Briner and employee of Hassall |
| **Sarah Fletcher** | Jacob's wife |
| **Mistress Johnson** | Sarah's mother and friend to Elizabeth Cheswis |
| **John Davenport** | Wich house owner and friend to Daniel Cheswis |

| | |
|---|---|
| **Bridgett Palyn** | Friend of the Davenport family |
| **Adolphus Palyn** | Bridgett's father |
| **Gilbert Robinson** | Head briner in Daniel's Cheswis's wich house |
| **Christopher Thomasson** | Physician |

*In Combermere (1644)*

| | |
|---|---|
| **George Cotton** | Elderly landowner, owner of the Combermere estate |
| **Thomas Cotton** | George's son |
| **Frayne** | Chief Steward |
| **Abraham Gorste** | Deputy Chief Steward |
| **Cooper** | A footman |
| **Martland** | A groom |
| **Joe Beckett** | A groom |

| | |
|---|---|
| **Sir Fulke Hunckes** | Governor of Shrewsbury |
| **Edward Herbert** | First Baron Herbert of Cherbury, owner of Montgomery castle |
| **Alice Furnival** | Widow of royalist spy, Hugh Furnival, and Daniel's childhood sweetheart |
| **Jem Bressy** | Royalist spy |
| **Geffery Crewe** | Steward in charge of the stables at Combermere |
| **Edwards** | Coroner of Whitchurch |

*In Nantwich (1572)*

| | |
|---|---|
| **Roger Crockett** | Landlord of The Crown |
| **Bridgett Crockett** | Roger's wife |
| **Thomas Wettenhall** | Friend of the Crocketts |
| **Roger Wettenhall** | Friend of the Crocketts |

| | |
|---|---|
| **Thomas Palyn** | Servant to the Crocketts |
| **Richard Hassall** | Gentleman and merchant |
| **Anne Hassall** | Richard's wife |
| **Thomas Wilson** | Friend of the Hassalls |
| **Edmund Crewe** | Friend of the Hassalls |
| **Richard Wilbraham** | Gentleman and merchant |
| **John Maisterson** | Gentleman and merchant, coroner, and brother-in-law to Wilbraham |
| **Thomas Clutton** | Deputy Steward |
| **Randall Alvaston** | Bailiff |

# Chapter 1

*Nantwich – Thursday, December 20th, 1572*

*T*homas Clutton stared with distaste at the naked and lifeless body in front of him. He inhaled deeply to stop the bile from rising in his throat. Prodding the cadaver gently with his walking stick, he watched as the left arm of the corpse fell from the trestle table on which it had been laid and swung from side to side before coming to rest with its forefinger pointing eerily towards the ground. It was as though the dead man were anxious to be laid to earth, rather than be displayed, as he was, like a slab of meat in the middle of the High Street.

It was a cold and frosty morning in Nantwich, one of those days when townsfolk trudged by with their heads bowed, minds focused only on reaching their respective fields, wich houses, or workshops. This particular day, however, was different, for crowds of onlookers had gathered in front of The Crown Hotel to behold a most curious sight.

*Tradesmen had pulled up their carts opposite the inn, steam rising from the flanks of their horses. Milkmaids loitered and chattered, their buckets clanking on the cobbles. Work stopped in a backhouse opposite, and the bakers emerged to view the scene, the waft of freshly baked bread turning the heads of the crowd momentarily, for it was not every day that the whole town got to inspect the body of a victim of murder.*

*"Have a care, Mr Clutton," said the hard-faced woman in her forties who was guarding the corpse. "It would not do for our deputy steward to be held responsible for the destruction of evidence that might convict those who killed my husband."*

*Clutton cast a swift glance to his side, where the bailiff, Randall Alvaston, was trying hard not to smirk, and rolled his eyes. Having been forced to miss his breakfast to attend this pre-organised sideshow, Clutton was in no mood to be trifled with.*

*"So, Mistress Crockett," he said, "it has come to this. It has long been said that mischief would be done here if your husband and Richard Hassall did not mend their differences, and so it has been proved."*

*"My husband was murdered," said Bridgett Crockett simply, her arms folded across her chest in a deliberate display of belligerence, "not just by Hassall, but by Richard Wilbraham, Thomas Wilson, Edmund Crewe, and diverse others. I trust you are here to make them accountable for their actions."*

"Mistress, I am here to apprehend the murderer," replied Clutton, "whoever he may be. No names have been provided to me by the constables. Guilt with regards to this matter has not yet been apportioned."

"Then take a look, sir," said the widow. "My husband has been sore beaten, not just by one man, as his persecutors would have you believe, but by many people. I urge you to inspect his body, for if you do, you will know the truth."

Clutton sighed with frustration, breathing out clouds of warm air into the frosty December morning.

"Master Alvaston," he said, turning to the bailiff, "you knew this man. Enlighten me, if you please, as to why the people Mistress Crockett accuses would want to see him in his grave."

Alvaston smiled thinly and drew Clutton to one side, where they could not be overheard. A short, greying man of middle years, the bailiff was dressed in a plain black doublet and cloak, and exuded an air of efficiency in keeping with his office.

"That I cannot say, sir," he began, "but it is a well-known fact that Roger Crockett was not a universally popular man. Many held him for a churl, albeit a rich one. Many folk say his dispute with Hassall proves he knew not how to behave in the company of gentlemen. And there is worse. There are also those that have him as a villain and a cut-throat, who would take any man's living over his head."

*Clutton nodded. This much he knew. Crockett had been the landlord of The Crown, Nantwich's largest and best-appointed inn. He was certainly a wealthy man, having made his fortune buying and selling land, and it was this which had led to his disagreement with Richard Hassall, a member of one of Nantwich's leading families.*

*The dispute had arisen over the lease to Ridley Field, a prime piece of pasture land to the south of Welsh Row on the opposite side of the River Weaver to The Crown. This land had been leased for years by the Hassall family, most recently by Richard Hassall, but also by his father before him. Crockett, however, had negotiated with the landlord and secured a new lease on the field before the old lease had expired or been offered for renewal. This had resulted in Crockett being accused of underhand dealing and had led to an ongoing feud between the two men, each of whom possessed a group of vociferous followers.*

*Indeed, the hostility towards Crockett had been such that he had scarcely dared to cross the bridge into Welsh Row, where Hassall lived, for fear of being assaulted by the latter's friends. The dispute had come to a head the previous day, when Crockett had been due to take possession of Ridley Field.*

*Clutton was well aware of the disturbance that had taken place the previous morning on Wood Street, a narrow lane which ran alongside the river* and consisted mainly of wich houses and workers' tenements. However, he had not known of the tragic consequence of the affray until he had been raised from his slumber by the bailiff at seven in the morning to attend the inquisitive crowd of spectators that had gathered on the street outside The Crown.

It was certainly an unusual sight. Crockett's battered corpse, totally naked, had been placed in full view outside the inn's front door. Next to it, bizarrely, sat a man with an easel, who was busy painting a portrait of the dead body.

"To bear witness to the injuries my husband sustained in this unprovoked attack," explained Bridgett Crockett, noticing Clutton's interest. "It is so that no-one may lie to the coroner about what happened here yesterday."

Clutton glanced down at the body and suppressed the urge to grimace. The victim had certainly sustained a considerable array of injuries. His ribs were covered in ugly purple bruises, his nostrils were caked in blood, and his left eye was nearly out of its socket. There was also a large wound in the centre of the dead man's chest. Clutton shuddered; Crockett was lying on his back, but the blood red pupil in his shattered eye socket seemed to follow him as he walked round the trestle table, inspecting the body.

"Mistress Crockett," said Clutton, "you make serious allegations against a number of respected gentlemen of this town. I trust you can substantiate your claims? Were you present when your husband was attacked?"

"Of course not," replied the widow, her voice betraying her impatience with the deputy steward. "I was busy here in the inn, but there are witnesses aplenty, as the bailiff is well aware."

Alvaston bowed slightly and turned to Clutton. "You might wish to speak to Thomas Wettenhall, sir," he said, gesturing to a balding, square-jawed man in his fifties, who was leaning nonchalantly against the wall of the inn, smoking a pipe. Clutton noticed that he was sporting a black eye.

"Master Wettenhall," said Clutton. "I see you bear the marks of this disturbance."

"Aye, sir, and my brother more so," replied Wettenhall. "He is badly wounded. He still lies abed and will do so for some time yet. He is fortunate to be alive."

"Can you tell me what happened?"

"Of course," said Wettenhall. "I was attacked on Wood Street by Thomas Wilson, who was carrying a long pike shaft. When my brother, Roger, heard this he came running to my aid, but he too was assaulted, this time by Richard Hassall and Edmund Crewe, both of whom were similarly armed. Roger was only able to save himself by escaping into a nearby garden, where I found him collapsed against a malt kiln."

"And you can explain this attack?"

"No, sir. I had no gripe with Thomas Wilson, at least not until yesterday. I asked him if he would kill me. He did not give me an answer, but I do not believe that was his aim."

"How do you mean?"

"It was a planned attack, sir. The idea was to entice Mr Crockett over the bridge. They've been trying to do it for a couple of days now. Richard Hassall's wife, Anne, was sat in Ridley Field for over a day armed with a quarter staff, threatening anyone who came near. And I understand there was a large gathering at Hassall's house after Roger was hurt, with all manner of weaponry on show. They are not so cock-a-hoop now I'll wager."

Clutton cast a glance over towards Alvaston, who pursed his lips and nodded.

"This is what I also hear, sir," said the bailiff, "and yet it cannot be denied Roger Crockett himself crossed the bridge yesterday equipped for a fight. Many witnesses have confirmed he was carrying a pike staff."

"Of course he was," hissed Bridgett Crockett. "What do you expect? He came to protect his friends, the Wettenhalls, who were being unjustly attacked by Hassall and his gang of delinquents."

Alvaston frowned, his face colouring slightly. "I would thank you to mind your tongue, mistress," he said, "lest you end up in Pillory Street gaol. If your husband was so innocent of intent to harm Mr Hassall and his associates, why, pray, has he steadfastly refused to have the peace of him, as has oft been offered to him?"

This, considered Clutton, was a fair point. The ill-feeling between the leading protagonists in the dispute had grown to such an extent that an extensive list of recognisances had needed to be drawn up binding them to keep the peace. The Wettenhall brothers had been forced to agree not to assault Hassall or Richard Wilbraham, whilst over a dozen people had been similarly bound not to assault Bridgett Crockett. Roger Crockett, however, had refused to become involved in any such mutual pledge.

"This, Master Bailiff, is because he had been consistently labelled a coward by Hassall and his ilk," explained Bridgett Crockett. "To resort to the law as a means of protection would have simply added fuel to that particular fire."

At that moment a low murmur began to rise among the multitude of tradesmen and ordinary townsfolk that had gathered in the street to watch the spectacle, and presently the crowd parted to reveal a short but distinguished-looking gentleman dressed in a fine pinked white doublet with heavily padded red hose. Over his shoulders hung a matching red cape to protect him against the cold.

"Good morrow, Mr Wilbraham," said Clutton. "You have chosen a most opportune moment to present yourself, and Mr Hassall and Mr Wilson too, I see."

The two less ostentatiously dressed gentlemen who had accompanied Wilbraham into the High Street nodded their greetings to the deputy steward. Both were attempting to portray an air of casual indifference, but from the beads of sweat which had appeared on Hassall's brow despite the frostiness of the morning, Clutton could tell that both were worried.

"Under the circumstances we felt it wise to be present," said Wilbraham. "We would not wish for our good names to be dragged through the mud by Mistress Crockett and her clique of brigands and fraudsters."

"Brigands, you say?" spat Bridgett Crockett, who made to step out from behind the trestle table, only to be held back by one of her servants. "You have a nerve, Mr Wilbraham," she continued, her voice shaking with anger. "You murdered my husband."

"Fie, woman," exclaimed Wilbraham. "You are in the wrong of it. I was still in bed when your husband was struck down, as many here will testify. Indeed, I came as quickly as I could with my hose in one hand and without my shoes, specifically to help your husband. It is a matter of sadness to me that I was unable to save him."

"You came for no other reason than to protect your brother-in-law, Richard Hassall, who would prevent *my husband from gaining access to land which he had lawfully leased."*

*Hassall opened his mouth to speak, but Wilbraham stopped him with a stern look.*

*"It is true, mistress," he said, smiling patiently at Bridgett Crockett, "that I wished to prevent Richard from going too far, but I understand that it was Edmund Crewe that struck the blow that felled your husband, not Richard Hassall."*

*"He was set upon by a crazed mob of people," cut in Thomas Wettenhall, "of which you, sir, are the ringleader. You are all equally responsible."*

*"And then," added Bridgett Crockett, "there is the additional matter of which we may not speak pertaining to Ridley Field. One of you has my husband's property; I demand you return it."*

*Wilbraham stared at the widow for a moment before breaking into laughter. "This woman is mad," he said. "I know not of what she speaks. Her husband brought the whole affair upon himself. It should come as no surprise that a man who is cheated out of his means of making a living by an unscrupulous rogue such as Crockett should wish to exact revenge. But Richard Hassall did not kill Roger Crockett. The fatal blow was struck by Edmund Crewe. That is not denied, nor is it in doubt."*

*"That, Mr Wilbraham, is the crux of the matter, and it is for the coroner to decide," said Clutton, after a*

moment's hesitation. "The question is whether Roger Crockett died from one blow delivered by Edmund Crewe or by many blows delivered by a number of people. It is not a small matter. However, there is enough evidence in this case for me to have to ask you, Mr Hassall, Mr Wilson, and all others who may be named by Mrs Crockett, to remain in Nantwich and to present yourselves here on Saturday morning, when the coroner will conduct an inquest. In the meantime," he added, now addressing Alvaston, "please instruct the town constables to arrest Edmund Crewe. Of all the people involved in this case, he would appear to have the biggest case to answer."

Alvaston bowed deferentially. "Certainly, sir," he said. "As you wish. However, there is but one minor difficulty. Edmund Crewe has left town. The man in question, it would appear, has flown the nest and vanished off the face of the earth."

# Chapter 2

*Nantwich – Friday, July 5th, 1644 – Seventy-two years later*

There were not many days during the first years of my marriage to Elizabeth Brett when I felt liberated from the spectre of the terrible civil war that plagued our country. God, it seemed to me, always managed to contrive a situation where I would be dragged against my will into the service of Sir William Brereton, commander-in-chief of Parliament's forces in Cheshire, in unending repayment for my release from my responsibilities as Nantwich's town constable.

Joshua Welch, the Puritan minister of St Mary's, would have considered my predicament to be a matter of pre-destination, a fate which I was powerless to alter. I'm not sure I agreed. I had little appetite for the kind of Puritan doctrine so prevalent in Nantwich in those difficult times. I enjoyed good sport and a jug of ale the same as any man. All I knew was that, during that worry-filled summer of 1644, days of pleasure for me and my young household seemed few and far between. And yet those three days following my wedding – they were somehow different.

Quite apart from the overwhelming bliss I felt at finally being united with the woman I had fallen in love with five months earlier, the war seemed to be moving slowly away from Nantwich, into Shropshire and the Welsh Marches – not that we could feel entirely at our ease, for the royalist strongholds of Chester and Shrewsbury were no more than a day's ride away. Nevertheless, the debilitating malaise which had hung over Nantwich like a shroud, instilling the fear that our town would be sacked and pillaged and our townsfolk murdered, had begun to dissipate following Sir Thomas Fairfax's victory over Lord Byron in the fields below Acton the previous January.

On the three days in question, Nantwich was even quieter than usual, for on July 1st the entire garrison, with the exception of the town companies, had marched with our garrison commander, Colonel George Booth, to join the Earl of Denbigh and Sir Thomas Myddelton. Sir Thomas had been tasked with relieving the recently established parliamentary garrison at Oswestry, which was being harassed by royalist forces from Shrewsbury under Sir Fulke Hunckes.

The streets of Nantwich, therefore, seemed almost devoid of military personnel. Only the massive earthen walls which surrounded the town were manned, musketeers stationed several yards apart, staring out into the wasteland of demolished cottages and burned-out barns, destroyed to prevent them offering cover to any would-be attackers, not that anybody harboured the fear that an enemy force would be able to approach undetected, for Sir William Brereton's network of scouts and agents had assured that Nantwich would be warned of any approaching royalist threat long before it came into view.

With Prince Rupert and Lord Byron engaged in Yorkshire, there seemed little chance of such a threat, and so, with my apprentice Jack Wade once more able to travel to the surrounding farms to collect cheese for our market stall, and with a new wife to keep me occupied, the days between 2nd and 5th July 1644 seemed the happiest of my life. I should have known this would not last.

It was the Friday afternoon when the chain of events began which would bring our all-too-brief honeymoon to an abrupt end and plunge me once more into the murky world of murder and espionage.

Elizabeth and I, as I recall, were clearing out one of the upstairs chambers in the substantial brick house in Beam Street which she had inherited from her husband the previous December. It was a room which Ralph Brett had used for storing some of his personal effects, and Elizabeth had not had the heart to move them out since his death. Now we were married, however, we both felt it important to make a fresh start and not to have any unfinished business from her old life hanging over us.

The room was covered in six months worth of dust and gave off an uncomfortable aura of another time and another marriage. I felt as though I should not be there, but I forced myself to enter and start sorting out the jumble of clutter that lay strewn across the floor, chairs, and the room's only table. The room was filled largely with rolls of fabric and assorted offcuts from Ralph Brett's mercers business, much of which could be thrown away, whilst the usable items could be passed on to Gilbert Kinshaw, the local merchant who had purchased the business from Elizabeth.

In the corner of the room, however, was a finely decorated oak chest, perhaps two feet wide, with an ornate iron lock and hinges. It was a fine piece of craftsmanship, and its presence in the spare room of a middling merchant from a small town such as Nantwich seemed somewhat incongruous.

"A gift from his lordship, the Duke of Hamilton," explained Elizabeth, who had noticed my interest. "In gratitude for Ralph's service in Germany. I had quite forgotten it was there. Ralph was always very secretive about it. I could tell he didn't want me meddling in his private business, so I left it be."

I nodded my understanding. "Then perhaps now is the time to take a closer look," I suggested.

With some effort, Elizabeth and I dragged the heavy box into the middle of the room. The act of moving it sent clouds of dust through the air, causing my nostrils to itch ferociously.

"Do you have the key?" I asked, trying to stifle a sneeze.

"I cannot be sure, but I think so," replied my wife, and she disappeared downstairs, returning a few moments later with a large metal key chain on which hung a single key.

"I handed over the keys to Ralph's workshop to Kinshaw," she explained. "This key was amongst them but didn't fit any of the locks, so I kept it. It didn't occur to me at the time, but the key must be for this chest."

I inserted the key carefully and turned it in the lock, the locking mechanism clicking gently as it released the hinge and bracket which held the chest closed. I opened the box and peered inside.

There did not seem at first sight to be anything out of the ordinary – a number of parchments and papers, some relating to Brett's business and others relating to the ownership of the house. There were also some personal letters bearing the seal of the Duke of Hamilton and, more unusually, a fine dagger wrapped in a white cloth, which I presumed was also a gift from the duke. Underneath all of it, neatly folded, was a tunic, which I assumed was the coat Brett had worn whilst serving in Germany.

I was about to ask Elizabeth what she would have me do with the contents of the box, when I heard a door slam and the unmistakeable sound of children's voices coming up the stairs. I also caught the hint of a rather unpleasant aroma, which reminded me of the inside of a cowshed.

A few seconds later the door swung open and in tumbled Amy, the ten-year-old granddaughter of my housekeeper, Mrs Padgett, closely followed by Elizabeth's son, Ralph, named after his father, who was giggling hysterically and chasing Amy with a small wooden sword. Both children were filthy, their clothes dishevelled and smeared with mud and dirt.

"By the saints," exclaimed Elizabeth, grabbing her son by the collar. "Where have you been? You smell as if you have been rolling in cow dung. You have ruined your new clothes."

Ralph, whose shoulder-length blond hair was making him look more like his father each day, stopped his giggling and looked solemnly at his clothes and then at his mother. The boy was wearing new breeches and a doublet that Elizabeth had bought for him Ralph's sixth birthday had been but a week before our wedding, and Elizabeth had thought to dress him for the ceremony in his first pair of breeches rather than the smock usually worn by small boys.

Ralph had been delighted with his new clothes. Breeching was an important rite of passage for a young boy and, having received his first set of grown-up garments before many of his contemporaries, Ralph had been the envy of his young friends. Now, however, he appeared distinctly sorry for himself.

"Amy and I have been in Ridley Field," said Ralph, as contritely as he could, "the stone pillar and water troughs make a fine castle."

I looked at the boy with surprise. "Then you have disobeyed us," I said, sternly. "We told you not to play there."

Ridley Field was a large pasture, which bordered the River Weaver in the area to the south of Welsh Row. It was separated from the town centre not only by the river, but also by the broad expanse of Mill Island, which split the flow of the Weaver in two. The field was unusual in that it contained a curious stone pillar used for tethering livestock, which was surrounded by a collection of pens and water troughs.

More importantly, it was outside the ring of defensive earthworks that had been thrown up the year before to protect the town from attack, which is why we had instructed Amy and Ralph not to play there. Although there had been no warning of approaching royalist forces, you could never be certain, and Ridley Field was certainly outside the area protected by the garrison.

"And how is it that you are so dirty?" I demanded. "Ridley Field was good green pasture land the last time I saw it. It is no swamp, but you are both covered in mud."

"Please, Master Cheswis," said Amy. "It was I who led Ralph there. If there is anyone to blame it is me. It is not usually so dirty in Ridley Field but there have recently been cows in the field, and there has been some digging around the stone pillar. There were holes everywhere."

"Digging?" I exclaimed, with incredulity. "That field is used for grazing cattle. Why would anyone wish to dig holes in it? Are you sure you are being truthful with me?"

"Of course. You may ask the soldiers guarding the earthworks; they saw us playing, as did Mr Maisterson and Mr Wilbraham, who were entering the field as we left."

"Then this also means you have walked all the way through the Beast Market and the length of Beam Street in that state," I said, pausing momentarily to wonder what business Thomas Maisterson and Roger Wilbraham, two of the town's most influential merchants, could have in a cow field. "You will put us all to shame," I added.

Amy bowed her head and her face began to crumple, but Elizabeth stepped in.

"Do not chide her so, Daniel," she said. "They are both children. Let them behave as such. God knows, there is little enough opportunity these days for them to act their age. In any case, Amy will be in enough trouble when Mrs Padgett sees the state of her clothing."

This, I conceded, was true enough. Amy was rapidly approaching the age when she might be expected to behave a little more like a young lady, but although a quiet girl by nature, she was also something of a tomboy, and I sometimes felt she would have preferred running around the fields in breeches like Ralph rather than being restricted by the bodice, waistcoat, and petticoat she was wearing. But I could not blame her. She reminded me a little of my old sweetheart, Alice, at that age, and how we used to spend our time in the fields around Barthomley, the village where we both grew up.

"I have some spare clothes she can wear," said Elizabeth. "They may be a little large for her but they will suffice until she gets home."

I nodded my acquiescence and was just about to leave the room so that Elizabeth could rid the two children of their filthy garments when I noticed that Amy's attention had been drawn to the box lying in the middle of the floor. She had lifted out Ralph Brett's battered tunic and was holding it up to the light. As she did so, a round metal object fell out from inside the lining and clattered onto the floor.

Amy picked up the object with curiosity and inspected it closely before handing it to me. It was a pewter engraving, about three inches in diameter.

On one side an image of the Virgin Mary had been stamped into the metal, whilst the other showed a coat of arms bearing a shield with diagonal stripes and several fleurs de lys.

"What is it?" asked Elizabeth.

"I was hoping you might be able to shed some light on that," I answered. "It looks like some kind of religious artefact. Where has it come from, do you suppose?"

"That, I cannot say," said Elizabeth, "but look, there is some writing underneath the coat of arms."

I squinted slightly in the gloom of the upstairs chamber and saw that Elizabeth spoke the truth.

"Cistercium Mater Nostra," I said, with a frown. "That is strange. This cannot have come from the Duke of Hamilton. Judging from the motto, this engraving has originated from a religious house, presumably of the Cistercian order. That means the engraving must be more than a century old, for it is over a hundred years since King Henry's time, when the monasteries were destroyed. What on earth would your husband be doing with something like this?"

"I don't know," said Elizabeth, "but wait... the Cotton family at Combermere live in the converted remains of a monastery. Perhaps it came from there. I know Thomas Cotton was a regular customer of my husband."

"Then this engraving should be passed onto Gilbert Kinshaw, along with the remaining papers belonging to the business. The tunic and the dagger we should keep. Ralph might treasure them when he is older."

With that, I placed the engraving back in the chest and left Elizabeth to change the children's stinking and filthy clothes. It was then that there was a knock at the door.

When I answered it I realised instantly that my honeymoon was well and truly over, for standing on my doorstep was Ezekiel Green, the fresh-faced young town clerk. From the apologetic look on his face, I could tell that the tidings were not good.

"Master Cheswis," he said. "Please excuse the disturbance, sir, but I have been sent by Colonel Croxton."

I groaned and glanced over my shoulder at Elizabeth, who was standing halfway down the stairs, her face a mask of barely suppressed rage, for she also understood the significance of Ezekiel's presence. I confess, I felt some sympathy for the lad, for Ezekiel was a pleasant enough young man, and it seemed it was always he who was lumbered with the task of breaking such news to me.

"I'm truly sorry, mistress," he said, before turning back to me. "Master Cheswis, the colonel asks that you attend him at the Booth Hall on Monday morning at nine. He also asks that you bring Master Clowes with you."

# Chapter 3

*Nantwich – Monday, July 8th, 1644*

Taken on its own, I would have still seen Ezekiel's visit as a forewarning of difficult times to come, for I was already becoming used to the idea that the involvement of Colonel Thomas Croxton in any aspect of my life was likely to result in demands on my time and loyalties which I was prepared only reluctantly to give.

But that weekend, there was also an undeniable feeling of change in the air, and it made me uneasy. The bright sunny weather of earlier in the week had stagnated into a stifling, sultry heat, and storm clouds loomed ominously on the western horizon, as though mirroring my own thoughts.

Many would not have understood my fears, for the news from Oswestry was undeniably good. On the same day as Elizabeth and I were making our wedding vows, Cheshire's parliamentary forces under Sir Thomas Myddelton had routed a significant part of the region's royalist army at Whittington, three miles from Oswestry, causing Sir Fulke Hunckes to abandon his siege and scuttle back to Shrewsbury.

However, this meant that the triumphant men of the Nantwich garrison would be back any day now, bringing the war once again onto our doorstep. Indeed, the latest scouts entering the town had told stories of Lord Denbigh and Colonel George Booth, the garrison commander, amassing forces at Cholmondeley, only a few miles away. On the Sunday, two troops of volunteers under Captains George and Thomas Malbon, the sons of the well-known Nantwich lawyer, had ridden out to join him.

Meanwhile, reports had begun to filter through of a much more significant victory for Parliament, which had taken place on the same day, in the moorlands to the west of York. The talk was of thousands of dead, and my first thought was for my brother, Simon, who had followed his hero, the radical writer and political activist John Lilburne, to serve in Fairfax's army in that part of the country. Had he survived, or would I have to tell my children that their uncle had died in battle on my wedding day?

I also thought about James Skinner, my erstwhile apprentice, now fighting on the King's side, and the many friends and comrades I had made during the Siege of Lathom House, men like Lawrence Seaman, himself newly betrothed to Beatrice Le Croix, who I had also met for the first time during those difficult weeks in Lancashire.

People were talking of a crushing defeat for Prince Rupert, saying that the so-called Duke of Plunderland might have escaped back over the Pennines. Of course, such an eventuality, if true, would not be good news for Nantwich, for it meant that Rupert, recently appointed President of Wales, would probably try to regain his strength in Chester and Lancashire before turning his attention once more on Shropshire and the Welsh Marches. Nantwich, of course, would be directly on his route south.

Despite this, the news from Oswestry had lent the town an air of expectation. The Saturday market was busier than usual. Vegetable sellers, milkmaids, and butchers lined the sides of Pepper Street, fighting with each other for space. A young woman walked up and down the length of the bustling line of stalls with a basket full of herbs – bunches of lavender, rosemary, and marjoram. Meanwhile, three doors away from me, Margery Clowes stood in front of her house with a table full of candles made by her husband, and my best friend, Alexander. Trade was brisk and the cheese brought the previous day from my father's farm in Barthomley by Jack Wade was almost fully sold by eleven in the morning.

However, despite the general mood of buoyancy in Nantwich that day, the good news did not seem to have filtered through to my own family. Elizabeth, who usually helped enthusiastically with the selling of our cheese, very quickly disappeared and spent much of the morning in earnest conversation with Margery, who kept looking at me with a sullen face and eyes like daggers. Alexander, meanwhile, was nowhere to be seen.

Amy too was housebound, having been forbidden by Mrs Padgett to leave the confines of the kitchen in punishment for ruining her petticoat in Ridley Field. Ralph sat glumly on the steps of the house, tapping his wooden sword against the door frame. Even Wade, normally an ebullient soul, caught the tension in the atmosphere after a while, and after several attempts to lighten the mood, gave up the pretence and concentrated on selling our cheese as quickly as he could.

"Forgive the impertinence, Master Cheswis," he said, "but everyone round here has a face like a smacked arse. And here's me, one leg short, with real reason to be grumpy, and I'm the only one smiling."

Wade had a point. I contemplated the youth as he hobbled around the table, cutting a whole cream cheese expertly with a wire and wrapping a piece of it for one of the goodwives listening to his good-natured chatter as they patiently queued. His wooden leg clumped noisily on the cobbles as he carried out this work. I felt a binding obligation to Wade, for he had lost his leg five months previously, after being shot in the foot whilst helping Alexander and me pursue the royalist spy and murderer Hugh Furnival across Beam Heath.

I liked Wade. He had never complained about the hand that fate had dealt him and had simply got on with learning the new trade that I had given him. He was a fast learner too. Under the able tutelage of Gilbert Robinson, he had spent Mondays to Thursdays in my wich house on Wood Street, learning the art of walling. Despite being unable to carry out much in the way of physical work, Robinson assured me his charge would soon be able to manage a kindling on his own.

On Fridays, Wade helped with my burgeoning cheese business, taking my horse and cart to local farmers to gather the best in Cheshire cheese and the occasional churn of butter, which we would sell at the Saturday market.

Every day I felt a pang of guilt that my good fortune in finding Wade was down solely to his terrible injury and the fact that my previous apprentice, the less than committed James Skinner, had been captured by royalists during January's battle.

"You are in the right of it, Jack," I said, "and as usual it is I, myself, who is the source of this unhappiness."

Wade looked at me carefully and put down his cheese wire. "You have been summoned once again by Sir William Brereton, I hear."

"By Colonel Croxton," I said, "but it amounts to the same thing. I may have rid myself of the responsibility of being a constable, but it seems to me that my current situation is much worse. Don't get me wrong, being free of the need to deal with drunkards, uncooperative landlords, and vagrants is a fine thing, but, as things stand, I never know when I might be called upon, and to what end."

"If I may be so bold, sir, you take your responsibilities too much to heart," said Wade. "If people are downcast and uncommunicative this morning, then maybe it is because people are concerned for you."

"Perhaps," I replied, wondering where the conversation was leading.

When he saw that I was not going to comment any further, Wade took a deep breath and opened his mouth once more. "If you are called into service by Brereton again," he said, "please do not forget that I am here. If I can be of service in any way, I am at your disposal. I may be a cripple, but I can still ride a horse, drive a cart, handle a musket... and I have eyes."

I stared at Wade with surprise. "But you have lost your leg on my account," I exclaimed. "Why would you want to risk more?"

"You are seeing it wrong, Master Cheswis. I followed you that night of my own accord, and it was some bastard malignant who shot me. You were not to blame. Indeed, by making me your apprentice, you have saved me from a life of begging on street corners. It is I who owe you, not the reverse."

I was not wholly convinced, but Wade's words gave me heart and strengthened my resolve that whatever Colonel Croxton had in store for me, I would face up to the challenge and succeed, if not for my own sake, then for the sake of all those who depended on me.

* * *

The Booth Hall was the large black and white wooden structure on the opposite side of the square to St Mary's Church, a stone's throw from The Crown. In my capacity as constable, I had become used to attending the deputy lieutenants there, but the meeting with Croxton to which I had been summoned was not of the same ilk, and the prospect filled me with trepidation. Alexander, I could tell, was feeling much the same way, for his normal cheerful countenance had been replaced by a mask of worry as we marched up Pepper Street and across the square.

Ezekiel Green was waiting for us outside, his hand clasped to his nose as a protection against the foul stench that was emanating from the drainage channel that ran directly in front of where he was standing. He removed his hand and gave a tight-lipped smile when he saw us approaching.

"Good morrow, sirs," he said. "Apologies if my expression is one of distaste. This weather, I swear, is sent to us by the very devil himself. This town has

45

begun to smell like the bowels of hell."

"Aye, you're not wrong there," said Alexander. "The gong farmers will be working overtime during these days, that is for sure."

It was true that the sultry weather had begun to be a cause for concern throughout the town. It was at times like this that thoughts turned to public health and the risk of disease. It had been so hot that one of the rulers of walling had cancelled all kindlings in the wich houses on Wood Street and Snow Hill until further notice.

"The weather is indeed unpleasant," I concurred. "I propose we go inside where the air is better."

Ezekiel acquiesced with a brief nod and led us inside the building.

"Colonel Croxton is engaged with another appointment at the moment," said the clerk, "but I believe he is almost finished. At any rate, he asked me to bring you directly to him."

Ezekiel led me to a small ante-room facing the square, where Croxton was sat. The colonel's black but stylishly cut doublet was unbuttoned, revealing his shirt, and his black, wide-brimmed hat lay on the desk in front of him. A bead of sweat dripped down the side of his forehead.

Opposite Croxton sat a slim, balding man in his forties, who, despite being dressed in plain, Puritan garb, seemed unbothered by the heat.

"Ah, Master Cheswis, Master Clowes," said Croxton, jovially. "Punctual as always, I see. I am more or less finished here, but before we sit down to discuss matters which concern us, I would introduce you to Marc Folineux. He is newly appointed as a sequestrator collector for Nantwich Hundred."

"But I thought we already had a sequestration committee in Nantwich," I said, somewhat surprised.

Since his return from London three weeks previously, Brereton had moved quickly to establish a committee to sequester the property of anyone suspected of helping or supporting the royalist cause. Trusted townsmen like the lawyer, Malbon, had been recruited to administer this process, but the man sat with Croxton was unknown to me.

"Mr Folineux has been personally recruited by Sir William," explained the colonel. "He has a reputation for being particularly assiduous in the pursuit of those who would seek to hide their assets from Parliament. He will be engaged to pursue the more affluent of our local delinquents."

"And there are plenty of those," I pointed out, thinking of the likes of Randle Church, Thomas Maisterson, and Roger Wilbraham, men of influence within the town, all of whom I had reason to be wary of. "But these are men just like you or I," I added. "Their conscience has instructed them not to be disloyal to their king, as they see it. Do they truly deserve to have their estate and

47

property confiscated?"

Folineux, who until now had said nothing, lowered his chin and stared at me with pinched mouth. "Sir, you speak as though you were a delinquent yourself," he whispered. "If Colonel Croxton had not already informed me of the good service you have given to our cause, I believe I would have grave doubts as to where your loyalties reside."

Folineux had a remarkably quiet voice, but it was one which carried an unmistakeable measure of menace. This, I was certain, was a man of ruthless efficiency, who was not to be taken lightly.

"Mr Folineux, you have me wrong," I said. "I do not question the need to act against our true enemies, but many of these people are men who have not raised arms in anger against the forces of Parliament. They are simply men who have remained loyal to His Majesty and have said as much in word. Perhaps not all have done so in deed. Some may have given funds, men, or goods to the royalist army, but not all of them. Is it right that we alienate such people even more than we have already done?"

"Sir, if that is your belief, then you are both naïve and a fool. Such men must be crushed and made to pay for their delinquency. With God's grace, this will be achieved in the coming months, and the completion of this process will hasten the end to the bloody conflict in which we find ourselves. If you have no stomach for doing what has to be done, then pray leave it to those who have. Good day to you, sir." With that, Folineux got to his feet, nodded to the colonel, and left the room.

"A man of conviction," said Croxton, as we watched Folineux's back recede down the corridor towards the entrance hall.

"Seems like a proper arsehole to me," said Alexander.

Croxton gave Alexander a sharp look, but let the comment go. "You will no doubt wish to know why your presence here has been requested," he said, pouring himself a cup of beer from a jug on the table.

"I can only assume it is a matter of the highest urgency," I replied, trying to hold back the sarcasm. "After all, it was deemed necessary to summon me within three days of my wedding."

Croxton sucked his teeth and raised his hands in submission. "For that I can only apologise, Master Cheswis, but this situation was not of my making. Indeed, the knowledge, which has necessitated my approach to you, has been in Sir William's possession since before your nuptials. I have deliberately given you a few days grace before calling on you."

"And I am supposed to be grateful for that?"

"Not necessarily, although one might have expected some degree of recognition on your part for the fact that Sir William has relieved you from your duties as constable. As I have explained to you, it is not our intention to tax you unduly, but a situation has arisen which you and Mr Clowes are best positioned to deal with – and your impetuous brother too, were he not trying his level best to get himself killed in Yorkshire."

"You have received word of Simon?" I asked.

Croxton nodded. "Your brother is safe, so I am told, but he will not be returning to Nantwich any time soon. He has expressed his wish to continue to serve under Major Lilburne."

It was bitter-sweet news for me. Although I could not hold back my relief that Simon had survived the battle, neither could I conceal my dismay that he had chosen to stay with John Lilburne and fight for his political ideals. I wondered whether he would have made the same choice if he had seen what I had seen on the night of my wedding – namely Simon's betrothed, Rose Bailey, walking arm in arm with young Edmund Wright, one of the apprentices at Roger Comberbach's tanner's yard.

"Thank you for this information, Colonel. My parents will be relieved to hear this news, I am sure. I hear the victory was significant."

"Indeed. Four thousand royalists dead, Newcastle's Whitecoat regiment decimated almost to a man, and a great victory for Lieutenant General Cromwell of the Eastern Association. Even Rupert's infernal dog perished in the action, although the whereabouts of his master are still unknown."

"So the tide in this war is finally turning?" I ventured.

"We must not count our chickens before they are hatched, Master Cheswis, but so it would appear. Even in these parts, the momentum is with us. As we speak, Colonel Booth and Lord Denbigh are bombarding Cholmondeley House. The enemy cannot last out for long, which is exactly why we must be vigilant."

"Vigilant, sir?"

"Certainly, a desperate malignant makes for a cunning foe, and word has reached us of a plot concerning one such malignant who is well known to you; one Jeremiah Bressy."

My heart sank as I realised there was truly no way out of the trap I now found myself in.

"Jem Bressy?" I said, desperately. "I thought he was in Chester. How can I possibly be of assistance with regards to him?"

"Bressy, it appears, has been less than discreet with some of the whores in The Boot in Chester. You will recall we have some friends in that particular establishment."

"Of course," I acknowledged. I did not mind admitting it. Alexander and I would be eternally grateful for the role played by Thomas Corbett, The Boot's landlord, his son Charles, and Annie, the brothel madam, in securing our escape from Jem Bressy's clutches in March. On that occasion, we had been forced to clamber through the back of a stinking privy and make good our escape disguised as churchmen.

"It appears that Bressy has been talking about a hoard of gold, plate, and other valuables, which he says lies buried somewhere in or near Nantwich. It sounds somewhat far-fetched, I know, but Bressy claims he has the means to locate this hoard and plans to travel to Nantwich in order to recover the valuables for the royalist cause. We cannot be sure how much truth there is in the story. However, we cannot risk funds as potentially significant as this being appropriated by His Majesty's forces in Shrewsbury. They have their own mint there, as you will no doubt be aware. It would be a disaster if he were to succeed in this endeavour."

"But how can Alexander and I be of help?" I asked.

Croxton smiled. "Bressy is an elusive fellow. Away from his own stamping ground in Chester he tends to remain very much in the shadows. But you and Mr Clowes know what Bressy looks like. Of course, a few others do too, such as those soldiers still here who served with Bressy when he infiltrated our forces at Beeston Castle – I believe your apprentice, Wade, is one such man – but we cannot entrust this kind of information to common soldiers.

"What is more, we know that you have been just as much of a thorn in Bressy's side as he has been in yours. So, if he is lurking somewhere in Nantwich, it may well be that he will come looking for you. All we ask is that you keep a lookout for him and, if he puts in an appearance, you alert us to the fact, especially if you find out where this treasure is located. If such a hoard truly exists, we cannot afford for it to fall into the wrong hands."

"And that is all?" I asked, not sure whether to be relieved that Croxton wanted us to do nothing more than a piece of surveillance or horrified at the thought that the murderous Bressy might once more emerge to blight my life.

I was busy contemplating this when there was a gentle knock at the door, and Ezekiel Green appeared.

"Excuse the disturbance, Colonel," said Green, "but Constable Sawyer is here, and he would speak with you as a matter of urgency."

Croxton tutted with indignation and waved his hand dismissively. "Sawyer?" he breathed. "What does he want? Tell him to come back later. I'm engaged in important business."

"Beg pardon, sir," said Green, "but you might want to hear what he has to say. He reports that there has been a murder. A body has been found in Ridley Field, so he says."

"But that is a civilian matter, Green."

"No, sir. The victim, although a local man, is a member of the garrison. In the absence of Sir William or Colonel Booth, Sawyer has asked that you attend the scene."

I flashed a glance across the table at Alexander. Another murder in Nantwich, and in Ridley Field too. I made a mental note to use this news to explain to Amy and Ralph why it was unsafe for them to play there.

"I see you are in demand, Colonel," I said, glad of the excuse to escape Croxton's presence. "If that is all, we will be on our way. We will keep our eyes peeled for Bressy as you asked."

I made to get up, but Croxton reached across the table and placed his hand on my wrist.

"Not so quick, Master Cheswis," he said, his eyes flashing dangerously. "You have displayed a remarkable aptitude in the past for identifying the perpetrators of crimes such as this. If this is indeed a military matter, then I will require someone with investigative skills to assist me. If you and Master Clowes would care to join me, we will attend to Constable Sawyer forthwith."

# Chapter 4

Alexander and I found Sawyer waiting in the vestibule, trying to fan himself with the corner of one of the tapestries hanging from the wall of the council antechamber. A small, wiry man, the constable was better equipped to deal with the stifling heat than most, but, judging from the large patch of sweat under his armpits, he too was suffering badly from the sultry weather. He dropped the corner of the tapestry as though it were a hot coal when he saw us coming and sighed irritably.

"God's Blood," he said, "I ask for Colonel Croxton, and I get a useless pair of canker blossoms like you two. What the fuck are you doing here? It is below the good colonel to deal with the likes of me, I presume?"

It was more or less the reception I was expecting. Sawyer was an ungracious and cantankerous fellow at the best of times, but since I had been relieved of my duties as constable he had become even more obnoxious than usual. It was down to jealousy, I knew, and for that I could not blame him, for both of us had found ourselves trapped in an office that was only supposed to be of one year duration, as the collapse of local government that had come with the onset of war had meant there was no system in place to relieve us. After two years' service, Brereton had replaced me with a corviser called Eldrid Cripps, but for Sawyer there was no end in sight.

I resisted the temptation to trade insults with my erstwhile colleague and decided to focus on the matter at hand. "I assure you I am not here by choice," I said. "Colonel Croxton will be here presently. In the meantime he has asked Master Clowes and myself to attend you. There has been an incident in Ridley Field, so I hear?"

Sawyer scratched his large, pock-marked nose and snorted in exasperation. "Jesus," he said, "you and the bellman seem to get bloody everywhere." He levelled his gaze at me momentarily, but quickly conceded defeat as soon as he saw the expression on Alexander's face. "Aye, all right," he said, "if we must. There's been a body found, discovered at first light by one of the sentries manning the earthworks. Trussed and bound like a suckling pig, he was. And tied to the pillar in the middle of the field too. Pretty bloody strange if you ask me, and not just because of the way the body was left."

"How do you mean?" I asked.

"Well, for a start, it looks as though the victim was drowned."

"But the pillar is only fifty yards or so from the river. What's strange about that?"

"The corpse reeks of brine," said Sawyer. "This was not someone who died in the river. The victim drowned in salt water."

"A local man, Green tells me."

"Aye. Don't know him meself, but those who found him say his name is Henry Hassall."

"Hassall?" exclaimed Alexander with surprise. "I know him. He owns one of the wich houses on Snow Hill."

I nodded. "That would explain the brine," I agreed, "but what was he doing in Ridley Field?"

"Nobody knows," said Sawyer. "That's what's strange about this. Hassall was a member of the town guard, but he was not on duty last night, so he had no reason to be near the earthworks. But I dare say Croxton will find out why he was there."

I was considering this when the colonel reappeared. Once Sawyer had repeated the basic facts to him, Croxton allowed himself to be led out of the Booth Hall, down the High Street, through the Swine Market, and across the Town Bridge, into Welsh Row. Alexander and I followed a few paces behind. Immediately after we had crossed the bridge, Sawyer turned left into a narrow lane bordered by blackberry bushes, which led us fifty yards along the river bank to a gate and a stile.

On the other side of the stile was a well-worn footpath, which skirted off a few yards to the right, where it stopped abruptly against the side of the four yard high earthworks. This was the point where the mud walls which rose above the western bank of the river turned sharply towards the west around the back side of the cottages and tenements which lined the southern side of Welsh Row.

At the point where the footpath met the earthworks, a set of steps had been fashioned within the side of the defences and bolstered with planks of wood. This led to the wooden platform which ran around the top of the earthen walls, against which a retractable ladder had been laid, leading to the open fields beyond.

It irked me to think that the construction of the town's defences meant there was no longer an immediately accessible route into Ridley Field from Welsh Row. Without the co-operation of the sentries lining the walls, the only way into the field was to walk to the sconce and gateway at the end of the street several hundred yards away, negotiate the guards that were on patrol there, and then double back along the outer edge of the earthworks.

Amy and Ralph must therefore have been explicitly allowed to descend the wooden ladder that led into Ridley Field and re-scale it once they had finished playing. The pillar in the middle of the field was only a hundred yards or so from the walls, and therefore the children would have been well within the supervisory range of the garrison men. Nonetheless, I resolved to ask Croxton to have a quiet word with the captain in charge to make sure they weren't allowed out again.

Today, however, this was not a priority, for there were more important matters at hand. Ridley Field, normally inhabited only by cows, was a hive of activity. Word had spread quickly about the death of Henry Hassall, and already two or three score people were milling around the pillar in the middle of the pasture. To my right, at least twenty more curious townsfolk were picking their way along the rough path, which ran alongside the ditch underneath the earthen walls, eager to view the grisly sight.

From atop the earthworks I could see that half a dozen soldiers were keeping the crowd at bay, whilst Eldrid Cripps inspected the cadaver, which was propped up on the stone steps surrounding the pillar, hands tied behind its back. The dead man's head was slumped unnaturally to one side.

Curiously, as Amy had described, a number of holes, each perhaps two or three feet deep, had been dug in the turf in the area around the pillar and its attendant water troughs. On the face of it, it looked as though someone had tried to dig a grave for the body, but had been forced to leave quickly, perhaps on sight of the farmer. This seemed possible, for the cows,

59

which usually roamed the field, appeared to have been removed as soon as the body had been discovered. But why dig several holes rather than just one, and how did the body end up in Ridley Field? Surely the murderer would have had to carry it down the ladder in full view of the sentries or, at the very least, through the checkpoint at Welsh Row End. It didn't make sense.

Descending the wooden ladder, Alexander and I followed Croxton and Sawyer across the field, taking care not to fall into any of the holes, many of which had been trampled by the crowd into a dusty mix of mud and cow dung.

As we approached the people gathered round the pillar, I detected a certain hostility in the air. Sawyer, however, did not stand on ceremony, barging a path through the onlookers.

"Make way, make way for Colonel Croxton," he shouted, digging a reluctant brine worker in the back with his club to encourage him to move to one side.

Once the crowd had parted I was able to see the reason for the onlookers' agitation. Sat between two of the soldiers, with his back to one of the water troughs so that he was invisible from the earthworks, was a broadly built man in his twenties dressed in the common work clothes of a briner. His black hair, cut short to just below his shirt collar, was streaked with dried mud, and blood oozed from a cut on his lip. One of the soldiers was pointing a pistol at his head. I did not miss the malicious grin on Sawyer's face when he saw the sight, but Croxton did not seem amused.

"Master Cripps," he began. "Perhaps you would care to explain the meaning of this. Constable Sawyer left you in charge of a crime scene, but you appear to have transformed it into a free-for-all."

"No, Colonel," said Cripps, whose pudgy, slightly florid face was beaming from ear to ear. "You are mistaken. I have managed to apprehend the murderer." Cripps gestured to the man sat on the floor between the soldiers.

"Had me beaten to a pulp, more like," snarled the prisoner, defiantly.

"Shut the fuck up, churl," hissed Sawyer, who made to strike the man across the cheek, but held back at the last moment. "Unless you want your bones raddled, I suggest you speak only when you're spoken to."

"Leave the man alone, Sawyer," warned Croxton. "Let him speak, and we might learn something. Well?" he said, turning to the prisoner. "What is your name?"

"Jacob Fletcher, sir, a briner of this town," said the man, his eyes flicking rapidly between Croxton and Sawyer, "or rather I was. As you can see, my master lies dead before you."

Croxton raised an eyebrow. "You worked for Hassall?"

The prisoner nodded the affirmative.

"The constable suspects you of killing your

master," continued the colonel. "What say you to that suggestion?"

Fletcher started scratching the back of his neck nervously. "I did not do it, sir. It is as I told the constable. I had an argument with Master Hassall over pay, but that is all."

"That is not what we have heard, Colonel," interjected Cripps. "We have a witness who says he saw Fletcher trying to drown Hassall inside his wich house."

"Inside the wich house?" My mind flashed immediately to the large salt pans used during a kindling, and to the 'ship', the hollowed out tree trunk used for storing the brine prior to boiling it. Both were suitable receptacles for drowning a man.

"Yes, sir. It appears Hassall has just completed a kindling, and the ship was still full of brine. The witness happened to be walking by and saw Fletcher depositing Hassall, head first, into the ship. As you can smell, sir, Hassall's body stinks of brine."

This, at least, was true. Large, white streaks had appeared on Hassall's doublet and breeches, where the salt water had dried out. I walked over and looked closely at Hassall's body. His face was caked with dried salt, but there were also dribbles of vomit on his neck, cheekbones, and shirt. I ran my hand carefully round Hassall's neck, which I noted was not broken, despite lying at a somewhat strange angle, and inspected his neck, scalp, and temples for signs of violence. At first

I could find nothing, but then I smiled to myself as I discovered what I was looking for.

"Who is the witness, Mr Cripps?" I demanded. "I should like to speak to him."

"It was I," responded a familiar voice from among the rabblement, which was watching these exchanges with increasing interest.

I initially couldn't make the speaker out, but then the crowd parted, and John Davenport stepped forward.

Davenport was my long-time friend, and the proprietor of the wich house adjacent to my own. It was he who I had saved from the suspicion of being the murderer of William Tench, the first victim in the spate of killings I had investigated in Nantwich in December and January. I had also been present when Davenport's daughter Margery had been killed during the siege, when Lord Byron had attempted to destroy Townsend House by showering it with red hot bullets from the demi-cannon he had positioned at Dorfold House.

"John," I said, with surprise. "You saw this? What were you doing in Snow Hill?"

"I was there merely on a business matter," explained Davenport. "There is a wich house owner up Wall Lane, who has a walling allocation which he cannot fulfil for health reasons. He wishes to sub-contract this work to me. I was there to negotiate the kindling rights."

"What time would this have been?"

"About eight-thirty in the evening. I was walking along Wall Lane, past Mr Hassall's wich house, when I noticed that the main door was open and Mr Fletcher was inside arguing with Hassall."

"Is this true, Fletcher?" cut in Croxton.

"Sounds about right, sir," said the prisoner. "I had been employed on Hassall's latest kindling, but he refused to pay me all I was owed. Said I had done less time than I had. I cannot afford to be cheated, sir. I have a wife and family."

Croxton nodded slowly and looked at me in anticipation of my continuing the interrogation. I pursed my lips and turned to Davenport.

"So what makes you think Mr Fletcher is responsible for Hassall's death, John?" I enquired. "An argument is not evidence of a murder."

"Correct. However, I was returning the same way no more than half an hour later, when I heard a commotion from within Hassall's wich house, more shouting, and a crashing sound, as though someone had knocked over a couple of salt pans. I walked over to the door to investigate and saw Fletcher holding Hassall over the side of the ship and pushing his head into the brine. Hassall was thrashing and kicking like a mad man."

"The m-man is lying," stuttered Fletcher, whose face had turned a ghostly shade of white. "I never did such a thing. I remember this man watching me arguing, but I was talking with Master Hassall for no more than five minutes, after which I returned straight home."

"And where is home?" I enquired.

"On Wall Lane, no more than fifty yards from the wich house."

"And there are witnesses to this?"

Fletcher stared at me for a moment, but then his face fell, and he slumped back against the water trough. "No, sir, my wife was attending her parents at their house on Beam Street. She did not return until after ten."

There was a murmur of interest from the crowd, most of whom had been listening to the conversation intently.

"Lock him up, Colonel," shouted someone from the back.

"Aye, hang the murdering whoreson," said someone else.

I began to sense trouble. I had experienced the power of a mob once before, as had Davenport, who had been the subject of the crowd's ire on that particular occasion. I could see from the horrified expression on Davenport's face that he was thinking the same as me.

Alexander, who had said nothing up to this point, nudged me with his elbow. "Fletcher may be speaking the truth," he whispered. "Half an hour is a long time for a violent altercation over a matter of pay. And has it occurred to you that Fletcher pays more than a passing resemblance to one who we know to be a murderer, and who we have just been told to expect in Nantwich any day now?"

I felt a shudder deep within my bones as I realised what Alexander was suggesting.

"Jem Bressy," I breathed. "You are right. It is time to stop this. Master Davenport," I said, raising my voice in order to attract the attention of the crowd, which had begun to push against the soldiers in an attempt to reach the petrified Fletcher. "Are you quite sure that this was the man you saw attacking Master Hassall?"

Davenport frowned and gave me a puzzled look. "Of course," he said. "At least it looked like him from where I was standing."

"Did you see his face?" I asked.

Davenport hesitated a moment and then shrugged. "No," he said. "He was facing away from me, but I'm sure it was him. Well built, short black hair. Yes, I'm sure of it."

"It was nine at night, so it would have been going dark."

"Daniel," said Davenport, who was now beginning to get agitated, "what are you suggesting? That I'm a liar?"

"Of course not," I countered, "but you may have been mistaken. Tell me, was the attacker wearing the same clothes the second time you saw him?"

"He had taken off his doublet, but I fail to see-"

"Cheswis, we have no time for this." Croxton's voice

cut sharply and with urgency through the noise of the rabble, who had started picking up clods of earth and launching them in the direction of Fletcher, who had been surrounded by soldiers for his own protection.

In an attempt to stave off the tide of angry onlookers, the colonel drew his pistol and fired a single shot into the air. It was enough to make the crowd hesitate.

"Enough!" shouted Croxton. "Return to your homes. We are arresting this man for the suspected murder of Henry Hassall. You may all sleep soundly in your beds tonight, but you will let justice take its course. I will tolerate no lynch mob under my jurisdiction. Do you hear me?"

There were a few mutterings amongst the crowd, but no-one dared say anything. I noticed that Fletcher was about to open his mouth to protest his innocence, so I stepped over to him and whispered in his ear.

"Say not a word, Mr Fletcher," I said. "I know you are innocent of this crime, but you must go with Constables Sawyer and Cripps for the time being. It is your safest option. I will call on your wife and inform her what is happening. I will have you freed once this hubbub has died down. It may take a few days, but do not fear."

Fletcher stared at me momentarily and then gave a thin smile. "You are said to be a good man, Master Cheswis," he said. "Now I know this to be so. It is a shame not all constables can behave in such a manner."

With that, Sawyer, who was standing nearby and overheard Fletcher's remark, grabbed the prisoner by the collar and hauled him through the jeering crowd, closely followed by Cripps and four of the soldiers, leaving Croxton, Alexander, the remaining two soldiers, and myself to await the arrival of the coroner.

The crowd of onlookers dissipated almost as quickly as it had assembled. Most followed Sawyer's procession down Welsh Row, across the bridge, and along the narrow path that lined the eastern bank of the Weaver towards the gaol on Pillory Street. The remainder either disappeared across the fields or headed back to the sconce at Welsh Row End.

Once they had gone, Croxton removed his hat and scratched his head thoughtfully.

"So you consider the young man, Fletcher, to be innocent, Master Cheswis?" he said, running his finger along the feather in the brim of his headgear.

"I believe so, sir," I replied. "Hassall did not drown in a ship full of brine. He walked here. Apart from the fact that there is no logical reason why Fletcher should murder Hassall in an argument over pay, and then drag his body several hundred yards to Ridley Field before tying him to a stone pillar, there are several indications that he is not the perpetrator. Think about it; firstly, from a practical point of view, how would a young man like Fletcher have transported a dead body from Snow Hill across the river and into Ridley Field

68

without the help of multiple accomplices and without being spotted? He would have needed to get it over the earthworks the way we have just come or along the length of Welsh Row and through the checkpoint at Welsh Row End. That is simply inconceivable."

"And you can prove this theory, I suppose?"

"I think so, sir. First of all, if Hassall had been drowned in the ship, it is highly unlikely that he would have vomited down his shirt. He probably did that on the way here. Secondly, you may wish to take a look at the back of Hassall's neck." I walked over to Hassall's body and pushed his head gently forward so that Croxton could see the base of the skull, where there was a vivid red mark.

The colonel put his fingers to the wound and pressed. "The bone is soft here," he acknowledged. "Hassall had a fractured skull."

"Correct. It's not immediately apparent, for the rest of his body is unmarked, but a single blow to the back of the neck can kill a man outright, especially if the killer is trained to do such a thing."

Croxton raised an eyebrow and looked at me quizzically. "You are suggesting that Hassall was murdered by a trained assassin?" he said. "The thought is preposterous, surely? Hassall was merely a local merchant, who happened to serve in the town guard. He volunteered to defend this town in Parliament's name and did so loyally as far as I am aware. Why would someone want to murder a man like that?"

"I have no idea," I replied, with honesty, "but what I do know is that, when viewed from behind, Fletcher bears a significant resemblance to the royalist spy you wish us to locate."

"Bressy?"

"Precisely. I cannot be sure, but I would hazard a guess that Bressy is already in Nantwich and that he paid a visit to Hassall shortly after Fletcher left. It is just possible, I suppose, that Fletcher assaulted Hassall by pushing him into the ship. However, a more likely scenario is that Bressy did this, half drowning him in the process. What we don't know is why Bressy picked on Hassall, how and why he led him out of the town, and why he decided to murder him in Ridley Field."

"That is an interesting theory," said Croxton, "but, if you are right, that means that Fletcher is innocent, and we must free him."

"Not yet," I said. "If I am right, and Bressy is indeed in town, then it is better that he does not suspect we know he is here. Apart from which, Fletcher is safer in gaol until we can prove he is innocent."

I was surpassing myself. I had spent six months regretting my involvement with Brereton, rueing the fact that I had been dragged unwillingly into the world of the intelligencer. However, I realised with surprise and some consternation that I was starting to talk like one. Consternation, not just because of the potential presence of Bressy, a man with whom I had crossed swords twice before, but because of the shocking realisation that I was beginning to enjoy myself.

"Very well," said Croxton, replacing his hat. "I will hold him without charge for a week. After that we will have to charge him or let him go. I suggest you make haste with your enquiries. If it is as you say, Bressy cannot have gone far, and, if he has not yet solved the matter of which we talked earlier, then he will surely return."

* * *

Jacob Fletcher lived in a ramshackle worker's cottage about halfway up Wall Lane, the main thoroughfare through the salt-making area of Snow Hill. The house was surrounded by wich houses, and, across the street, brine workers loitered around the door of one of them, smoking their pipes and chattering.

A wooden theet ran from the entrance in the direction of 'Old Biot', the town's brine pit, denoting that a kindling had been scheduled, but there was no activity, for the kindling had been cancelled owing to the weather. There was no celebration on the part of the briners, for a cancelled kindling meant no money.

When I knocked on the door of the cottage (alone, for Alexander had returned home to face the ordeal of explaining our latest task to Margery), several people looked warily in my direction, and a shutter closed noisily behind me, a pair of curious eyes disappearing behind the wooden slats.

After a few seconds, the door was opened by a careworn young woman with two small children attached to her skirts. From the look of the swelling in her abdomen, it was clear that another child was on its way. To my surprise, a flash of recognition crossed the woman's face as soon as she opened the door.

"Master Cheswis," she said, "what brings you here?"

"You know me, mistress?" I asked.

"But of course. My name is Sarah. My mother you know as Mistress Johnson, who has oft times helped your wife keep house, as and when she has needed to earn money to make ends meet. These are difficult times, as you know, and my mother has been grateful for the work. To what do I owe this courtesy?"

It was clear that not one of Sarah Fletcher's neighbours had possessed the courage to inform her about her husband's arrest, even though, judging from the looks I was being given, the whole street was fully aware of what had happened in Ridley Field.

"It would be advisable if we were to talk indoors instead of in full view of your neighbours," I said.

The inside of the Fletchers' home was as one might expect – small and cramped. It was well-maintained, but palpably the home of a poor family. There was a plain oak table and several chairs in the hallway, but very little else. I also noticed a hole in the thatched roof.

"That needs mending, but we cannot afford to pay the thatcher," explained Sarah. "We must hope that this weather does not break with a storm, otherwise it will get wet in here."

I smiled in sympathy and turned to the matter at hand. There was no easy way to inform the woman about what had happened to her husband, so I told her with as little ceremony as I could get away with, taking care to state my belief in his innocence and Croxton's pledge to allow me a week to prove it.

I watched as her expression changed, not to one of horror, as I expected it might, but to one of anger and resentment.

"I know it is a sin," she said, "but I cannot bring myself to be sorry that Mr Hassall is dead. I know he put bread in our mouths, but he took it away too. He was not a good man."

"Your husband said he tried to cheat him," I ventured.

"He was always doing that," replied Sarah. "Not just to Jacob, but to others too. If there was a way for him to avoid paying for all the work carried out, he would find it. If any salt was wasted or fell from one of the barrows, you could be sure someone would pay for it. If too much ale or cows' blood was used during the kindling, the same would happen, and if there was any opportunity to lengthen the kindling by an hour or so,

73

then he would take it, putting everyone at risk of being fined by the Rulers of Walling."

"So was anything different about yesterday?"

"Not really," said Sarah, pushing wisps of sandy hair back under her coif and wiping a tear from the corner of her eye, "other than the fact that Jacob was drunk when I returned from my mother's at ten o'clock. He was so upset at the way he had been treated by Hassall that he had half emptied the barrel of ale we had bought the day before."

"So tell me what happened?"

"Jacob, being young and strong, had been placed in charge of moving the barrows of salt into the store room. With the kindling finished, there was only a limited amount of salt to move, and Jacob is good at this work, so he finished his task half an hour quicker than he expected. Master Hassall, however, wishes to pay by the half day, and as Jacob was half an hour short, he was docked a full half day's pay. This is money we cannot afford to lose."

I made a quick mental calculation. If Fletcher had been seen arguing with Hassall at eight-thirty and was next seen by his wife at ten, it was theoretically just possible for the person seen attacking Hassall at nine to have led the victim to Ridley Field, committed the murder, and returned to Snow Hill by ten, but certainly not enough time to have got roaring drunk too. Although I was personally convinced that Jem

Bressy was the person seen at nine, this was going to be difficult to prove, as the only person who was witness to Fletcher's drunkenness and his presence in Snow Hill at ten was his own wife. I had a feeling her testimony would not cut much ice if Fletcher were forced to face a trial. I had the suspicion I was going to need to locate Bressy before I could prove Fletcher's innocence.

"Can you account for why Hassall behaves in this manner?" I asked.

"I could not say," replied Sarah. "Perhaps he feels he needs the money too. Historically, the Hassall family has been a family of high status in these parts, but Henry Hassall was a younger son, and has only his wich houses to his name, plus some land which he leases to tenant farmers. In fact, he hasn't been the same since he lost the lease to Ridley Field."

I looked up sharply. "Ridley Field?" I said. "I thought Ridley Field was farmed by Robert Hollis from Welsh Row End. I did not know Hassall was the leaseholder."

"He was until recently. The Hassalls have leased Ridley Field on and off for generations. However, last year, Master Hassall was outbid by Master Hollis, who had sub-let the field from Hassall for several years. Those close to him say it was a shock for Master Hassall, for the income made all the difference to him. And now he is dead. It is a well-known story that the last time the Hassall family lost the lease to Ridley

Field, it also resulted in a murder. It is as though the field were cursed."

I gazed in amazement at Sarah Fletcher. The conversation had taken an entirely unexpected turn.

"A murder?" I exclaimed, with incredulity. "When was this?"

"Many, many years ago, long before I was born. It was in Queen Elizabeth's time. The landlord of The Crown was murdered in a dispute over the lease of Ridley Field. It is a story often told by Nantwich folk, but I am not aware of the finer details. I am only young. However, there are Nantwich people still alive who knew those involved. The murderer, I believe, was never caught."

I whistled quietly. It seemed rather too much to expect that a tale from seventy years ago could have anything to do with a crime that had just taken place, but it was worth finding out – and I knew just the person who might be able to help.

* * *

"The murder of Roger Crockett?" said Mrs Padgett, inquisitively.

In addition to being a fine cook, my housekeeper was the font of all knowledge as far as Nantwich history was concerned, and she looked at me now with raised eyebrows.

"That is a murky tale, which is best left buried in the past," she opined. "It is a story which affected many of the leading families in this town and created ill feeling which lasted for a generation. Why would you want to go delving into such matters, may I ask?"

Mrs Padgett was surrounded by pots and pans, and clouds of steam almost obscured her from view. Vegetables lay chopped and ready for cooking on the table, and a shoulder of mutton bubbled away in a pot on the stove, giving off an enticing aroma of meat and herbs. I had to concentrate to keep my mind from wandering towards thoughts of lunch.

"I don't know," I said, truthfully, and recounted the events of that morning, including the grisly discovery of Henry Hassall's body. "It is probably nothing, but I understand that Crockett's murder also involved a member of the Hassall family, and, like today's killing, occurred shortly after the Hassalls lost the lease to Ridley Field. It seems unlikely, I know, but I wondered whether there might be some connection."

Mrs Padgett put down the knife she was using and wiped her hands in her apron.

"It happened a long time ago," she said, "before the Great Fire, when Nantwich was a very different place, but my grandmother told me the story – she was alive at the time these events occurred. Crockett was a local businessman, who had grown rich on the profits made by The Crown Inn, but he was considered somewhat uncouth, as was his wife, who was commonly held for a loud-mouthed slattern. As a result neither was accepted by the town's elite."

"But that is no grounds for murder," I interjected. "I understand there was a dispute over the lease to Ridley Field, though."

"That is true. Master Crockett was an acquisitive sort, and when the lease to Ridley Field was up for renewal, he negotiated the lease directly with the landlord without allowing the existing leaseholder, Richard Hassall, the opportunity to renew. The argument over the field went on for months, splitting the town down the middle and causing much unpleasantness. Most of the town's leading families, the Maistersons and Wilbrahams amongst them, sided with Hassall. On the day he was supposed to take possession of the field, Crockett was set upon by a crowd of Hassall's supporters and beaten so badly that he died of his injuries."

"I understand the murderer was never apprehended," I said.

"That's right. My grandmother always told me that a friend of Hassall's named Edmund Crewe struck the fatal blow, but he was spirited away by Hassall's friends and family and never seen again. Crockett's wife, however, tried to blame the majority of the crowd who had attacked her husband, and attempted to have Hassall and several others, including Richard

Wilbraham of Townsend House, indicted for murder."

"But she failed?"

"That's right. The coroner, who was a Maisterson, found that Crewe alone was responsible for the killing, and so the matter was brought to a close. The Crockett family continued to run The Crown, and Bridgett Crockett lived well into her eighties. I remember her from my youth; a bitter old woman, and not without reason, I suppose. Anyway, when she died, the Crockett family left Nantwich. I have no idea what happened to them."

It was a fascinating tale, but, of course, it shed no light on what might have happened to Henry Hassall that morning.

"That is all I know," said Mrs Padgett, somewhat apologetically. "However, the record of the inquest may still exist. I do know that some of the records from that time survived the Great Fire which destroyed this town in fifteen eighty-three. Young Ezekiel Green would know. There may also be records in Chester. It is said that after the inquest, Bridgett Crocket did not give up in her quest for vengeance and bribed one of her servants to testify that Richard Wilbraham was among the crowd who killed Crockett. The servant, it is said, only recanted his story when accused of perjury and threatened with the hangman's noose."

I thanked Mrs Padgett for her help and left her to her cooking, making a mental note to speak to Ezekiel

Green at the first possible opportunity. It would not be the first time I had asked Green to guide me through court archives in pursuit of the truth.

Deep in thought, I wandered over to the front door and opened it to let the air circulate within the house. As I did so, I noticed that the sky had darkened ominously and a soft rain had begun to fall. Behind the building in the square, a jagged fork of lightning illuminated the sky, followed immediately by a sharp crack of thunder. A storm would be much welcomed, I thought. Perhaps it would clear the atmosphere.

As I stood in the doorway and watched the globules of rainwater growing steadily larger, I glanced the opposite way down the street towards the Beast Market and Beam Street, and was surprised to see Jack Wade limping his way up the street, his wooden leg clunking loudly on the cobbles. He gave a grimace of pain and rubbed the area around his stump as he reached me, gasping heavily with the effort.

"You must come quickly, Master Cheswis," he breathed. "There has been a break-in at your house on Beam Street."

"A break-in?" I exclaimed, with concern and disbelief. "How can that be? And Elizabeth? She was at home?"

"No, sir. She had been accompanying me to deliver the items you had put aside for Gilbert Kinshaw. We took the horse and cart, and we had just returned. The sound of Mistress Cheswis opening the door must have disturbed the perpetrator, for he charged down the stairs and barged his way out through the front door before we could react."

"And how is my wife? She is hurt?"

"No, sir. A little shaken, perhaps, but that is for reasons other than the mere intrusion."

"What do you mean?" I asked, catching a strange look in Wade's expression. My apprentice hesitated a moment before fixing me with a penetrating stare.

"The intruder," he said, "he was no casual burglar. Both Mistress Cheswis and I recognised him instantly, a man who neither of us wished to see again. Tell me, Master Cheswis, what in the name of Jesus is going on, and why is Jem Bressy walking the streets of this town?"

\* \* \*

That evening, at dusk, I sat out in our back yard with a tankard of ale and watched the stars appear one by one in the northern sky. It was a calm, cooling evening, the storm of earlier in the day having washed away the sultriness in the atmosphere. I had invited Elizabeth to join me, but she had declined, being unable to rest until the mess left by Jem Bressy had been cleaned up.

Bressy had ransacked the house from top to bottom. Cupboards and drawers had been opened and searched, clothes strewn everywhere. Curiously, the spare room used by Ralph Brett for storage had come in for particular attention, and I was thankful that much of the contents had been delivered to Gilbert Kinshaw earlier that day. Nonetheless, Brett's ornate chest had been smashed and the contents strewn over the floor. Oddly enough though, nothing had been taken, not even the Duke of Hamilton's knife, which surely must have been worth something.

I sat and pondered what Bressy was doing back in Nantwich and wondered at the chaos which one man could create in such a short space of time. What, I wondered, was this treasure that Bressy had spoken of? Did it exist, and, if so, where had it been secreted? What, if anything, did Henry Hassall have to do with this, and why would Bressy want to kill him – and why take the trouble to take the wich house owner to Ridley Field to meet his death?

More interestingly, might there really be a connection with the seventy-year-old murder of Roger Crockett, the erstwhile landlord of The Crown, or were the apparent connections between the two killings just coincidence?

Finally, and most crucially for Elizabeth and myself, what on earth did her deceased husband, Ralph Brett the elder, have to do with all of this? A professional like Bressy, I acknowledged, did everything for a reason. So what, I wondered, did Ralph Brett possess that Bressy needed so badly?

I sighed, drained my tankard, and headed back inside the house. The summer storm might have cleared the atmosphere, but I perceived storm clouds of an entirely different kind on the horizon, and I had no option but to wait for them to break.

# Chapter 5

*Montgomery – Thursday, July 25th, 1644*

*I*t was not what she was expecting. Squeezed into the confines of the middle ward of Montgomery Castle, this half-timbered mansion was the main abode of Edward, Lord Herbert of Cherbury, and it seemed somewhat incongruous set against the backdrop of the castle's forbidding stone towers, which flanked the gateway to the fortification, itself standing atop the steep, rocky ridge to the west of the town.

But that was Herbert all over, Hunckes had said. His lordship was a man who had stood out from the ordinary throughout his life and was still an eccentric now he was in his dotage.

In truth, despite her reticence about the task she had been given, Alice Furnival had been looking forward to the prospect of meeting Lord Herbert, who, in his youth, it was said, had been irresistible to women, although this, Hunckes had pointed out, was a reputation largely of Herbert's own report.

"An egotist, then?" she had said, betraying a hint of a smile. "How interesting. But why me?"

"Precisely because you are a woman, Alice," the governor of Shrewsbury had replied. "Herbert may be old and in ill-health, but in the presence of an attractive woman, he cannot help himself, which is precisely what we need. For months he has prevaricated over his support for the King, to the point where we can no longer be sure where his loyalties truly lie, other than to that confounded library of his.

"Your task will be to persuade his lordship that we can find a suitable repository for his precious books for the duration of this conflict, such that he may permit us to garrison Montgomery Castle, thereby preventing Sir Thomas Myddelton from continuing his march through the countryside hereabouts. Myddelton has already captured Oswestry, and, thanks to the beef-wittedness and insubordination of Colonel Marrow, inflicted a damaging defeat on us at Whittington. The last thing we need is for him to capture Montgomery too."

"And you know of such a place, where his lordship's books can be safely concealed?"

Sir Fulke Hunckes had stroked his greying beard thoughtfully and given a wry smile. "I believe I do, Alice," he had confirmed, "but it will necessitate *a return to within striking distance of a place that brought bad fortune to both of us. You are aware of the Cotton family at Combermere?"*

*"I am," Alice had replied, frowning. "George Cotton was an acquaintance of my husband, when he was alive. But Combermere is only six miles from Nantwich. I cannot go back there."*

*"Oh, but you will, my dear, you will, and I shall accompany you there personally, for more is at stake here than a few books. I do not exaggerate when I say that the very future of the royalist cause in these parts hangs from a thread. Since his defeat in Yorkshire, Prince Rupert is in desperate need of money and ammunition. There is no aid from Ireland, as he had hoped, and we can only tax the local populace so much before we start to alienate them. His Royal Highness is now on his way to Chester, where he plans to make his winter quarters, but it is not easy for him."*

*Alice nodded. She could see that Hunckes was right. Rupert had been in Shrewsbury only a few days previously, and, although he had arrived with his customary pomp and ceremony, she had been struck by a look of desperation in the prince's eyes, a recognition, perhaps, that he was not going to be able to ride roughshod through every parliamentarian force he crossed swords with.*

*Then Hunckes had explained about Jem Bressy and the riches he had promised to acquire for the royalist cause, and Alice had realised that a visit to Combermere would be unavoidable.*

*First, however, she had Lord Herbert to deal with. And so, dressed in her best blue outfit with embroidered under-petticoat and matching lace coif, kerchief, and cuffs, she had ridden the twenty miles from Shrewsbury to Montgomery equipped with a personal letter of recommendation from Hunckes.*

*She had arrived in Montgomery the previous evening and immediately sought out the town bailiff, a short, sour-faced man called Bennett, who, on viewing the governor's seal, had reluctantly helped her find accommodation at The Old Bell, a comfortable if unprepossessing inn, which nestled under the escarpment that led to the castle.*

*That morning, Bennett had accompanied her to the castle, grumbling the whole way, partly because it was market day, and the town was bursting at the seams with market traders, but also because she had refused to walk up the inordinately steep track that climbed up behind the black and white timbered market hall. Instead, she had attracted the bailiff's ire by insisting he accompany her along the street leading to the Kerry Gate and past the tanners' yard, before doubling back and approaching the castle from a much gentler gradient.*

*Fortunately, the letter from Hunckes and the intervention from Bennett, who was known to the* guards at the castle gates, had served their purpose. It was with some relief that she had found herself led over the wooden drawbridge that spanned the ditch between the outer and middle wards and into Herbert's home, where a servant had directed her into the library.

Alice was not an avid reader, but she could not fail to be impressed by Lord Herbert's collection of books, which lined three complete walls of the room from floor to ceiling. The wall opposite the entrance was panelled with oak and contained a large leaded window, which provided a view over the town below, the wide thoroughfare of Broad Street and its drainage channel, the appropriately named Shitebrok, the market hall, the spire of St Nicholas' Church, and beyond that the ruinous medieval wall and ditch which surrounded and purported to protect the town.

Next to the window stood a grey-haired man of around sixty, who winced noticeably as he turned to acknowledge her. Lord Herbert, Alice noted, still bore the finely chiselled features of his youth, his carefully groomed silver beard and moustache lending him an air of authority and wisdom, but there was also a certain pallor about his complexion as he limped forward to greet her. Herbert, it was clear, was not a well man.

"Forgive me, madam," he said, noticing Alice's concern. "It is merely a touch of gout, which ails me from time to time. It is a little painful, but I tolerate it, for it reminds me of all the excellent French wine I have had the good fortune to drink in my time."

"Ah, yes, my lord," acknowledged Alice, "I understand you were once England's ambassador to France."

"Indeed I was, but that was in King James' time, and it was a role which ended rather abruptly, as I recall. Despite having secured the present king's marriage, my reward was dismissal, a mountain of debt, and arrears of payment that persist to this day. Still, it is good to see I am in demand again. Sir Fulke Hunckes is indeed a persistent fellow."

Alice ignored the blatant sarcasm. "Then you know why I am here," she said, patiently.

"Of course, it is not difficult to hazard a guess. At least this time he has sent me something to brighten my day. The view of Corndon Hill from this library is one of my greatest pleasures, but today it is naught compared to the view within this room."

Alice felt herself flushing at the compliment, and she made sure Herbert noticed her pleasure. "You flatter me, my lord," she said, giving a slight curtsey.

"Not at all," said Herbert. "But tell me, Hunckes would have me fill this place with his musketeers. I have told him before that my sons and I are perfectly capable of defending our own home. Why would I turn the castle over to Hunckes and risk incurring the wrath of Parliament?"

"Because you are loyal to His Majesty and would wish to demonstrate that loyalty, why else?"

Herbert smiled inscrutably. "It is true," he said, "that I have no love for the bunch of churlish cropheads who imprisoned me not two years ago, merely, I might add, for adding the words 'without cause' to the resolution that the King violated his oath by making war on Parliament. Nonetheless, I do not want to see this place destroyed, so self-preservation is my primary aim, as well as the saving of my library, which is very dear to me. It is something I pray for daily."

"And do you believe God answers your prayers, my lord?"

Herbert gave Alice a sharp look and opened his mouth as if to say something. However, he then changed his mind and smiled benevolently. "He answers them every day," he said. "However, it is for us to interpret the signs he sends us and act accordingly."

"And have you seen these signs?"

"Indeed. For example, many years ago I was considering whether to publish my treatise on religion, 'De Veritate', so I prayed to God for guidance. Even though it was a clear, sunny day with no wind, no sooner had I uttered my prayer than I heard an otherworldly, yet gentle noise in the sky, that was so comforting I took it as an affirmation of my petition to the Lord and so proceeded to print my book. If you *pray for something, God will always answer."*

Alice smiled. She had heard this story before from Hunckes, who had prepared her well. "Herbert never tires of the suggestion that he has a direct path to God," he had said. "Humour him, and you will get what we want."

"Then perhaps you would consider a practical suggestion from an earthly source as a sign of the path you should take?" she suggested.

"I might," said Herbert, warily. "What did you have in mind?"

"My lord, perhaps you are aware of a family called Cotton from Combermere, between Nantwich and Whitchurch. They are strong for the King and would provide good and loyal service to him whenever it is required."

"I know of them," said Herbert. "Why do you ask?"

"Combermere," said Alice, "is built on the site of an abbey that was destroyed a hundred years ago by King Henry during his purge of the monasteries. Only the abbot's house survives, and this has been converted into the Cotton family's private residence. However, we have managed to ascertain that somewhere on the estate there is an underground repository that dates from the time when the monastery was active.

"The location of this repository is known only to Cotton and his direct family. This would be a perfect site to store your library in safety. We have already spoken to the Cotton family, who have indicated their willingness to host your library until such a time as it is safe to return it to Montgomery."

"Madam, I do not know the Cotton family personally. How could I possibly entrust such a valuable collection to an unknown entity?"

"You wouldn't have to," said Alice. "I would propose you travel to Combermere with Sir Fulke and myself in order to view this repository for yourself and to make the acquaintance of those who would be the custodians of your collection. What do you say, my lord?"

# Chapter 6

In the event, nearly three weeks passed before I was able to secure the release of Jacob Fletcher. The difficulty was not so much in persuading Croxton that Jem Bressy was the man who had murdered Henry Hassall, for the colonel had declared himself convinced of Bressy's presence in Nantwich thanks to the testimony of Jack Wade and Elizabeth. He had also accepted without question the suggestion that Bressy's likeness to Fletcher could have conceivably placed him at the murder scene.

The problem lay more in John Davenport's stubborn refusal to renounce his claim that the man he had seen immersing Hassall's head in the brine-filled ship was indeed Fletcher – that and the self-righteous insistence of Constables Sawyer and Cripps that they had arrested the right man.

Sawyer had even gone so far as to petition the high constable to intervene in an attempt to force Croxton to put a stop to what my erstwhile colleague saw as an interference in civilian matters. This, in turn, had forced the colonel's hand, and he had written to Brereton in London with a view to bringing an end to the impasse.

In the meantime, Croxton had told both the bailiff, Andrew Hopwood, and the high constable that they would be personally answerable to Sir William Brereton himself if Fletcher was tried before Brereton's response arrived from the capital.

The situation was not helped by the fact that Bressy had disappeared without trace. Despite Croxton asking Elizabeth, Jack, Alexander, and myself, as well as all those soldiers who had served with Bressy in Beeston Castle the previous year, to keep a watchful eye out for the royalist intelligencer, it seemed Bressy had once again surpassed himself in merging seamlessly into the background, a skill, I had to admit, in which he was particularly adept.

I conceded it was unlikely that Bressy had gone to ground within the walls of Nantwich itself, but as he had clearly not found what he was looking for when ransacking our home, I could only assume he would be back in his own good time. I had no option but to be patient and wait for his return.

As it turned out, Fletcher's ordeal was brought to a rapid conclusion when I rather fortuitously came up with the idea of trying to persuade John Davenport to return to the gaol in Pillory Street in order to make absolutely sure Fletcher was the man he saw attacking Hassall in his wich house.

"But why would I want to do that, Daniel?" my friend asked, when I called on him at his wich house one morning in late July. "I know what I saw that day. I was not mistaken." Davenport was stripped to the waist, his broad shoulders glistening with sweat as he heaved the heavy barrows of salt around the store room.

"Because," I said, "there was a day, not so long past, when you sat rotting in that gaol house yourself, similarly accused of murder with no-one to believe your story but me. I stood by you when the rest of the town would have seen you hang. The least you can do is humour me and do me the courtesy of taking one final look."

Davenport grimaced and grumbled, but he saw my point, and so the next morning he accompanied me reluctantly to call on Andrew Hopwood, who I found in his cramped office by the entrance to the gaol house, devouring a trencher of bread and ham. The pungent smell of cheap tallow candles filled the air, disguising a second aroma that emanated from the corridor leading to the cell block, a mixture of mould, sweat, human waste, and hopelessness. The tall, gaunt-looking official looked up from his table with raised eyebrows and gave a poorly disguised smirk when he saw who I had brought with me.

"Well, Master Davenport," he said, spraying the table with breadcrumbs in an attempt to suppress a snort of amusement, "you seem to have trouble staying away from this place. Am I to assume you are anxious to enjoy some more of our hospitality?"

On hearing Hopwood's mocking tone, Davenport gave the bailiff a scowl of contempt and made to march back out into Pillory Street, a move which forced me to grasp my friend's arm to make him stay.

I was glad I did, for I saw the transformation in Davenport's face as Hopwood led him into the dark, dingy interior of the gaol block, towards the stinking, rat-infested cell he had shared not six months previously with the unfortunate Thomas Steele, the soon to be executed governor of Beeston Castle. I could see the set, determined shape of his jawline begin to disintegrate as he realised the implications of his testimony for the man slumped against the stone wall of the cell.

Three weeks in gaol on prisoners' rations had done little for Fletcher's appearance. His face had a hollow, cadaverous look about it, with the exception of his cut lip, which had become infected and had swollen to twice its normal size. His white shirt, still stained with blood, was now covered in dirt and sweat and was barely recognisable. He tried to struggle to his feet when he saw us coming, but I signalled for him to remain seated. Davenport took one look at the sorry figure before him and turned to me.

"You know what, Daniel," he said, "you are right. I cannot be sure that this man was the person I saw that night, after all. It was dark, and the attacker was facing away from me. I only caught the briefest of glimpses, so it could easily have been someone else."

And so that was that. After a brief explanation, the bewildered Hopwood allowed me to lead Fletcher out of the cell towards freedom, just in time for us to encounter Sawyer and Cripps coming in the other direction.

The two constables were roughly manhandling a terrified-looking youth, each holding onto the young man's collar with one hand and one of his arms with the other. The youth, wide-eyed and trembling, was poorly dressed, his clothes almost in rags, and his hair, matted and unkempt, hung in thick clumps over his shoulders.

"A bloody thief," growled Sawyer by way of explanation, when he saw the quizzical look on my face. "Caught pilfering bread from Tom Horrocks' bakery."

Cripps, however, his face even more flushed than usual, said nothing, for he had just caught sight of Fletcher, who was being led by Hopwood, just behind Davenport and myself.

"Master Cheswis," he hissed, fixing me with a hard,

flinty glare. "What, pray, is this man doing out of his cell? He is a murderer and should be locked away. What do you suppose gives you the right to poke your snout into affairs that are no longer any of your business?" The constable's dangerously protruding eyes bored into me, a muscle at the corner of his mouth twitching in irritation.

I stared at Cripps with a degree of curiosity. I did not know the man well. Indeed, the most I had ever had to do with him was when I had purchased a pair of boots from him some months previously. Nevertheless, I had not taken him for a man capable of such a display of suppressed anger.

"Calm yourself, Master Cripps," I said, in an attempt to placate him. "We mean nothing untoward. It is simply that Master Davenport has withdrawn his witness statement. He admits he was mistaken in identifying Mr Fletcher as the man who attacked Hassall. Fletcher is free to leave. Surely you would not wish to see an innocent man languish in gaol?"

Cripps pursed his lips and took a sharp intake of breath, wheeling round to face Hopwood, who shrugged apologetically.

"It is as Master Cheswis says," admitted the bailiff. "There is no longer any evidence that Fletcher is your man. I have no option but to release him."

Cripps hesitated for a moment before fixing me with a baleful stare. "You are wrong, Cheswis," he snarled, in a manner that reminded me of a wounded dog. "You have not heard the last of this. Fletcher will hang for this crime, you can be sure of that. He is a guilty man, and I will prove it yet." Cripps was breathing heavily, his head making strange, jerking movements in my direction. "And as for you," he added, "you will be sorry that you interfered in this matter."

"Ah, for fuck's sake," said Sawyer, grabbing his colleague by a shirt sleeve in an attempt to calm him down. "Don't be such an addle-brained clotpole. Leave the bastard alone, there's nowt more to be achieved here."

Unfortunately for my erstwhile colleague, by attending to Cripps, Sawyer had been forced to loosen his grip on the youth, who, scarcely believing his luck, swung out wildly with his spare arm, causing Sawyer to howl with agony as he caught his knuckles against the stone wall of the gaol house. Now completely free, the youth scuttled out into the street and disappeared into the crowds.

There was no time to tarry. Whilst Sawyer was bellowing in pain and anger, Davenport, Fletcher, and I took our leave as quickly as we could. But as we did so, I could have sworn I caught the hint of a smile on Fletcher's face – relief, perhaps, or was it self-satisfaction that I saw?

I gave the briner the benefit of the doubt, but I could not help but wonder what had made Cripps so intent on seeing Fletcher convicted for Hassall's murder, and why such hatred and anger? There was more to the relationship between Fletcher and Cripps than met the eye, I was sure, but what? I resolved to find out, but first I had an appointment with someone who, not necessarily through any fault of his own, had proved to be most elusive during the previous three weeks.

When we reached the corner of Hospital Street, I thanked Davenport for his honest, if somewhat belated, testimony, sent Fletcher back to his wife and family, and headed straight for the Booth Hall.

\* \* \*

I found Ezekiel Green hunched over a desk in a dimly lit room towards the rear of the old court house, writing notes in what looked like a large register. In a sconce on the wall, a single candle cast flickering shadows against a large, half-filled bookcase. A small window opening to the west was shuttered, suggesting Green had deliberately tried to hide himself away from the summer sun.

Around him lay books, scrolls, and various other documents in a jumble uncharacteristic of the normally assiduous clerk, who I generally found to be an open, reliable, and good-natured fellow. His fingers, I noticed, were stained black with ink, and he carried the demeanour of a man who was suffering from exhaustion. To my surprise, he scarcely lifted his head as I entered the room.

"You will damage your eyesight, if you persist in working in such gloom," I said by way of greeting.

Green gave me a wan smile. "Ah, Master Cheswis," he said. "You are a welcome sight, sir. Anything to provide some relief from this drudgery."

I eyed the young clerk with concern. Green was a studious, pale-skinned young man, barely into his twenties, but he was generally helpful and enthusiastic, with an air of understated assurance that belied his years. Today, however, he looked as though he hadn't slept for a week.

"How do you fare, Ezekiel?" I asked. "You don't look too well. What ails you? You have not been an easy man to track down of late."

"It is true," admitted Green, blinking at me in the half-light. "I have not left this room for two days." The young clerk gestured to the pile of paperwork strewn across the desk. "All work of the Sequestration Committee," he explained. "The Lord knows, I'm no royalist, but this work is not to my taste. It has the whiff of vindictiveness about it."

"You are right, Ezekiel," I said, realising why Green had been so difficult to pin down during the previous days. More than once I had presented myself at the Booth Hall only to find him under the watchful gaze of Thomas Malbon, Marc Folineux, or one of the other sequestrators. "Grinding people into the ground as a punishment for supporting the King will serve no purpose whatsoever, save to nurture further discontent and ill-feeling. They are working you hard, I see."

"They are indeed. Especially Folineux, who is a man without mercy. He has a touch of the fanatic about him."

I gave Green a smile of sympathy. I could only agree with him. I glanced at the register in front of him and realised I was looking at a list of sequestration assessments for the Nantwich Hundred. Green saw me looking and graciously flicked through the register for me – there were pages and pages of it. No wonder the clerk looked tired.

I looked closely at Green's entries and realised the assessments covered many of the area's main royalist families – the Walthalls, the Wicksteads, and the Wilbrahams of Woodhey (although curiously the Townsend House branch of the family seemed so far to have avoided assessment).

I also noticed that the estate of Lady Norton, barely three months in her grave, had been sequestered for a significant proportion of the annual rents on her land and property. Easy prey, plundering the inheritance of a dead woman, I thought. I added up the list of properties and realised that almost £70 per annum was being taken from her estate. The rent taken relating to her substantial mansion on Beam Street alone was over £10.

Thomas Maisterson, I noticed, had not escaped Folineux's attention either, sequestered for over £30 per year on his various properties in Welsh Row and Beam Street, whilst Lord Cholmondeley had been similarly hit.

"You see what I mean," said Green. "Folineux and his ilk have kept me occupied for days with these assessments. I scarcely have time to eat." He leafed backwards through the register for several pages and smoothed down the paper. "And it's not just the rich either," he continued. "Take a look at this."

I examined the page closely and realised Green was showing me an assessment of John Saring, the previous minister of St Mary's Church and a noted delinquent, now imprisoned for his royalist tendencies, but still a man who had served Nantwich well for many years and was highly respected in the town. I read the assessment with a growing sense of dismay.

"But Saring has been sequestered of almost everything he owns," I said, reading through a long inventory of furniture, pottery, and other personal possessions, which had been sold.

"Aye, they've even taken his chamber pot, so if he ever gets released, he won't even be able to take a piss at night." Green fingered his tufty brown beard and sat thoughtfully for a moment. "But I'm glad you came to see me today," he continued, suddenly becoming more animated. "You bring a welcome respite from this unpleasant work – and I think I know why you're here."

I glanced sharply at Green, who responded with an enigmatic smile. "Indeed?" I said, somewhat taken aback. "Pray elaborate."

"Of course. You wish to find out more about the affray which took place here in fifteen seventy-two, which resulted in the death of one Roger Crockett. Am I getting warm?"

I stared at Green in open-mouthed astonishment. "Well, yes," I flustered. "You are right, of course, but how could you possibly know that?"

The young clerk replaced his pen carefully in the inkwell on his desk and wiped his hands on his breeches.

"Come, sir," he said. "It is not so difficult to deduce. The town is awash with rumours about the death of Henry Hassall, and several of the town's older residents who remember such things have remarked on the coincidence that Hassall had just lost the lease to Ridley Field, just like his ancestor.

"I am fully aware that Colonel Croxton has tasked you with uncovering the truth behind this matter, and, as far-fetched as a real link between these two murders may seem, I realised your thoroughness would not permit you to leave any stones unturned. I guessed you would eventually wish to view the original documents relating to Roger Crockett's inquest."

I regarded Green with renewed respect and admiration. "We are not so very different, I think, you and I," I said. "I take it you have already unearthed these documents?"

Green beamed with pleasure at the compliment. "Indeed I have," he said. "Won't you follow me?"

Green lit another candle from a taper and led me out of his room and down a corridor towards a solid-looking door set underneath the stairwell that led to the Booth Hall's upper floors.

"Here, hold this," he said, handing me the candle and extracting a key from a pocket sewn into his breeches.

He unlocked the door, which led to a set of wooden steps spiralling downwards into a wide stone cellar. As my eyes grew used to the light, I could see that the walls were lined with bookshelves filled with old documents. In the centre of the room was a plain oak table and a couple of chairs.

"The people who built the Booth Hall learned from experience," explained Green. "Many of the town's records were destroyed in the Great Fire of fifteen eighty-three, but fortunately the custodians of the records at that time had the presence of mind to save some of the more recent documents, and they made sure that a cellar was built in the new building to minimise the risk of damage should such a disastrous event recur in the future. It is God's providence that the Court Rolls from the early fifteen seventies were among those documents preserved." Green indicated two heavily bound volumes lying on the table.

"You have extracted these documents already?" I asked.

"I have. One of the volumes contains the record of the inquest held in St Mary's Church on the Saturday following Crockett's death, the other records the proceedings of the subsequent Nantwich Sessions Trial. I think you will find them interesting."

I stepped forward and gently opened one of the books, disturbing a thin layer of dust on the spine. I could see that Green was itching to talk me through the documents, and so, loath to disappoint him, I invited him to continue his explanation.

"You have been most thorough in your work," I said. "You are to be complimented. But, tell me – what is there to learn from these accounts that may have some relevance today?"

Green frowned. "That, Master Cheswis, is not so easy to say, for the testimony recorded is both contradictory and confused. However, what can be stated with some degree of certainty is that the murder of Roger Crockett was a most curious affair indeed."

The crime, Green went on to explain, had centred on a disagreement between Roger Crockett, the landlord of The Crown, and Richard Hassall, a member of one of Nantwich's leading families, over the lease to

Ridley Field. On the face of it, the dispute appeared straightforward enough. Hassall's lease had been up for renewal, and Crockett had negotiated a new lease with the owner of the field without paying Hassall the courtesy of allowing him to negotiate a renewal himself.

This, in itself, I decided, was not particularly noteworthy. Such disagreements happened all the time. However, this specific dispute had turned out to be unduly bitter in nature, continuing for months and splitting the town in half. This, in turn, had resulted in a series of threats and counter-threats of physical violence, which had resulted in many of the protagonists having to 'swear the peace' against one another. Crockett, interestingly, had refused to have anything to do with such undertakings, preferring simply to keep his distance from Hassall and his followers.

"It is difficult to tell from these documents what is the truth, what is bluster, and what is downright lies," said Green. "There are two documents here. One, we must assume, is an accurate record of what happened at the inquest, which was carried out behind closed doors on the Saturday after the murder. The coroner at those proceedings was a member of the Maisterson family – one John Maisterson, who was a supporter of Hassall and closely related to Richard Wilbraham, the most prominent of the accused.

"The second document is a collection of witness statements gathered during the aftermath of the inquest.

There are statements from well over a hundred people, a fair cross-section of the population of Nantwich at the time. You may be interested to note the names of the town's constables recorded in the documents."

Green opened up one of the volumes to a page which listed the names of all the witnesses interviewed at the time of Crockett's murder. I scanned the page, and my heart lurched as I saw the names of the two constables – John Wickstead and John Brett. Was the latter an ancestor of Ralph Brett perhaps, and, if so, what was the significance of that? I inspected the list further, and my eyes focused on another name I recognised. Almost hidden away among all the briners, tanners, and corvisers was the name of Thomas Bressy.

I had to force myself not to jump to conclusions, but was Bressy's name present on the list merely by chance, or was there a more sinister explanation? It was all very confusing, but I tried to remain circumspect.

"Brett was the name of my wife's first husband," I said, "and Bressy is the name of one of his murderers, but surely this is just a coincidence. What can you tell me about Crockett's murder?"

"Well, firstly, the attack on Crockett appears to have been co-ordinated, probably sometime in advance. Indeed, it looks as though Crockett was lured to the west bank of the Weaver by Hassall's cohorts, who had carried out an unprovoked assault on one of Crockett's friends, a man by the name of Thomas Wettenhall.

"When Crockett arrived on the scene, he too was set upon, by a large crowd of bystanders. Hassall's supporters do not actually admit to collusion, but there appears to be plenty of evidence that this was the case, not least the fact that there was a significant gathering at Hassall's home after the attack.

"Where there are discrepancies, however, is in the various accounts of who was responsible for striking the blow which killed Crockett, and how implicit various people were in the events surrounding this act. Crockett's wife and friends insist that a large melee of people was responsible for the killing, whereas Hassall's followers lay the blame squarely at the feet of a single person, Edmund Crewe, who was subsequently spirited away, never to be seen again. Of particular importance is the attempt by Bridgett Crockett to implicate Richard Wilbraham in the murder, when most of the witnesses say Wilbraham arrived on the scene still dressed in his night clothes."

"Not the actions of a man who was expecting trouble," I ventured.

"Precisely. Indeed, Wilbraham is said to have helped Crockett to a nearby house for treatment. Hassall's wife, Anne, also comes in for conflicting treatment. Some have her shouting at Crockett like a crazed harridan, whilst others have her tending the injured man as though she were a caring nurse."

"It all seems very strange," I agreed.

"And it becomes even stranger," said Green, warming to his task. "After Crockett's death, his widow, Bridgett, appears to have mounted a vigorous campaign to prove that her husband died by more than one hand, attempting, in the process, to frame Richard Wilbraham, among others, for the murder. She even employed a local artist, a man by the name of Hunter, to paint a portrait of the body to show that her husband had sustained many injuries. The painting and the reported state of Crockett's body apparently bore her argument out. Then, during the inquest, she tried to persuade the coroner to subject those accused to the ordeal of the bier."

"The ordeal of the bier?" I said with surprise. "That is nothing more than an old wives' tale. A bizarre request to say the least."

"But still common even seventy years ago," pointed out Green. "Bridgett Crockett tried to persuade the coroner to have the Hassalls and Wilbraham brought before Crockett's corpse in the belief that it would bleed afresh in the presence of his murderers. The coroner unsurprisingly refused the request and found that Crockett died exclusively at the hands of Edmund Crewe."

"And the coroner was a Maisterson, you say?"

"Yes. John Maisterson, brother-in-law to Richard Wilbraham. The whole case opened Maisterson to charges of corruption."

I sat down on one of the chairs for a moment whilst Green waited in anticipation for my comments. The candle, I noticed, was burning low on its wick, and so, after a few moments reflection, I closed the book and signalled for Green to follow me back upstairs.

"I have to say, I tend to agree with you," I said, eventually. "The behaviour of all parties in this case is most unconventional, as though something else were at stake beyond a simple disagreement over a lease. Why on earth did Crockett risk alienating all the town's elite just to lease a field? On the other hand, why were Hassall and his followers prepared to go as far as to commit murder in order to prevent Crockett gaining control of the field, why did Bridgett Crockett go to such extraordinary lengths to try and frame Richard Wilbraham for the murder, and did John Maisterson deliberately manipulate the findings of the inquest to protect his brother-in-law? And if so, was loyalty his only motivation? It is a complicated puzzle, but we are still missing one element."

"You are right," agreed Green. "We still have no proof of a connection to the present day, but I would like to help you find it, if you will allow me."

I considered the young clerk's suggestion for a moment and offered a grateful smile. "You enjoy this kind of investigative work, don't you, Ezekiel?" I said.

"It is certainly more rewarding than transcribing countless court documents," came the reply.

"But considerably more dangerous, I think you'll agree."

Green nodded in acknowledgement. "Perhaps so," he said. "I confess, I would not be much use in a tavern brawl, but I do know one end of a court document from another. I can be of help to you in this matter."

I looked at Green and tried to suppress a growing sense of foreboding. The last time I had involved someone as young as him in my affairs, they had ended up losing their leg. Nonetheless, I gritted my teeth and made the decision I knew I had to make.

"Very well, then," I said, reluctantly. "Why don't you go through the list of witnesses and see what connections can be made, if any, between their descendants and Henry Hassall. In the meantime, I will try to continue my investigations, although I confess I am at a loss as to where to look next."

Green smiled broadly and thanked me profusely for my confidence in him. Then, almost as an afterthought, his face turned serious once more.

"If you are looking for a new direction in this investigation, you might try Thomas Maisterson and Roger Wilbraham," he said, stroking his beard. "It may be nothing, but both of them were seen in the vicinity of Ridley Field just before Henry Hassall's death. A discussion with them may prove to be more fruitful than you might expect."

# Chapter 7

*Nantwich – Thursday, July 25th, 1644*

I must confess, there have been occasions when I have been forced to contemplate whether God has a singularly wicked sense of humour, so when I arrived home to find both Maisterson and Wilbraham seated at the table in my hall, being served by my wife and sampling the delights of Mrs Padgett's almond cake, I felt as though he might be having a laugh at my expense. It was almost as though the two gentlemen had been eavesdropping on my conversation with Ezekiel Green and had rushed to intercept me before I could change my mind.

The prospect of having to deal once again with Thomas Maisterson and Roger Wilbraham was not something which I looked forward to with a great deal of pleasurable anticipation. I had not forgotten how the two men, together with their colleague Randle Church, had attempted to compromise my integrity the previous December by suggesting my business might gain their favour if I were to turn a blind eye to the nature of their relationship with the murdered tanner, William Tench. The repetition of such a scenario was something I keenly wished to avoid.

The two merchants made an incongruous looking pair. Maisterson, in his forties, tall, thin, and soberly dressed, looked like he could have been a lawyer rather than the prominent gentleman that he was. Wilbraham, on the other hand, still in the full flush of youth, was short and squat in build, and wore his fair hair short. Although he was one of the town's most prominent royalists, his hairstyle would have marked him out as a puritan, were it not for his clothing: a fine silk doublet in purple with matching breeches.

Elizabeth gave me a knowing glance as I entered the house. "We have guests, my dear," she said, as Maisterson and Wilbraham rose to greet me. "I will take the children somewhere where they can play, and leave you to your business."

Amy and Ralph, I noticed, were sat quietly and respectfully at the table; quite unlike them, I thought. A spinning top and whip lay discarded on the wooden floor, and I realised they must have been playing when the two men arrived.

"There is no need for that," cut in Maisterson. "What we have to say concerns you also. We would prefer that you stay." There was something about Maisterson, with his hooked nose and sharp eyes, which reminded me of a bird of prey, and just for a second Elizabeth's expression took on the look of a startled field mouse, but she quickly pulled herself together and shooed the children out into the garden, telling them not to stray too far.

"I cannot imagine why you gentlemen would wish to speak with me," she said. "I am no more than a simple goodwife."

"Our information is that you have been rather more than that," said Maisterson, casting a meaningful smile at his companion, who extracted a small velvet pouch from the inside of his doublet and laid it on the table.

Wilbraham pulled the tiny bag's drawstring to open it and took out a small metal object, holding it between thumb and forefinger in the light of a candle, so that both Elizabeth and I could see it.

"Do either of you recognise this?" he asked.

Elizabeth gasped, and I felt a pit open up inside my stomach, for Wilbraham was holding the small pewter engraving that we had found in Ralph Brett's tunic.

"How the devil did you get hold of that?" I asked. "It belongs to my wife."

Wilbraham smiled and flicked the engraving over so we could see both sides of it. "Not this one, Master Cheswis. This particular engraving has been in my family for generations. Mr Maisterson has a similar one, and, judging by your reaction, you appear to have one too."

Neither Elizabeth nor I were ready to admit that the pewter coin was now in the hands of Gilbert Kinshaw, so Elizabeth merely asked,

"These engravings are clearly of some importance, Mr Wilbraham. What are they exactly?"

"Now that," said Wilbraham, his face breaking into a broad smile, "is a very good question. There is no short answer, but the story needs telling, for I believe we may all be in grave danger."

"Danger?" I exclaimed. "How so?"

"It is a long, convoluted tale," said Maisterson. "May we be seated? This may take some time."

I glanced at Elizabeth, who shrugged and gestured for the two men to make themselves comfortable. Maisterson turned his chair round to face us and sat demurely with his hands in the middle of his lap, one on top of the other. Wilbraham elected to remain standing, with his back to the window.

"How much do you both know about the history of Combermere Abbey?" asked Maisterson, eventually. My mind flashed immediately to the coat of arms we had seen on Brett's engraving. My wife, I realised, had correctly identified its source. Elizabeth stiffened, and, judging by the look on her face, she had also recognised the significance of Maisterson's words.

"It was a Cistercian house, was it not?" I said, trying to lighten the mood a little.

Maisterson raised his eyebrows slightly and

nodded. "You are well-informed," he acknowledged. "Combermere was indeed affiliated to the Cistercian order, although it was not always so. The place was founded in the twelfth century by Savignac monks, but it eventually became a daughter house to the Buildwas Abbey in Shropshire.

"Combermere never had a particularly salubrious reputation. It ran into financial difficulties on many occasions and picked up an unfortunate habit of attracting scandal. In the fifteenth century, one abbot was accused of counterfeiting gold coins, whilst another was murdered, shot dead with a bow and arrow. There was also another murder in the fifteen twenties, when one of the monks was killed by the abbey's tanner, who was protected and hidden away by the abbot himself until the fuss had died down.

"It sounds like a veritable nest of delinquents," I conceded.

"Yes, but the monastery was never very large. At the time of the Dissolution, only twelve monks resided there. Nonetheless, its impact on the local economy cannot be underestimated. Combermere owned numerous fields, properties, and wich houses in Nantwich, from which it exacted tithes. The abbey, therefore, had considerable influence over the lives of the folk who lived hereabouts, even the more prosperous families. Indeed, at the time, the families of both Mr Wilbraham and myself rented wich houses and other property from the abbey."

"How does any of this concern us, Mr Maisterson?" interjected Elizabeth, who was leaning against the door to the kitchen with her arms crossed.

Maisterson smiled indulgently. "Patience, madam," he said. "I am getting to that. The story which concerns us involves the very last abbot at Combermere, a man named John Massey, who had acceded to his post in fifteen twenty-nine.

"The Dissolution, it should be pointed out, was not something which happened overnight. It was something which had been brewing for a number of years, and Massey, who was a shrewd fellow, had been wise enough to notice that the writing was on the wall for the monasteries.

"So what did Massey do?" I asked.

"He knew that if the abbey was closed, the crown would confiscate all its property, so he started to secrete away money, gold, and plate over a period of time. I suppose his plan was that once Henry was dead, England would revert to the old religion, and the abbey would be able to reform. Of course, as everyone knows, England did revert to Catholicism for a short time during the fifteen fifties, and with bloody consequences too, but it didn't last, and in any case, by this time Henry had torn down the monastery to its very foundations, something which Massey had clearly not anticipated.

"But I digress. By fifteen thirty-five, when Cromwell's auditors first descended on Combermere to assess its value, Massey had already managed to hide away valuables of considerable worth, and by fifteen thirty-eight, when he was called to London to surrender the monastery, he was in a strong position. Of course, Massey did make a token attempt to persuade the King to allow him and his monks to remain in the monastery, but he had no wish to have his head nailed to the abbey door like Abbot Whiting at Glastonbury, and so Combermere was eventually surrendered. The monks all left quietly, and Massey himself lived out the rest of his days on a comfortable pension of fifty pounds a year. He died in fifteen sixty-five."

"An absorbing story," I conceded, "but what happened to the money?"

"That is the interesting part," said Maisterson. "Massey was the only person who knew of the whereabouts of this treasure. For some reason, he kept its location a secret from his monks, possibly because he thought some of them might covet it for themselves. However, in the months preceding his death, when he knew he was dying, he began to make plans for how best to reveal the treasure's location and how to assure it would be put to use in a manner and at a time of which he would have approved.

"His solution was to pick seven prominent individuals from the local community who would be custodians of this knowledge, people who he had considered to be both pious and trustworthy."

"Trust can be a dangerous thing," I suggested. "How could he be sure one of these people would not be tempted to steal the whole lot and disappear?"

Maisterson emitted a low chuckle. "That," he said, "was a conundrum which had occupied Massey for several months, but his solution to make sure nothing was ever done without the consensus of all seven custodians was most ingenious. Firstly, he made sure that the individuals he chose were recruited in secret, so that each man was unaware of the identities of the other six. He then had six almost identical pewter engravings cast, which were distributed individually to six of the seven men. Each of those given an engraving was told that he should guard it with his life, for it contained information which would reveal the location of the treasure he had put away, but only in conjunction with the other six.

"Now, you may ask about the role of the seventh man. Well, he had a particularly privileged position, for he was the individual who Massey trusted above all the others. It was he who was entrusted with the task of making a judgement on when the time was right to recover the treasure. This man was not given an engraving. However, he was given the names of the other six men and told to bring them together when the old religion was re-established in England, and the opportunity was there to re-establish the Cistercian order within the abbey. Of course, his vital mistake was to assume this might take somewhat less than the eighty years that have passed by since his death."

Wilbraham, I noticed, had started shifting uncomfortably from foot to foot at the mention of religious orientation, as though the talk had begun to touch on matters which he would rather not discuss.

"I did not take your family to be closet Catholics, Mr Wilbraham," I said, guardedly. "I always saw you as being fiercely loyal to the crown, loyal enough to attract the patronage of King James not one generation past. His Majesty was once a guest at Townsend House, so I'm told."

Wilbraham bridled slightly and his cheeks took on a faint russet hue. "So he was, Master Cheswis, and I assure you, I am no ally of Rome. My family were always loyal to the monarch of the time, but for my ancestors this was more about loyalty to Combermere Abbey and to the abbot in particular, who had brought much business my family's way. The leading families always worked closely with the abbey. We were obliged to, for, as you have heard, the monastery was not without influence here."

This, of course, made sense, and I conceded the point to Wilbraham, but there was still one thing I did not understand.

"Forgive me," I said, "but if Massey only revealed

121

to one man the identity of the other six who had been given engravings, how is it that you and Mr Maisterson are aware of each other's position in this regard?"

Wilbraham gave a quiet snort of derision. "I thought that would have been obvious," he said. "The Maistersons and the Wilbrahams have always been close. It did not take many years after Massey's death before our respective ancestors realised they had both been chosen by the abbot as custodians. Over the years, we have identified one or two others, but not all of them. For several years we had suspected that Ralph Brett was in possession of one of the engravings, for reasons which will become clear. However, until today we could not be certain."

At this point, Maisterson reached inside his doublet and took out a second engraving, placing it on the table next to Wilbraham's.

"Take a closer look at the two engravings," said the older man. "What can you tell me about them?"

Elizabeth walked over to the table, and we both inspected the two pieces of pewter. At first sight they looked identical, but it was Elizabeth who spotted it first.

"Look, between 'Cistercium mater nostra' and the coat of arms," she said, triumphantly. "It's very small, but there is another word engraved into the metal; a different word on each piece."

"Very good, mistress," grinned Wilbraham. "That is

most observant of you."

I picked up Wilbraham's engraving and squinted at it, trying to read the minute detail of the lettering that had been cut into the pewter with considerable skill.

"It reads 'Assumption'," I said, confused, "but that means nothing at all. What does the other one say?"

"'Evensong'," said Elizabeth, equally nonplussed.

"We don't know for certain," replied Maisterson, "but it is our belief that each of the six engravings carries a different word, and that when placed together, the words will help reveal the location of Massey's hoard of valuables."

I stared at Maisterson in disbelief. This was getting increasingly bizarre. A hidden treasure, secreted away over a hundred years ago, of which Ralph Brett appeared to have been a custodian. If that were not strange enough, I suddenly remembered Wilbraham's opening remark.

"You suggested we might be all in danger," I said.

"Indeed," said Maisterson, grimly. "We believe Henry Hassall was in possession of one of these engravings and that he was murdered for it. We believe the murderer may well be seeking to acquire the remaining engravings and that at least some of the answers to this puzzle are to be found at Combermere Abbey. We think you may be of some assistance in helping us to identify the murderer, particularly as you have a personal interest in the matter, and that Colonel

Croxton has tasked you with pursuing this case. We have more information to share with you, but first we would ask that you share the information that you have and produce your engraving."

Elizabeth and I stared apologetically at Maisterson. "We would if we could, sir," said my wife, sheepishly, "but I'm afraid it is no longer in our possession. It is already in the hands of Gilbert Kinshaw."

\* \* \*

The two of us sat in silence for some time after Maisterson and Wilbraham had left. As soon as they had ascertained that we were not in possession of Brett's engraving, Maisterson had wasted little time.

"I do not wish to know why you have given the engraving to one such as Kinshaw," he had said, sternly, "but it is not his to keep. The custodianship was granted to the Brett family, and so it should remain. Apart from which, if the fact that Kinshaw has the engraving becomes common knowledge, it could put him in serious danger. You need to make haste and recover your property. We will give you until Wednesday next to retrieve the engraving, but then we must head for Combermere. We will divulge more information once the engraving has been returned to your possession."

With that, the two gentlemen had taken their leave,

leaving Elizabeth and I to contemplate the implication of the latest hand that fate had dealt us.

"I was under the impression that your first husband shared all his secrets with you," I said, eventually. "It seems I was mistaken."

Elizabeth glared at me for a moment, anger flashing in her eyes, but she then seemed to have second thoughts and sighed deeply, banging her palms on the table in frustration.

"I had no knowledge of this, Daniel, I swear," she said. "Ralph once told me that when our son was grown, he had a secret he would share with him, but it was made clear from the start that I was not going to be made party to this knowledge. I presume the engraving is what he was talking about."

"So there's no further light you can shed on the matter?"

"None, I'm afraid. All I know is that we must recover the engraving from Kinshaw."

"But how?" I asked. "Kinshaw is not a man to readily give up anything he believes to be legitimately his, and once he realises the engraving is of value to us, he will surely try to exact a high price for its return."

"You forget, Daniel, that I hold a signed agreement from Kinshaw to sell Ralph's business back to me at the original selling price. Now we know that the engraving has nothing to do with the affairs of the mercers business, he must return the engraving to us, as it was not included in the original purchase. If he refuses, I could always threaten to exert the right to buy the business back."

I shuddered at the thought of the can of worms that would be opened if such a scenario came to pass. The previous January I had accused Kinshaw of deliberately colluding with his sister Marion Tench and her husband William to blackmail John Davenport for fraudulently claiming walling rights he was not entitled to. Conversely, Kinshaw had accused me of turning a blind eye to Davenport's misdemeanours because he was my friend. A resolution that neither of us would talk openly about these issues had been a part of Kinshaw's agreement to buy Brett's business.

"My dear," I said, incredulous. "That is one thing we cannot do. Such an action would have to be the very last resort."

Elizabeth formed her hands into a steeple on the table and lowered the tone of her voice. "Then in that case," she said, "if he refuses to do the right thing, perhaps he will need some physical persuasion. Who do we know who is good at that sort of thing?"

Before I could express my horror, and as if on cue, there was a sharp knock on the door, and Alexander strolled in, clutching a wicker basket full of candles.

"For Simkins' workshop," explained my friend. "Boots are much sought after by the garrison at the moment, and Simkins says he is working into the night in order to meet demand. He is fast running out of candles. I was on my way to see him, but I bring a message from Mrs Padgett. She wishes for Amy to return home without delay to help with the washing."

"She will be outside playing with Ralph," said Elizabeth.

I strode into the kitchen and looked through the window to see if I could see the children, but the back yard was empty. I had been so preoccupied with Maisterson and Wilbraham that I had failed to notice the lack of noise from the garden.

"They cannot have gone far," I said. "I will send her home as soon as she comes back."

Alexander nodded, but then he looked at us both closely, having noticed the tension in the air.

"Is something amiss?" he asked, edging closer to where I was sitting. "You seem somewhat preoccupied."

I gestured for Alexander to take a seat and poured him a mug of ale. I then recounted the details of Maisterson and Wilbraham's visit and watched as Alexander's eyes grew wider. A smile began to spread across his features.

"That is indeed an enlightening tale," he said, cupping his chin in his hands and focussing on me intently, "but are you any the wiser as a result of this knowledge?"

"I am not certain," I admitted. "Let us analyse the facts. Firstly, we have Maisterson and Wilbraham's assertion that Henry Hassall was murdered on the assumption that he owned one of the engravings and because of his connection to this so-called treasure."

"So-called?"

"Yes, of course," I said. "We do not know for certain that this collection of gold and plate actually exists. However, we do know that Jem Bressy was planning to come to Nantwich to recover a hoard of valuables. We know that he has ransacked our home, because he was seen by Elizabeth and Jack Wade, so he is presumably aware that we own one of the engravings. He was also seen attacking Hassall in his wich house."

"Which makes him the likely murderer."

"Well, yes, of course, that is the most likely explanation, although we have no witnesses who actually saw Hassall being led to his death."

"But someone must have seen him," said Alexander.

"Indeed. My guess is that one or more guards were bribed to let them through and are now keeping their mouths firmly shut for fear of being implicated in the murder."

Alexander scratched his chin thoughtfully and frowned. "Very good," he said, "so what do we have?"

"The biggest puzzle," I said, "is the seemingly strange connection with the murder of Roger Crockett over seventy years ago. Members of the Hassall, Maisterson, and Wilbraham families were all involved in some way in the events of that day. A Bressy is also on the list of witnesses at Roger Crockett's inquest, as was Ralph Brett's great-grandfather, who was one of the town constables at the time. And what on earth is the connection with Ridley Field?"

"Well, that is simple," cut in Elizabeth. "Ridley Field must be where this treasure is buried."

I sat and considered that suggestion for a moment. Elizabeth was probably right. "Maisterson and Wilbraham will have known this," I reasoned. "They were spotted loitering around Ridley Field after the murder."

"And don't forget," added Alexander, "the field was like a rabbit warren – full of holes. Someone has obviously already been digging for this treasure. Perhaps they've already found it."

"I doubt it," I said. "Whoever dug the field up had no real idea where to look, for the field was covered in holes, and without exact co-ordinates, looking for the precise location of this hoard would be like searching for a needle in a haystack. My guess is that someone with one or two clues, Bressy perhaps, tried to take a calculated guess as to the location of the treasure but failed miserably. He will now have realised that he cannot hope to be successful by digging the whole field up. It's simply too big. The treasure could be absolutely anywhere. He will therefore have realised that his only hope is to discover more of the six clues."

I paused for a moment to let the effect of this

statement sink in. I could tell by the expressions on Alexander and Elizabeth's faces that they had come to the same conclusion as me. There was only one way to solve this. We had to pay a visit to Gilbert Kinshaw.

# Chapter 8

*Nantwich – Thursday, July 25th, 1644*

Gilbert Kinshaw lived in a finely appointed, half-timbered town house about half way up Hospital Street. It was not a long walk, but the sun was already low in the sky by the time Elizabeth and I were able to venture forth to seek him out.

Amy and Ralph had not returned, neither to Beam Street nor to my old house on Pepper Street, but in the end we could wait no longer, so we left a grim-faced Mrs Padgett in the company of the children's by now stone cold dinner and walked over to Pepper Street, where we left word with Jack Wade to remain at home, lest the children show up.

"This is truly the last time Amy and Ralph are allowed to run free like this," I said, bristling with anger at their disobedience. "They will be confined at home until they learn to obey instructions."

Elizabeth smiled at me indulgently, but she merely said, "Let us just pray that they are safe and that our business with Kinshaw does not detain us too long from finding out where they are."

Once we had given our instructions to Wade, we called on Alexander, who emerged into the street, brandishing a half-eaten mutton pie.

"Do you not even have time to stop for dinner these days?" called Margery, raucously, from somewhere inside the hallway. Alexander closed the door with a sheepish grin, ignoring his wife altogether. We could still hear her berating him fifty yards up the street.

"That, my friend, is what all men can expect from their wives as the years pass by," said Alexander, wearily. "Present company excepted, of course," he added, hastily, when he saw the look on Elizabeth's face.

It was a fine, warm evening in Nantwich. Householders sat on their doorsteps, enjoying the last of the evening sun. Men spilled out of the taverns into the street, drinking and laughing. On the green in front of the church, several off-duty soldiers from the garrison were carrying out sword practice, the clash of metal upon metal reverberating across the square. Food vendors mingled with the crowds, touting their wares and filling the air with the smell of fresh baking. It was a happy scene and hard to imagine that only six months ago these were freezing and worried people, not sure whether to expect starvation or slaughter at the hands of the hordes of besieging royalists.

Despite the cheerful mood of the townsfolk, something indeterminate filled me with unease as we walked towards The Lamb at the start of Hospital Street. I could not be certain, but I had the oddest feeling I was being watched, and as I glanced over towards the Booth Hall, I thought I saw a figure disappear furtively down one of the alleyways that led down to the river. Was I imagining things, or had he been observing my movements? Elizabeth, sensing my unease, gave me a curious look and squeezed my hand reassuringly.

When we arrived at Kinshaw's house, the scene outside was not what I expected. A sizeable crowd of onlookers had assembled on the street outside Kinshaw's front door. I could not see much, but I could hear raised voices emanating from somewhere in the middle of the gathering. The three of us pushed our way forcefully through the crowd, to be met by the strangest of sights.

Kinshaw, dressed only in his breeches and a torn white shirt, was arguing in an animated fashion with Constables Cripps and Sawyer. Seething with anger, he hitched up his breeches in a vain attempt to prevent rolls of milk-white flab from bulging out through the tear in his shirt. Kinshaw, I realised, had been involved in a fight and had clearly come off second best. He sported a huge fat lip and an angry-looking red mark on his cheekbone, whilst blood dripped from a cut on the side of his neck. The overweight merchant, red-faced and pompous, was taking Cripps to task over something, but the constable was having none of it, repeatedly jabbing Kinshaw in the chest with his finger.

As soon as he saw me emerge from the crowd, Cripps stopped what he was doing and fixed me with a rancorous stare.

"Ah, Cheswis," he growled, "I might have expected you to be in the vicinity. You arrive at an opportune moment. This man and members of his household have been assaulted, and yet he would speak only to you about what happened here. Perhaps you can clarify to me why that should be so? I have explained to him that you are no longer a constable of this town, and yet he takes no notice. I thought I told you to keep your nose out of business which is no longer your concern."

I gave Kinshaw a quizzical look, but my attention was quickly drawn to the scene inside his house. Although my view into the interior of Kinshaw's hall was largely restricted, I caught a glimpse of upturned chairs and a painting which had been torn from the wall. Meanwhile, at the bottom of a stairwell, Kinshaw's footman lay slumped against the wall, clutching a blood-stained rag to a wound on his forehead. Cowering by his side was a young parlour maid, her face white and streaked with tears.

"Master Cripps," I began, "I assure you, none of this is of my doing. I came here to see Mr Kinshaw on a private matter."

"Aye, and I would speak to you," interrupted Kinshaw. "There is nothing here that cannot be dealt with privately between you, your wife, and myself. However," he added, gesturing towards Cripps, "this ignorant oaf would force me to discuss such matters with him."

Cripps, barely containing his anger, made to take a step forward, but Sawyer put up an arm to hold him back.

"Mr Kinshaw," said Sawyer, with more patience than I thought him capable of, "we were told by your own neighbours that there had been a disturbance here, and we came forthwith to find you and your staff had been assaulted. That makes it our business. You should be grateful for our quick response, not berating us."

I looked at Kinshaw, who showed no sign of conceding the point and was continuing to stare belligerently at Cripps.

"Constable Sawyer is correct," I said, trying to calm the situation down. "You will need to give the constables a statement, but if you agree to do that, I am sure Constable Sawyer will permit you a few moments to speak to me in private first."

Sawyer harrumphed loudly, and Cripps said nothing, but both men stepped back reluctantly and began to clear the crowd. Meanwhile, I followed Elizabeth, Alexander, and Kinshaw into the latter's hallway.

"What is all this about, Mr Kinshaw?" I asked, closing the door behind me.

"I might ask you the same question," retorted Kinshaw. "What is it about the engraving you gave me that makes it so valuable?"

"The engraving? Valuable?" I responded. "That was what we had come to see you about. It was part of Ralph Brett's personal property and not associated with his mercers business as we first thought. As such, it was given to you in error, and we have come to request that you return it to my wife."

Kinshaw smiled sardonically. "You'll be lucky," he said. "It is now in the hands of the bastard who did this to me."

"You gave it to him?" I exclaimed, astonished.

"Of course. What do you expect? He strolled in here, clobbered Samuel, my footman, on the head and had me up against the wall, threatening me with a knife. Said he'd slit my throat if I didn't hand it over. What alternative did I have?"

"Can you describe this man for me?" I asked. "Let me guess – athletic build, jet black hair, short, well-groomed beard?"

Kinshaw looked at me with curiosity.

"Not really," he said. "Athletic for sure, but then most people are athletic in comparison to me. However, the man who attacked me was clean shaven, and his hair seemed more brown than black, but I could have been mistaken. Who is he, as a matter of interest?"

"That," I said, with a degree of haughtiness I usually reserved for people I didn't like, "is a matter which I am not at liberty to divulge. Needless to say, the man I describe is a dangerous individual, who we believe may have been responsible for the murder of Henry Hassall. You are fortunate indeed to have met his acquaintance and escape with such superficial injuries."

"Is that all you can say?" spluttered Kinshaw, extracting a kerchief from inside his torn shirt and dabbing it against his neck. "I get sore beaten by this man, solely because you chose to pass this engraving onto me. I could have been killed and you suggest I am fortunate? And what, may I ask, has Henry Hassall got to do with this?"

When I didn't answer, Kinshaw merely smiled at me knowingly.

"No matter," he said, waddling over to the door to let us out. "The truth will eventually emerge. Good Day, Mistress Cheswis, gentlemen. You know where to find me if you require my services."

* * *

Alexander, Elizabeth, and I trudged our way back to Beam Street in a state of dejection. Cutting in between the houses on Hospital Street, we walked past the makeshift campsite that had been erected on Tinkers

137

Croft for those soldiers who had not been able to find indoor billets, through the churchyard, and onto Churchyardside. We then headed across the fields to emerge opposite Lady Norton's residence, at the place near the earthworks where Ralph Brett had been murdered by Bressy, Hugh Furnival, and Nathaniel Hulse several months before.

I felt Elizabeth tense as we passed the spot. She was married to me now, but I could not blame her for still shuddering at the thought of an event which had changed her life so dramatically. Alexander, I sensed, had also noticed Elizabeth's mood, and so he hung back a few yards behind us to allow us a little privacy. I squeezed my wife's hand to show her I knew what she was thinking.

As we turned the corner into Beam Street though, all thoughts of Ralph Brett left me, for as soon as we came within sight of our home, a white-faced and frantic Mrs Padgett came flapping across the street to meet us, panic etched on her face, and she thrust a piece of paper into my hand.

"A young boy delivered this letter," she said, gulping back tears. "It's Ralph and Amy. They've been taken."

"Taken?" gasped Elizabeth, blanching noticeably. "What do you mean?"

I took the sheet of paper from Mrs Padgett and unfolded it. On it was a hastily written message in a barely legible scrawl.

*If you want to see your daughter, you know what you must do*

I looked at Elizabeth and Mrs Padgett with a mixture of horror and guilt. What manner of a mess had I managed to get myself embroiled in this time? So long as things only affected me, I had found that I was becoming used to the role of an intelligencer, I was able to more or less cope with the stresses placed on me by the role – but now it was different. My family was involved. Bressy had kidnapped Amy – and what about Ralph? Was he alive or dead? I had no idea. The letter made no mention of him.

I detached myself from the two women in my life and sat slumped on my doorstep with my head in my hands, wondering what to do next.

# Chapter 9

*Nantwich – Thursday, July 25th, 1644*

*S*tifling a sob, young Ralph Brett crouched low amongst the reeds that lined the bank of the River Weaver and watched as the man, who had taken Amy away, cursed and stomped his way through the nearby undergrowth.

*"Come out, you little bastard," growled the man. "I know you're in there somewhere. Show yourself, or you'll feel the edge of my sword." As if to illustrate his point, the man swung his weapon through the grass and bushes like a scythe until it clanged against a tree trunk.*

*"Fuck," he cursed, more desperate this time. "Where the hell did you go? If you don't show yourself, I'll cut off your miserable little pizzle and feed it to the crows."*

*Ralph shuddered and hunkered down further. Why had he not trusted his instinct and refused to follow the man into the trees?*

Ralph was soaking wet, knee-deep in river water. He was also beginning to get cold, despite the fact that the evening was still sunny and bright, he had lost his prized wooden sword, and his new breeches were ruined. His mother would tan his hide when he got back home, that was for certain, and he would be back in his skirts in no time. His friends had been so jealous when he had shown off his new breeches, but now he only had their ridicule to look forward to.

How he wished he'd run for it when the evil man had dragged Amy away. He would have had ample time to run back to the earthworks and alert the friendly sergeant who had let them pass into the field, and his clothes would have stayed clean, but instead he had hesitated and sought refuge amongst the reeds.

And how he wished he had not listened to Amy, who had insisted they go to play in Ridley Field in the first place. When his mother had ushered them out of the house so she and Master Daniel could speak to the two gentlemen in private, Amy had given him a sly smile and led him down Beam Street towards the bridge. Ridley Field was an exciting place, she had insisted. Only a few weeks ago a man had been murdered here, a grisly event, which they could act out in a game, and Ralph enjoyed such games. She could be the murderer and Ralph the constable who catches the killer, just like Master Daniel himself.

"Aye, off you go," the sergeant had said, when they

presented themselves at the foot of the steps leading to the top of the earthworks. "We'll keep an eye out for you. Just don't stray any further than the pillar, mind, just so as we can see you." And with a ruffle of the boy's hair, the sergeant had let the two children climb over the top of the earthen defences and down the ladder on the other side.

"Make sure you kill one of those malignants for us, mind," the sergeant had shouted, gesturing towards Ralph's sword, and the boy had swished his weapon a few times in mock combat before trotting off in Amy's wake towards the pillar in the middle of the field.

They had first seen the man outside Lady Norton's old house, but had thought little of it. He had been leaning against the stone wall that marked the boundary of Lady Norton's property; a tall, well-built man, perhaps the same age as his Uncle Simon. Athletic in build, Ralph knew the type. He looked just like one of the strapping farm boys that came into town on market day.

They had been surprised to see him once again as they talked to the sergeant, hanging back along the track that led back to Welsh Row. He had disappeared behind a hedgerow when he'd realised he had been noticed. The man made Ralph feel uneasy, but he had said nothing, and once he and Amy had begun playing, and he was chasing Amy with his sword around the water troughs and through the holes dug around the *pillar, he had soon forgotten his misgivings.*

*It had come as quite a shock, therefore, when they had suddenly become aware of a lone figure standing on the stone steps. The man wore dark grey breeches, a plain white shirt, and no hat, which allowed Ralph to notice his piercing blue eyes, which, despite the toothy grin he offered to the children, were hard and flinty.*

*"That's a fine sword, young man," the man had said, once it was clear he had been noticed.*

*"Yes, sir," Ralph had replied, warily.*

*"He's going to kill some royalists with it," Amy had chipped in, and she had skipped over to where Ralph was standing.*

*"I'm sure he is," the man had said. "He looks like a strapping young fellow."*

*At this, Ralph had pulled himself to his full height and stood to attention. "But today I'm going to catch the murderer," he had announced, "just like my stepfather."*

*"Murderer?" the man had replied, under raised eyebrows. "What murderer would that be?"*

*Ralph and Amy had looked at each other in surprise.*

*"You mean you don't know?" Amy had gasped. "I thought everyone knew Henry Hassall was murdered here only a few weeks ago. We were looking for clues."*

*"Then you might want to have a look in the bushes and trees by the river bank," the man had said, conspiratorially. "I'm sure I found a hidey-hole there*

*earlier today. It might have been where the murderer hid after he carried out this terrible deed."*

*"Really?" Amy had said in wonderment. "Where is that?"*

*"Come with me," the man had urged, with a smile. "I'll show you." And he had headed off across the grass towards a line of trees and thick undergrowth about fifty yards away.*

*Amy had followed him with an excited squeal, but Ralph had not been so sure. He did not trust the man. There was something in his eyes which promised danger. Ralph had taken an anxious look over towards the earthworks, but the sergeant had disappeared, gone to smoke his pipe, no doubt.*

*"Come on, Ralph," Amy had shouted. "What is the matter with you? Let us find out where the murderer hid."*

*And despite his misgivings, Ralph had sighed and followed Amy into the undergrowth.*

*Once they were out of sight of the earthworks, the man had pointed to a gap in between a hawthorn bush and a tangle of brambles, to what looked like a flattened area of grass.*

*"In there," he had said.*

*But as Amy stepped into the gap, he had given her an almighty shove, which sent her flying headfirst into the grass. Then, before Ralph could fully comprehend what was happening, he had grabbed the boy by the* waist and lifted him off his feet.

"Right, you little bugger. You're coming with me," he had snarled, the toothy smile vanishing instantly. "Make a noise, and you'll regret it."

But Ralph was not going to be dragged away without a fight. He still had his wooden sword, which he swung as hard as he could, catching the man fully on the side of his knee, sending both of them crashing to the ground. The man had breathed heavily as he tried to stifle a howl of pain. Not that it mattered, for Amy had pulled herself to her feet and had started screaming at the top of her voice.

"Ralph, Ralph," she had yelled, "run for it." But that was as far as she had got, for the man had struggled to his feet and lurched through the undergrowth before swinging his arm and catching her a fearful clout on the side of the head. Amy had collapsed, motionless, on the grass, whilst Ralph, driven by sheer panic, had dropped his sword and run headlong through the trees, in desperate search of a hiding place.

Ralph knew he could not outrun the man and had been preparing himself for discovery, but to his amazement, the man had hesitated and said, "You'll do," to Amy's lifeless form, before hoisting her over his shoulder and wading through the trees and bushes towards the wall at the southern end of Ridley Field.

It was then that Ralph had pushed further into the undergrowth and had found himself among the reeds *on the riverbank. Here he had crouched down onto his knees in the river water and held his breath for what seemed like an eternity.*

*He had expected all the shouting to have brought the sergeant running with some of his charges, but the soldier was obviously more interested in his pipe than the children's safety. Eventually, though, he had heard the sound of footsteps and the crackling of twigs, and he had realised with horror that the man had returned, this time without Amy.*

*He was, however, carrying a large sword, which he waved through the grass and bushes as he trampled his way through the vegetation.*

*Ralph pushed himself further down in the water, for the man was getting closer and closer. Only a few feet away, he could almost smell his breath. With a sigh, Ralph buried his head into the reeds and waited for the inevitable.*

# Chapter 10

It was past midnight before we found Ralph. He had been hiding amongst the reeds by the riverbank and had only emerged into the view of the search party assembled in Ridley Field when he heard me calling his name. Cowering, shivering, and soaking wet, he cut a sorry sight, and he was immediately swaddled in a blanket by Elizabeth, who had accompanied us into the field. Were it not for the pressing need to locate Amy, he would undoubtedly have been shepherded away into the safety of our home in Beam Street. Instead, he sat on the steps of the stone pillar, huddled in his mother's arms whilst we searched the rest of the pasture.

In truth, we had been fortunate to find either of the children, for the sergeant who had let them pass into Ridley Field had, for the most part, been singularly unhelpful, and it was not until Thomas Croxton had arrived on the scene and explained the gravity of the situation, namely that he had allowed a royalist spy to kidnap a child from under his very nose, that he began to realise the potential consequences for himself and started to co-operate.

It had not been too difficult to guess where Amy and Ralph had gone to play, and their exit point into the field had also been self-evident. When the hapless sergeant eventually began to talk, a picture gradually began to emerge of what had happened.

The children, it appeared, had been playing in the area around the pillar in the middle of the field, when the sergeant had descended from his look-out position to smoke his pipe. However, when he returned, the children had vanished. Several other soldiers stationed along the earthworks reported having seen a man talking to the children but had thought nothing of it, nor could they say where the children had gone, only that the unidentified person had been observed leading a horse away across the fields in the distance.

A garbled account from Ralph, who was in a state of shock, suggested that a tall man with blue eyes had struck Amy violently across the face and carried her away through the trees that lined the riverbank. Ralph himself had run into the undergrowth and had refused to move until he heard a voice he recognised.

The sergeant, it emerged, had carried out a brief search of the field once he realised that Amy and Ralph had disappeared, but, finding nothing, had initially determined to protect his own skin by denying point blank that he had seen the children at all.

Croxton, annoyed at having been disturbed from his dinner and incandescent at the breach in security, immediately ordered the sergeant to be detained, and he was led away, white-faced and thoroughly chastened, towards the gaol in Pillory Street.

This solved nothing, however, for Amy had completely vanished, and the only clue I possessed was the note that had been delivered into Mrs Padgett's hands and which I now held concealed in the lining of my doublet.

"You seem something more than vexed, Daniel," said Alexander, who came to join me on the steps of the stone pillar once the search party had begun to disperse. "What is it, aside from the obvious, that troubles you?"

I looked up at my friend and smiled by way of acknowledgement. For a big man, he could be remarkably perceptive at times.

"I am not certain," I admitted, "but there is something about this whole business that does not sit right. Logic says that Jem Bressy must be involved in this kidnap, but the description Ralph has given is not a match for Bressy. Kinshaw has also intimated that the man who attacked him was brown-haired and clean shaven. Bressy has black hair and a beard."

"Ralph is but a child, and Kinshaw may have

been mistaken," ventured Alexander, not entirely convincingly. "Or," he added, "perhaps Bressy has an accomplice – a replacement for Nat Hulse."

"That is a possibility," I conceded, "but it still doesn't make sense."

I took the scribbled note that Mrs Padgett had given me and showed it to Alexander.

"The person who wrote this thinks Amy is my daughter," I said. "Bressy is a skilled intelligencer. Surely he knows enough about me by now to be aware that I do not have any children of my own?"

"I suppose so."

"And, of course, you already know my views on the digging that has taken place in this field," I continued.

Alexander looked around at the deep holes and piles of earth that had been dug at various points around where we were sitting. "You said they look as though whoever dug them had no idea what he was doing."

"Precisely," I said, rising to my feet. "They are randomly distributed and too numerous. Do you really think a professional like Bressy, or even one of his lackeys, would dig up this field without knowing exactly where he was looking? Surely this is the work of someone else?"

Alexander strode over to the nearest hole and swished his boot around thoughtfully in the loose earth at the edge. "That is an interesting conjecture," he said. "As you have said yourself, Bressy must be involved, but, if that is the case, why does he continue to hold Amy? The message you hold suggests he wants us to surrender the engraving to him, but he has already taken that from Kinshaw."

"Exactly. So where is Amy now?"

"I don't know," said Alexander, with a grimace, "but one thing is clear. To find the answer to these questions, we have but one course of action open to us."

I nodded grimly, for I knew what my friend was alluding to. "We must seek out Maisterson and Wilbraham and persuade them to take us to Combermere," I said.

# Chapter 11

The road from Nantwich to Combermere crosses the Weaver at Shrewbridge and rises slowly as it leaves the proximity of the river, passing through green fields surrounding the hamlets of Sound, Broomhall Green, and Aston as it weaves its way into Shropshire and eventually to the town of Whitchurch. Just after Newhall, a track leads off to the right towards the two lakes which sit either side of the Cotton family's magnificent house, converted from the residence of the abbot of the monastery that once stood there, the long, slender Combermere on the west, bordered by mature oak trees, and the smaller Danesmere on the eastern side.

The route is one with which I am not overly familiar, for most of the farms which supply my cheese sit on the opposite side of the river, closer to my home village of Barthomley. My travelling companion seemed much better acquainted with the landscape than I, which, on balance, was a good thing, although it would have been preferable if he had been a little less taciturn. Roger Wilbraham, however, had said very little to me since the previous Friday, when I had revealed to him and Maisterson that Brett's engraving was lost.

This revelation had led to a series of curses on the part of the two merchants, the like of which I had seldom heard before from gentlemen of such breeding. This, however, had turned to concern when they were told that Amy was still missing. Maisterson had berated us for our carelessness, but ultimately both gentlemen agreed that I needed to travel to Combermere with at least one of them, and so a rider was despatched, asking the Cottons to prepare for our visit.

In the end, it was decided that Maisterson would stay behind in Nantwich and I would borrow his engraving, pretending it was Brett's. I would present myself as representing the interests of Brett's estate, hoping that the Cottons, as regular customers of Brett's, would be willing to help Wilbraham and myself cast some light on the history behind the engravings.

The two gentlemen had made it clear that they had not yet divulged all they knew about the engravings, and Maisterson promised that Wilbraham would reveal more to me during the ride. However, by the time I steered my bay mare, Demeter, down the track that led to the former abbey, the young gentleman had still not ventured any further information, and I was beginning to wonder whether the ride might end up being something of a wild goose chase.

In truth, though, I did not mind the diversion. I was pleased to be able to escape from Nantwich for a while, for the five days since Amy's disappearance had been fraught with anxiety.

Firstly, there had been no trace whatsoever of Amy, nor – and this was the most worrying aspect – had there been any further communication from her captor. I did not dare voice the opinion openly, but I began to wonder whether the kidnapper, having managed to secure the engraving from Kinshaw, had decided to dispose of Amy in the cruellest way possible; after all, he had already committed one murder.

Croxton, to his credit, had all the hedgerows for two miles on the eastern bank of the river searched for signs of her, and when that produced nothing, he sent a search party downriver as far as Beam Heath to check whether a body had been washed up among the reeds, but there was no sign of her.

All this had made Mrs Padgett more and more frantic, although she busied herself as best she could by cooking up warming broths and potions for Ralph, who had caught a fever as a result of the time he had spent kneeling in the river.

Alexander, meanwhile, was in a mood because Maisterson and Wilbraham had refused to allow him to travel to Combermere with Wilbraham and myself.

Instead, I asked my friend to monitor the movements of Jacob Fletcher and to see whether he could discover a reason for the antipathy shown to the briner by Eldrid Cripps. Alexander's grumpy acquiescence was a sign that I should leave him to his own devices for a while, and consequently I had not seen him for several days.

And if all this were not enough, I had been summoned the day before to Colonel Booth's quarters in The Lamb to receive a letter from Simon. The letter, I noticed, carried the seal of the Eastern Association. I broke the seal carefully and began to read;

*My dear brother,*

*I write to you from our quarters in the town of Doncaster, where our unit of dragoons rests, following our momentous victory near York. I am well and in good spirits, buoyed by the fact that I serve under such a committed officer as Lt. Colonel Lilburne.*

*We are keen to press home our advantage in these parts, and today we march on the castle at Tickhill at the Lt. Colonel's own behest, where it is believed the incumbent malignants are low in morale and ready to surrender. I therefore hope to have more good news to impart the next time I write.*

*In the meantime, I am pleased to be able to tell you that James Skinner survived the slaughter on Marston Moor without injury and now serves amongst our number. I discovered him, weak and hungry, among a group of prisoners outside York. He was happy to switch his allegiance to our cause, for which I thank God heartily.*

*Please remember me to Mother, Father, and George, should you pass by Barthomley, and to Elizabeth, to whom I understand you are now wed. It is a matter of great regret that I was not able to be present on that day.*

*Please also tell Rose she is always in my thoughts and that I will write to her separately.*

*Your loving brother,*
*Simon*

It was, of course, an unexpected pleasure to hear the news about Skinner, even more so for my erstwhile apprentice's brothers, Jack and Robert, who, as good parliamentarians, were as delighted that their younger sibling was no longer under the influence of royalists as they were that he was still in one piece. Unsurprisingly, though, the reaction I received from Rose Bailey to news of Simon's letter was not quite so positive, and I was curtly informed that, as far as she was concerned, it would be of no consequence if she never set eyes on my brother again, let alone received a letter from him.

From this I deduced that Rose had not yet had any kind of direct communication from Simon, and so I was forced to compose a letter to my brother explaining that he was no longer betrothed and that his intended wife was now seeing someone else.

The change of scenery had therefore come as a welcome relief, and as Wilbraham and I rode through the countryside, my mind began to turn once again to the question of the curious engravings from Combermere, and I remembered that Wilbraham had not yet told me the full story of their origin.

"We cannot ride the whole way to Combermere in silence," I said, eventually. "You told me you had further information to impart about these engravings. Now would be a good time to tell me."

Wilbraham brought his horse to a stop and looked at me carefully. "Very well," he said. "I have little choice but to put my trust in you, although God knows I wish there was an alternative."

I looked askance at my young companion and decided there was nothing to be gained by ignoring the young gentleman's lack of courtesy.

"It is a great comfort to know I have your full confidence," I replied, making sure my tone conveyed an appropriate degree of sarcasm.

"You may have wondered," said Wilbraham, disregarding the barb, "why Maisterson and I considered it so important for you to accompany us to Combermere and why we are so confident that the solution to the riddle of Abbot Massey's engravings is to be found here."

"I had assumed that the Cottons, as current owners of the abbey, might have some historical knowledge about the engravings that we are not party to. George Cotton, the owner of the Combermere Estate, must be in his eighties. His father would have known Massey. An interview with him might prove enlightening."

"You may well be right," agreed Wilbraham, "and we shall certainly speak to George Cotton, but that is not the real reason we are here. The person we need to speak to is one of the stewards at Combermere, and his name is Geffery Crewe."

The shock of hearing this surname, the name of the accepted murderer of Roger Crockett, must have made me jolt in the saddle, for Demeter whinnied in protest, and I had to stroke her neck gently to calm her down. Wilbraham, meanwhile, smiled in amusement.

"I see from your reaction that this name is familiar to you," he said. "This does not surprise me, I must confess, for you are a shrewd investigator. I knew it would not be long before you started to draw a connection between the various people entrusted by John Massey with engravings and the unfortunate death of Roger Crockett over seventy years ago."

I nudged Demeter into a slow trot and gestured for Wilbraham to do likewise.

"It is not difficult to deduce," I said. "The whole town is now abuzz with stories of how the Hassall family losing the lease to Ridley Field was an omen – a portent of a violent death in Nantwich."

"Old wives' tales," said Wilbraham, dismissively, "but there is plenty to tell about that particular event. You must understand, it has had a profound effect on my family, for my great-grandfather was very nearly put on trial for the murder of Roger Crockett."

"Unjustly, of course."

"Of course," scowled Wilbraham. "He was the target of a vendetta by Crockett's wife. As you know, Edmund Crewe was the name of the man who killed Crockett."

"Indeed; so what is the connection between this historical murder and what is happening today, and who is this Geffery Crewe who is employed at Combermere?"

"To answer that," said Wilbraham, "I need to take you back to the fifteen seventies and explain the relationships between the leading families in Nantwich at that time. The Wilbraham and Maisterson families have always been close, and in those days my great-grandfather Richard Wilbraham was married to the former Elizabeth Maisterson, while Richard Hassall was married to Anne Maisterson, both John Maisterson's sisters.

"Our three families were therefore closely related by

marriage, and it did not take long for the three men to realise that each of them was one of Massey's trustees."

"So I presume you are also aware of the secret word on Hassall's engraving?" I ventured.

"Unfortunately not. At that time, the three families kept to Massey's wish and did not attempt to work out the significance of each other's engravings. Their loyalty to Massey was such that they would have dutifully waited for a call from the seventh trustee before revealing their engraving to the group. It is only recently, in fact, that Thomas Maisterson and I have realised the significance of the secret wording on each engraving."

"I see," I said. "So where does Crockett come in?"

"Crockett was an up-and-coming merchant, who had made his own money. He was very successful, but he was also very indiscreet and not used to conducting himself in the way expected of a gentleman. He was, however, very good friends with a man called Thomas Wettenhall, who was from another prominent local family. Wettenhall, as it happened, was married to another of John Maisterson's sisters.

"When the dispute broke out between Crockett and Hassall over Ridley Field, Wettenhall supported Crockett, which caused a rift within the Maisterson family. Crockett's mistake, however, was to inform Wettenhall that he was one of Massey's trustees. What was more, he let it slip that his pursuit of the lease to

Ridley Field was in some way connected to this. This information, of course, found its way back to John Maisterson, through his sister, fortunately before the rift had got to the point where they were no longer talking to each other.

"At this point, John Maisterson, Richard Hassall, and my great-grandfather deduced that Massey's treasure must be buried somewhere in the field, and suspected that Crockett planned to try and find the treasure and keep it for himself, contrary to Massey's wishes."

"So Crockett's plan to drain the field was presumably part of a strategy to make it easier to find the treasure," I suggested.

"So it was suspected," confirmed Wilbraham, "and so our three families swore to try and protect the field, in order to preserve Massey's legacy."

"But they would have failed, were it not for Crockett's death."

Wilbraham did not answer, but the silence was enough to confirm my suspicions. I rode in silence for a few moments while I tried to process this new information. The implications of Roger Wilbraham's words were truly shocking.

"Are you telling me," I asked, eventually, "that Richard Wilbraham, John Maisterson, and Richard Hassall conspired to murder Roger Crockett?"

"No, no," exclaimed Wilbraham, his face paling. "You misunderstand what I am saying. The plan was to teach Crockett a lesson, once and for all, to bring him into line and make him realise that if he tried to break the pact made between Massey and his trustees, he would regret it."

"But the plan went awry?"

"Unfortunately so. Edmund Crewe was rather too enthusiastic in his approach and hit Crockett so hard on the head that it was clear he was going to die. Hassall's wife tried to help, but saw that the cause was hopeless, and so my great-grandfather was summoned from his bed. You already know the story from there. Crockett was helped back to The Crown by my great-grandfather and others, but unfortunately he died later that day."

"So what happened to Crockett's engraving?" I asked, already knowing the answer.

"The story passed down by my great-grandfather was that, in the face of his approaching death, Crockett became rather penitent and realised his greed was the cause of his predicament – not only that, he came to the conclusion that his fate was divine providence – God's judgement on his behaviour. He therefore repented and gave the engraving to my great-grandfather to find a new trustee.

"When Bridgett Crockett found out about this the following morning, however, she was incandescent with rage and demanded the engraving back, but my great-grandfather refused. It was the beginning of her attempt to have my great-grandfather and several others brought to trial for her husband's murder.

"In the meantime, Edmund Crewe was spirited away, first to Wrenbury and then out of the county, but not before Maisterson, Hassall, and my great-grandfather had made the decision to make Crewe the new trustee. He was the obvious choice considering that he would have had to abide by the others' wishes in relation to the engraving, for fear of his location being betrayed by them and being brought back to face justice in Cheshire.

"Crewe escaped down to the West Country and spent several years at sea, as far away as possible from justice. He was said to have served under Sir Francis Drake for many years, but after that, all contact was lost with him.

"For fifty years our family had no inkling of what had happened to Edmund Crewe or whether he had any descendants. About nine months ago, however, I happened to be visiting the Cotton family at Combermere. George Cotton's son, Thomas, was, at that time, attempting to curry favour with other prominent royalist families in the area, with the aim that his family might benefit should Lord Byron's forces eventually take Nantwich. In the event, he allowed Combermere to be used as a base for royalist forces in the lead up to the battle in January.

"During that visit, I learned that the steward in charge

at the stables was called Geffery Crewe. I considered this to be a coincidence I could not ignore, and so I took pains to get to know him. I managed to ascertain that Crewe, who is now in his forties, is the grandson of Crockett's killer. He was born in Devon but says he had always felt a calling to come to Combermere, that his destiny was somehow linked to the abbey and the story of Massey's engravings. He had no idea who any of the other trustees were, so, you can imagine, he was pleased to have made my acquaintance. As a result, we have stayed in touch ever since.

"A few weeks ago, I received a letter from him, saying he felt he was in danger. He did not elaborate, other than to say an attempt had been made on his life and that his lodgings had been ransacked. He wondered whether this might have some connection to Massey's engravings. When Henry Hassall was murdered, I put two and two together and wrote to him, telling him to be vigilant."

At that moment, Wilbraham and I rode around a bend in the track, and a wide vista opened up, showing that we had almost reached our goal. To the right, the long, thin stretch of water that was Combermere shimmered in the sunlight. Next to it, in the distance, stood a large, white, half-timbered mansion, in front of which was a walled courtyard. This was approached by a wide grassy avenue, which lead through orchards interspersed with man-made fish ponds. In the foreground stood a large farm building, which guarded the entrance to the Combermere Estate. I realised that we were approaching the Cotton family residence from the rear.

"It seems we have arrived," I said, "so we must guard our words, once we reach the gates. But tell me, if you have taken the trouble to become acquainted with this Geffery Crewe, surely you will have been able to ascertain the secret word that is on his engraving?"

Wilbraham smiled enigmatically and dug his knees into his horse's flanks to hurry him up. "Master Cheswis," he said, "I believe you already know the answer to that question. The word on Crewe's engraving is 'Ridley'."

# Chapter 12

*Combermere – Wednesday, July 31st, 1644*

At the entrance to the estate, Wilbraham and I were met by a lone gamekeeper, who directed us towards the collection of farm buildings which stood between the lake and the wide avenue leading to the rear of the main house. We were asked to wait in the farm steward's lodge, a round brick building with a pointed slate roof, where, after a ten minute delay, we were attended by a smartly dressed but hurried-looking member of the household, who Wilbraham seemed to know. He introduced himself to me as Abraham Gorste, personal assistant to the head steward.

"Please accept my apologies, Mr Wilbraham," he said. "We were not expecting you quite so soon, and, as you will soon see, we have several guests on the estate tonight."

"It is of no import," said Wilbraham, waving his hand dismissively. "We have made good time. The road here has been dry and clear, although we are a little tired."

"Then I will show you to the house," said Gorste. "Please bring your horses and follow me. Grooms are waiting at the front gates, and they will take your mounts to the stables. I will then show you to your rooms. Mr Cotton is looking forward to receiving you."

Instead of leading us back to the grassy avenue which cut through the middle of the orchards, Gorste directed us towards a narrow and dusty track lined with apple trees, which skirted the orchards and the side of the walled courtyard, before emerging at a jetty and a large boathouse at the edge of the lake.

The assistant steward, having recovered his composure, chatted to us in a genial manner as we led our horses down the track. In his early thirties, Gorste was a tall man with an athletic build and a loping stride. Wilbraham, I noticed, being short in stature, had to quicken his step to keep up with him.

"The main avenue to the rear of the house is currently closed," explained Gorste. "In January, the grounds of the house were used as a temporary camp for the King's army, and his artillery units churned up the ground to the point where it became unusable. The avenue has been levelled and re-seeded, but it is still not ready to be walked upon, even though the soldiers are long gone."

"The Cottons have been strong supporters of His

Majesty," said Wilbraham, "as have many of us."

"Aye, that they have, sir," concurred Gorste, "not that it will do them much good, I suspect. Now that Parliament has the upper hand hereabouts, I hear Brereton has already put his sequestrators in motion."

"There is a man called Folineux," I said, "who is charged with dealing with the most prominent royalist households. It seems he is not a man to be trifled with."

Wilbraham nodded grimly. "I have met this Folineux," he said. "He is the very epitome of infuriating Puritan righteousness. I have long resigned myself to the likelihood that I will be punished for my support of the King, but this man is like a dog with a bone. For your master's sake, you would do well to keep him at bay for as long as possible."

"Yes, sir," said Gorste. "It would be a shame to see this place reduced by the sequestrators."

Wilbraham, I noticed, was watching me carefully, studying my reaction to the blatantly political statement, but I was not going to reveal my views on such matters in a place steeped as deeply in royalist sympathies as Combermere, especially to one of the household staff. Instead, I changed the subject.

"This seems like a well-managed estate," I said. "You are self-sufficient here?"

"Not completely," said Gorste, "but we are well catered for. As you can see, we have extensive orchards and grow most of our own vegetables. There is also a herb garden in front of the house. We have our own fish breeding ponds to keep the lake fully stocked, and livestock are kept in the fields on the other side of the orchard."

As Gorste was saying this, we walked past a white picket fence, which ran alongside a narrow path leading to a wooden building by the lakeside, in front of which stood a huge circular tank made of wood, perhaps fifteen feet high, from which an intermittent banging noise was emanating.

"The building down by the water is our washhouse," explained Gorste, when he saw me looking. "The water tank which feeds it is usually filled from a conduit, which leads from one of the ponds on the higher ground behind us, although, as you can hear, the tank is currently being re-lined. Maintaining the buildings on an estate like this is a never-ending task."

I nodded and stared across the lake, which shimmered in the sun reflecting off the smooth surface of the water.

"It seems very peaceful here," I said.

"Yes, but it is not always so," said Gorste. "When the wind gets up, it whips across the water and turns the water choppy very quickly. It is no fun being caught out there when that happens, I assure you."

As if on cue, at that moment a rowboat came into view on the other side of the lake, having emerged from behind a small, wooded island close to the opposite bank. On the island was a curious looking hexagonal building with a pointed roof and arched windows, almost like a chapel.

"What is that?" I asked.

"That," said Gorste, "is Mr Thomas Cotton's summerhouse, often used at this time of year to entertain guests to the house. As you can see, that is exactly what is happening today."

I looked more closely at the small wooden craft, which was splashing its way slowly across the lake towards the boathouse. Two men in blue coats, clearly servants, were rowing vigorously, whilst three other men and a woman were relaxing and chatting to each other.

"Who are the guests?" asked Wilbraham.

"You will meet them tonight, sir. They are Lord Herbert of Cherbury and Sir Fulke Hunckes, governor of Shrewsbury. We are honoured to have so many prominent and esteemed gentlemen here at the same time." Gorste cast a pointed look in my direction to let me know that I was excluded from this comment. "I'm afraid I do not know the name of the lady accompanying Sir Fulke."

As the boat came closer, I caught the sound of laughter drifting across the water, and I froze, my mind instantly transported back to my youth, to a meadow near Barthomley, where I had heard that same staccato giggle before. Although the rowboat was still a hundred yards away, I focused my eyes on the woman sat up in the stern, and there was no mistaking it: the same blonde ringlets, the same wave of the hand.

Wherever I was, whoever I was with, she always seemed to have the same debilitating effect on me, and fate, it seemed, had decreed that whenever I least expected it, and whenever I least needed it, she would always be there. What in the name of God, I wondered, was Alice Furnival doing at Combermere?

I must have been staring into space for several seconds, for I suddenly felt Gorste touch me lightly on the shoulder.

"Are you quite alright, sir?" he asked. "You seem somewhat discomfited."

I quickly pulled myself together and tugged lightly on Demeter's reins to walk her back towards the house.

"I'm sorry," I said. "I felt a little faint all of a sudden. It must have been the exertion of the ride. It is a warm day."

Gorste nodded his understanding and began to lead the way past the boathouse towards the front of the main building, where I could see two grooms were already waiting for us. The steward had seemingly noticed nothing unusual in my reaction, but Wilbraham had not missed its significance, and he gave me a questioning look.

"Later," I said, once Gorste was out of earshot. "The stakes, it seems, have just been raised."

"So what was that all about?" demanded Wilbraham from the doorway of my chamber. Twenty minutes had passed since I had seen Alice being rowed across the lake, and in the meantime Wilbraham and I had been shown to separate rooms on the first floor of the main house. Wilbraham, I realised, must have exaggerated my importance to the Cottons, for I was quite unused to being granted a room so well-appointed. Once Gorste had left me, I had gone over to the window and realised that my chamber had a fine view across the mere.

Directly below my window, Alice was stood talking to Lord Herbert, Sir Fulke Hunckes, and the third man, a broad-built fellow in his thirties, who I took to be Thomas Cotton. Perhaps the shock of seeing my first love again had addled my brain and caused it to play tricks on me, but I could have sworn Alice looked up towards where I was standing and smiled.

"Come inside and close the door, Mr Wilbraham," I said. "I am not sure what is going on here, but our circumstances appear to have changed."

"Changed?" said Wilbraham, an edge to his voice. "What do you mean?"

It was a moment for decisions. It was common knowledge in Nantwich that Hugh Furnival had been a royalist spy and had been the man responsible for the murder of Ralph Brett, but few knew the full story.

Wilbraham, although he had met Alice, would not have been aware of the degree to which she had been implicated in the plot, and Bressy, Furnival's partner in crime, was only known to a limited number of soldiers, with whom he had served. To the townsfolk he was an unknown, and Colonel Booth had insisted on keeping it so.

I realised I was faced with a stark choice. I would either have to confide in Wilbraham, a known royalist sympathiser, or abort the visit to Combermere and return to Nantwich empty-handed. I took a deep breath and went with my gut instinct.

"The woman in the boat," I said. "I recognised her. It was Alice, the widow of Hugh Furnival."

"The man who murdered your wife's first husband?" Wilbraham shrugged, nonplussed. "I can see how that might present an awkward situation for you," he said, "but surely it is not so surprising she is here. She was only in Nantwich for a month. I fail to see why that presents such a difficulty for you, unless–"

Wilbraham had been watching me closely as he spoke. It must have been something in my expression that gave me away, for there was a sudden change in Wilbraham's eyes as suspicion dawned.

"Good God, Cheswis," he exclaimed, his face lighting up. "She was your lover, wasn't she? How the devil did you manage that? You are a fast worker, and that is the truth of it."

"No, no," I protested, my face reddening. "You misunderstand me. There was no impropriety when Mrs Furnival was in Nantwich, I assure you."

And so I told Wilbraham how I had known Alice since I was a child, how I had been betrothed to her, and how she had left me for Furnival all those years ago. I then explained how she and her husband had used me to gain information about the murder of William Tench in order to try and dupe me into believing that the murders of Ralph Brett and James Nuttall were carried out by the same person who had killed Tench. What I did not mention, of course, was how I had rescued Alice from St Mary's Church after the battle and helped her escape back to Shrewsbury.

When I had finished, Wilbraham slapped his thigh and guffawed loudly. "That is some story," he chuckled. "You are something of a dark horse, Cheswis. I would not have credited it, but you have gone up in my estimations."

"Wait," I added. "That is not all of it. There's still the matter of Jem Bressy."

Wilbraham frowned, pulled out a chair from under an ornately carved oak desk that stood in the corner of the room, and rested his forearms on the back of it.

"Bressy? Who is he?" he asked, serious once again.

"Jem Bressy," I replied, "is a royalist spy. He was Hugh Furnival's accomplice in the murder of Ralph Brett and Lady Norton's footman, James Nuttall, but, unlike Furnival, he managed to escape to Chester after the battle in January."

"But what relevance is that to our current situation?"

"Bressy, I believe, may be one of Massey's six trustees. He has been seen recently in Nantwich both by my wife and by my apprentice, Jack Wade, with whom he once served; he bears a striking resemblance to Jacob Fletcher, who was originally arrested for Henry Hassall's murder, and, as I have since discovered, a Bressy is listed among the witnesses at Roger Crockett's inquest back in fifteen seventy-two. Furthermore, although I have no idea what Alice Furnival is doing here at Combermere, my guess is that Jem Bressy is not far away."

Wilbraham give a derisive snort. "That is mostly circumstantial evidence and supposition," he said. "What makes you so sure that this Bressy is connected to the search for Massey's treasure?"

There was no escaping it now. If I was to have any chance of finding out what had happened to Amy, I was obliged to place my full trust in Wilbraham and hope that he would not betray me.

"Because," I said, "Bressy is known to be searching for a hoard of plate, gold, and other valuables, located somewhere in Nantwich, which he intends to purloin for the royalist cause."

Wilbraham said nothing, but sat down on the oak chair and looked at me intently. I could see the young

175

gentleman working out the implications of what I had just said. When he spoke again, his voice was quiet but assured.

"If you are privy to this kind of information," he said, "then that can mean but one thing. You must be an intelligencer yourself. One of Brereton's men, I presume. How long has this been going on for? Since before the battle at Nantwich?"

"No," I said, "after that, and not on my own instigation either, I assure you. And in case you were thinking it, betraying me will serve little purpose. There are plenty in the King's service who already know who I am."

Wilbraham laughed sardonically. "I may be many things, Mr Cheswis, but I am no fool. If I were to ride to Combermere with one of Brereton's agents and betray him to the royalists, what do you suppose would happen? I live in Nantwich, man! If I were to betray you, it would not look good for me, and that is the truth, especially with Brereton's collector, Folineux, sniffing around Townsend House."

"He's already been there?" I asked, surprised.

"Of course. My family is among the most prominent in Nantwich. It did not take long for him to come knocking. My head footman managed to stall him by pretending I was not at home, but he will be back."

"So what do you propose?" I asked, realising my position was not quite as weak as it seemed.

"A partnership of convenience, of course," said Wilbraham, proffering a hand for me to shake. "We are both in danger as long as Hassall's murderer is at large. We must also try and find out what happened to Amy Padgett and locate your wife's engraving, with a view to finding the treasure before Bressy does. Let us deal with priorities and focus on why we are here."

I nodded in acknowledgement and took Wilbraham's outstretched hand.

"So, what do we do now?" I asked.

"We go and talk to George Cotton," said Wilbraham. "He will see us in the library in five minutes."

* * *

George Cotton was already waiting for us when we arrived in the library. Standing by one of the windows which looked out over the courtyard at the front of the house, he cut a sprightly figure, despite his age. Quite unlike his son, Cotton was thin and wiry in build, with a sharp, intelligent face and a neatly trimmed grey beard. He smiled genially as Wilbraham approached.

"Mr Wilbraham. It is indeed an honour to welcome you to Combermere once again, and so soon after your last visit," he said, extending his arm.

"The honour is all mine," replied Wilbraham. "It is always a pleasure to visit you in such fine and inspiring surroundings."

This much, at least, was true. The view from Cotton's library was indeed impressive. Immediately below the window was a finely mowed lawn, dissected by the broad brown sweep of a carriage turning circle. In the middle of the lawn stood a marble sundial, behind which were a set of white entrance gates and a wide boulevard lined with poplars. Beyond that stood a further set of gates fronted by a large statue of a naked man wielding a sword. To the right of this was the boathouse and the shimmering expanse of Combermere Lake – to the left a walled formal garden, beyond which stood the stables and the smaller lake known as Danesmere.

I looked over towards the stables, where there appeared to be something of a disturbance. A horse was being led out into a pathway whilst several grooms appeared to be rushing around in a concerned manner. I was curious to find out what was going on, but my attention was drawn away by Cotton, who responded to Wilbraham's comment with mock dismissiveness.

"Tush, sir," he said. "The Wilbrahams are always welcome here. And this must be Master Daniel Cheswis," he added, turning to me. "A man of some investigative talent, so I hear, and a merchant with growing interests in salt and cheese. Welcome to Combermere, sir."

I shot a glance at Wilbraham, who appeared to be trying to stifle a grin.

"You flatter me, sir," I said, making a mental note of the fact that Cotton appeared well aware of my former status as a constable.

Cotton said nothing, but shepherded us past a large dining table towards an oak-panelled settle situated in front of an elaborate fireplace on the opposite side of the room. I looked above the hearth and realised there could be no doubt how the Cotton family had come about its wealth. Ornately designed, with an eclectic mixture of Celtic motifs and images from the New World, set above the more familiar sight of the coat of arms of England, the fireplace was dominated by four portraits lined up horizontally. Those on the far left and far right were of gentlemen I did not recognise, but the other two subjects were unmistakeable. Next to the sharp features and red hair of Queen Elizabeth hung the thin-lipped corpulence of Great King Henry.

"We have much to thank the Tudors for," said Cotton, reading my thoughts. "The portraits above the fireplace reflect that truth. The man on the left wearing the ruff is my father. The other portrait is of me as a young man."

"It is a long time since King Henry was alive," I said, "but there are many in Nantwich who have not forgotten that Queen Elizabeth made a personal contribution to rebuilding the town when it burned down in fifteen eighty-three."

"Indeed," agreed Cotton. "If it had not been for

Her Majesty's generosity, Nantwich would not have developed into the wealthy town it is today. There are those that would say it is a shame that the town's current generation of inhabitants appear to have forgotten the contribution of the monarchy to their town's well-being and have chosen to side with the rebels."

I was rescued from being dragged into a political debate by Wilbraham, who had reached inside his doublet and pulled out his pewter engraving.

"Mr Cotton," he said. "Your family were granted this estate after King Henry dissolved the abbey, but the last abbot of this place must have still been alive when you were in your youth. Do you remember him at all?"

"Abbot Massey? I'm afraid my memories of him are very vague. I was still a small boy when he died. He came here once to see my father, though, as I recall. There was something sad and broken about him, but that is not surprising, I suppose. By that time the abbey had been demolished and his own residence converted into this house as it is today."

Wilbraham pursed his lips and placed his engraving on the table in front of him. "Do you recall ever seeing anything like this before?" he asked.

Cotton frowned and picked up the engraving, turning it over between his fingers and inspecting it closely.

"What is it?" he asked, with suspicion. "It carries the mark of the Cistercian order. It looks like some relic from the abbey."

"That may well be the case," admitted Wilbraham, "but is it familiar to you? That is what I would wish to know."

"I believe so. It is a most curious artefact, so I would not easily forget. Several months ago our head groom, Geffery Crewe, came to me with such a thing and asked me similar questions to those you are asking now."

Wilbraham exhaled and aimed a self-satisfied smile in my direction. I chose to ignore my companion and stepped in with a question of my own.

"That is most illuminating, Mr Cotton," I said. "Tell me, a few years after Abbot Massey's death, the landlord of The Crown in Nantwich was murdered. Do you recall anything about that from your youth? I believe at the time it was treated as a most infamous occurrence."

"You mean Mr Crockett? You are right. His untimely death was the talk of Nantwich. I was still only twelve, but I recall my father being deeply shocked, for he was known to Roger Crockett, but I do not understand what that has got to do with – oh, I see," he corrected, light suddenly dawning, "you wish to draw a connection with my head groom. Geffery Crewe's grandfather, whose name was Edmund, was accused of having committed the murder."

"And you knew this?" I asked, dumbfounded.

"Of course. Crewe told me his history when he first

asked for work here. I had no reason to deny him a living. It was not he who was a murderer, after all, and he certainly knew how to handle horses. Such men are not so easy to come by nowadays. Tell me, Mr Cheswis, where is this line of questioning heading?"

"I'm not sure," I answered, honestly, "but I believe having possession of one of these engravings may be a dangerous thing at present, and both Mr Wilbraham and I stand to be affected. We would speak to Mr Crewe as soon as is sensibly convenient."

At that precise moment there was a gentle knock on the door, and a young footman entered.

"Yes, what is it, Cooper?" snapped Cotton. "I thought I said I was not to be disturbed."

"I k-know it, sir," stammered the servant, "but begging your pardon, you are to come straight away, sir. To the stables. There has been a terrible accident."

Wilbraham and I looked at each other, and a dark sense of foreboding began to overwhelm me.

"Accident?" said Cotton. "What kind of accident?"

"It-it's the head g-groom, sir. Mr Crewe," blurted the youth, who was trying hard to stop his words tumbling out over themselves. "He has been kicked in the head by one of the horses. I fear he may be dead."

# Chapter 13

*Combermere – Wednesday, July 31st, 1644*

The stable block was in a state of some confusion by the time Cotton, Wilbraham, and I arrived on the scene. A small crowd of footmen, grooms, housemaids, and other servants had gathered around the entrance to the far left hand building of a group of four timber-framed brick barns, which lined the bank of Danesmere.

Abraham Gorste was stood in defensive posture by the doorway, trying manfully to keep the crowd at bay. He looked relieved when he saw Cotton coming, and the melee of curious onlookers began to part.

"He's in here, sir," said Gorste. "In the farrier's workshop. Seems he were treating a lame horse."

Without being asked, Wilbraham and I followed Cotton into the barn. There, lying flat on his back, his hand still gripping a pair of clinchers, was a dark-haired man of medium build, quite plainly dead, the left side of his face covered in blood. As my eyes became accustomed to the light inside the workshop, I noticed that there was an ugly-looking dent in the side of his skull, just above the left temple. His eyes, one blue, the other blood red, stared up at the rafters and conveyed only astonishment at his sudden demise.

"May God have mercy," exclaimed Cotton through clenched teeth, his voice rising a notch. "How did this happen?"

"I cannot say, sir," said Gorste. "Martland found him. I was going to the bakehouse nearby and came running as soon as I heard the shouts."

"Is that true, Martland?" asked Cotton.

It was then that I noticed one of the young grooms, who had taken our horses, sitting on a bale of hay, his neck tucked into his chin and clearly in shock.

"Aye, sir," he said, his voice little more than a whisper. "I noticed one of the gentlemen's horses appeared to have turned lame, so I brought it in here for Mr Crewe to take a look at. I'd only been gone a couple of minutes when I heard a commotion and a loud cry coming from in here. I came back straight away and found Mr Crewe like this. He were stone dead, sir."

"Wait a minute," interjected Wilbraham. "You say he was kicked to death by one of our horses?"

"I'm afraid so, sir. It was the bay mare. She was all het up and sweating, so I calmed her down and put her in the stable next door."

"Demeter?" I gasped, disbelieving. "Are you saying

my mare did this?"

"Yes, sir. I'm sorry, sir. I left her with Joe Beckett, the other groom, to try and quieten her down. I'll get him to fetch her in. She might be a bit calmer now."

With that, the young groom hauled himself to his feet and shuffled his way out of the door.

As soon as Martland had left, Cotton directed Gorste to clear the curious crowd of servants, maids, and gardeners from the immediate environs of the farrier's workshop and get them back to their work, after which he was tasked with riding to Whitchurch to locate the coroner.

I got the strange impression that Gorste was keen to remain in the stables and follow our discussions, for I thought I caught a slight twitch of irritation touch the corner of his mouth. Nonetheless, he bowed deferentially to Cotton and set about shooing the onlookers back to the house and the various workshops that lay in between Danesmere and the orchards.

A few moments later, Martland returned with the other groom, who was leading a clearly agitated Demeter by the reins and stroking her neck in an attempt to pacify her. She had, I noticed, clearly gone lame in one of her hind legs. It always pained me to see my mare in distress, and so it was now. She whickered quietly in recognition as I took the reins from Beckett.

"She wasn't lame when we arrived," I said to Martland.

"I know," replied the groom. "I can't understand it myself. There was nothing wrong with her when I brought her into the stables. Here, see if you can keep her still a minute. I'll take a look at her hooves.

I nodded and blew gently into Demeter's nostrils to keep her calm, whilst Martland inspected her left hind hoof.

"That's strange," he said, after a couple of moments. "She has a piece of flint jammed in her hoof."

I felt Demeter wince as the groom extracted the sharp piece of stone, but fortunately she stayed calm and did not struggle.

"Strange?" I said. "How so? These things happen, surely?"

"Aye, sir," said Martland, "but this kind of flint is only used in the walled garden, and we did not take the horses through there. I cannot imagine how she got an injury like this."

I handed Demeter's reins to Wilbraham and moved round to where Martland was holding Demeter's foreleg between his own legs. Her hoof was oozing blood where Martland had removed the sharp piece of stone. The implication of the groom's words were that someone had deliberately jammed a piece of flint into the hoof. I already had my suspicions as to who might have been callous enough to do such a thing.

It was then that I noticed something else. On Demeter's hind quarters was a red mark the size of a coin. I touched it and was astonished to see a few flecks of dried blood on my fingers.

"God's death!" exclaimed Martland. "Is that what I think it is?"

"I don't know," I said, grimly, "but wait a minute." I looked at where the prone body of Geffery Crewe was lying and then tried to picture where Demeter must have been standing when she kicked him. I cast my eyes down towards the stone floor, and my eyes immediately focussed on a dull, metallic object lodged between two of the stones. I got down on my knees and prised the object out from between the slabs.

"Here," I said. "Demeter must have stood on it after she kicked out."

Cotton, who, during this interchange had been looking from Martland to myself in a bemused fashion, suddenly realised the importance of what I had discovered.

"Good Lord, man," he breathed. "A musket ball! Are you suggesting that someone shot your horse?"

"Not shot, sir," I said. "Firstly, no-one heard a gunshot, as far as I can make out. If they had, someone would have already mentioned. Secondly, if you look at right angles to where Demeter would have been standing, you can clearly see where the musket ball must have originated from."

Cotton glanced over towards the rear of the workshop, where an open barn door led out to a small yard. Beyond this lay a jungle of trees and untended vegetation, which lined the banks of Danesmere.

Cotton stared at me in bewilderment, but Wilbraham immediately understood my meaning.

"The trees are too close," he said. "The musket ball has only scratched your mare's skin. If someone had shot her from that range, she would have been in no condition to kick Crewe."

"Maybe someone threw the musket ball, or used a stone-bow, or some other such weapon," I said. "But truly, it is of no import, for the intention was not to hurt Demeter, but to murder Crewe."

Cotton blanched and stared at me as though he had been shot himself. "Murder?" he croaked. "At Combermere?"

"Yes, Mr Cotton," said Wilbraham, warming to the task. "By making Master Cheswis's mare kick Mr Crewe in the head. Very clever," he added, turning to me with a wry smile. "If it works, the murderer achieves his aim. If it doesn't, and the horse's kick misses Crewe's head, there is very little to prove that there was a deliberate attempt to kill him, and the perpetrator survives to try again later."

"So it would seem," I agreed.

Cotton, meanwhile, was regarding us both with a frown. "Something," he said, "makes me suspect you both already knew Geffery Crewe was in danger. Please tell me that is not the case."

"I'm afraid you are right, Mr Cotton," admitted Wilbraham. "It is connected with the engravings we showed you, although more than this we cannot tell you."

Cotton bridled. "You cannot tell me?" he protested. "A man is murdered on my property, and you suggest I do not have the right to know why? I suggest we bring the local constables here and conduct a full investigation."

At this point, I held up my hand to intervene. "Mr Cotton," I said, "I'm afraid that would not be the most appropriate course of action at the moment. I would suggest it would be more sensible if we let the murderer think he has got away with it and let the coroner, at least for the time being, conclude that this was merely a tragic accident."

"You mean hide the evidence – the horse's injuries and the musket ball?"

"Precisely. This murderer is a dangerous man, but he is also determined, and he may well reveal himself again soon. I would ask, in the meantime, that no-one outside these stables discusses what has happened here with anyone else."

"Except with my son, of course," said Cotton. "He will need to know."

"Especially your son, sir," I said. "At the risk of sounding disrespectful, your son's movements have not yet been accounted for, and he has guests here who we would rather not be made aware of these developments. Do you know, incidentally, why they are here?"

Cotton looked at me with astonishment. "Of course not," he said. "What are you suggesting? They are guests of my son. That is his business. What does it have to do with you?"

"In all probability, absolutely nothing," said Wilbraham, sensing trouble. "I promise you we will reveal our reasoning in due course, but in the meantime we would appreciate your discretion. I assure you it will be in your best interests."

Cotton hesitated a moment, but then nodded. "You have my word," he said. "I would not accept this from anyone but a Wilbraham. But what about the two grooms?"

Martland and Beckett had been stood listening to this exchange with incomprehension on their faces.

"They will need to be sworn to silence too," I said.

"But your mare has been in their care since we arrived here," pointed out Wilbraham. "How can you be sure they have nothing to do with this?"

"I can't," I admitted, "but I have seen enough of them to be convinced that they care for the horses under their charge. I may be wrong, but I do not get the impression that either of them would deliberately hurt a horse. In any case, apart from we three, they are the only two others who know of my suspicions with regards to Mr Crewe's death. If word gets out, it will not be too difficult to track down who is to blame.

Martland looked at me nervously. "I know not of what you speak, sir," he said, "but Joe and I know how to keep our mouths shut." The other young groom, Beckett, nodded enthusiastically.

"Then let us see what transpires," said Cotton, addressing Wilbraham and myself. "I invite you both to join us for supper this evening, where you will have the opportunity to meet the rest of our house guests."

# Chapter 14

Supper, as it happened, was a rather sombre affair, which, although not surprising given the circumstances, was undoubtedly a shame, for the Cottons had gone out of their way to impress their guests with a generous array of delicacies. There was a herring pie, a shoulder of mutton cooked with thyme, and a soup with ox tongues, followed by nuts, cheese, freshly baked bread, and a syllabub.

Due to the disturbance caused by the events in the stables, the kitchen staff had been late with their preparation, so it was fully seven o'clock before we took our seats in the library. By this time, having not eaten properly at midday, both Wilbraham and I were famished.

There were eight of us in total – George and Thomas Cotton, the latter's wife, a demure woman who said very little all evening, Lord Herbert, Sir Fulke Hunckes, Alice, Wilbraham, and myself. Thomas Cotton and his guests, it emerged, had been taking a stroll through the orchards at the time Crewe had been attacked, and all seemed genuinely shocked at the turn of events.

Alice, I was surprised to find, showed no sign of being in the least discomfited by my presence at the dinner table in such exalted company. This I took to mean that she had already been given prior notice of my status as an invited guest and had had sufficient time to get used to the idea. To my amusement, she began treating me as those I were a new acquaintance.

Wilbraham, to his credit, once again introduced me as an up-and-coming merchant from Nantwich, exaggerating my status beyond its true level. Both Hunckes and Thomas Cotton eyed me with suspicion, especially when I explained that Alice and I had been acquainted with each other since childhood. This revelation, I noticed, caused Alice to purse her lips in irritation.

"Nantwich has not been a happy place for me," remarked Hunckes pointedly, as he peered across the table at me. "To my mind it is full of rebels and traitors."

I smiled evenly at Hunckes. In truth, I did not begrudge the governor of Shrewsbury his viewpoint, for his most recent memory of our town would have been limited to the despoiled interior of St Mary's Church, stinking of the sweat, vomit, and excrement of royalist prisoners. Hunckes, I recalled, had been in command of the regiment of foot that had been tasked with guarding the exit to the sconce at Welsh Row End during January's battle. His unit had been hopelessly outnumbered by the men of the garrison flooding out of the town to aid Fairfax's army, and as a result he and all his men had been captured in a rather ignominious manner without being able to put up much of a fight.

"That particular time was not a happy experience for many of us," agreed Wilbraham. "For my part, I did not particularly relish my house being bombarded with red hot iron bullets by my Lord Byron's artillery. I support the King as you do, Sir Fulke, but we have all had our crosses to bear during this conflict. As for Mr Cheswis, he did not sign the Remonstrance which was circulated in Cheshire prior to the conflict, and which identifies Parliament supporters. That should be enough to demonstrate his good faith."

I had to suppress a smile, for this was a clever move by Wilbraham designed to diffuse a potentially uncomfortable situation. It was true that I had not signed the document Wilbraham was referring to. What he had failed to say, however, was that, at the time, I would not have been considered important enough to have been approached as a potential signatory. Whether Hunckes fully accepted what Wilbraham had said, I could not tell, for the governor of Shrewsbury merely offered an impenetrable smile and remained silent.

Thomas Cotton, however, flashed Hunckes a warning glare. "I must apologise to you, gentlemen," he said. "You are most welcome at Combermere. I think Sir Fulke was merely trying to express his surprise that in such difficult times as these, you would take the trouble to come out of your way to visit us here."

Hunckes emitted an almost imperceptible snort, but Wilbraham did not miss it.

"Sir Fulke, Mr Cheswis and I are here on personal business with Mr Cotton on an issue relating to an inheritance matter that concerns both of us, but not you," he said. "That is all I will say on the matter, unless, of course, you would like to discuss the intimate details of your own business affairs."

Hunckes exchanged glances with Thomas Cotton and reddened, but he bowed his head slightly in acquiescence.

"You are quite right, Mr Wilbraham," he said. "That was most ignoble of me. I apologise unreservedly for my lack of tact, but these are difficult times, and sometimes it is not easy to know with whom you are dealing."

"On that we can all agree," said Lord Herbert, speaking for the first time, "but by the same token, not everyone is desperate to make his choice by casting his lot definitively with one side or the other."

Cotton, I noticed, frowned at this, and Wilbraham looked at the ageing lord with interest.

"Do you speak from experience, my lord?" he asked. "I understand you refused a request from his Highness Prince Rupert to garrison Montgomery earlier this year."

"Of course," replied Herbert. "In sixteen forty-two I was imprisoned by Parliament merely for advocating moderation in their language pertaining to their judgement of the King for making war on Parliament. Ever since that day I have been wary of antagonising either side. It does not pay to pick a fight needlessly.

"It has been clear for some time that Sir Thomas Myddelton, major general for the six counties of North Wales, together with the Earl of Denbigh, has harboured ambitions to push south into the Severn Valley. The only thing that has stopped him has been the need to provide support to Sir William Brereton in Nantwich and, more recently, to Sir Thomas Fairfax in York, but now, with Prince Rupert defeated and licking his wounds in Chester, you can be sure Myddelton will be looking at Montgomeryshire with more interest. He has already taken Oswestry, to Sir Fulke's detriment."

"That is true," agreed Hunckes. "The Committee of Both Kingdoms gave him the permission to resume his plans not two weeks since. If it were not for the fact that he has been detained with the issue of what to do about Prince Rupert in Chester, he would already be in Wales."

"Exactly," Cotton continued. "Don't misunderstand

me. I have no love for Myddelton, but my interest is in preserving my house intact and protecting my valuable library from being plundered. Sometimes it is better to sit on the fence. As things stand it is now Lord Powys at Red Castle near Newtown who has sided most visibly with the King, and consequently it is he who is now in the firing line."

"Yes, my lord," agreed Hunckes, "but reinforcements are on their way. We have it on good authority that Sir Thomas Dallison has been sent south from Chester with a portion of the Prince's own regiment of horse to support Lord Powys, to fortify the area, and raise troops and money for the King."

"Indeed. Which all goes to prove that life will become more uncomfortable, if not intolerable, for the inhabitants of Montgomeryshire in the near future."

I felt sorry for the eccentric old aristocrat. He had spent most of his life in the service of the monarchy, had even been responsible, during his time as ambassador to France, for helping arrange the marriage of the present King to Queen Henrietta Maria. He was quite clearly a royalist, and yet he was now an old man, who wanted nothing more than to live out his days in peace and avoid unnecessary conflict.

Fortunately, George Cotton had noticed Lord Herbert's reluctance to discuss politics, and so the discussion was moved on to more mundane things. I was asked about my ambitions within the cheese business and about my recent marriage to Elizabeth, a subject, which, rather disconcertingly, appeared to interest Alice greatly. Herbert entertained us at length with anecdotes from his youth and from King Henry's court in France, and Alice explained that since her husband's death she had continued to publish and print Hugh Furnival's newssheet, The Public Scout, in Shrewsbury, thanks to the help and co-operation of her husband's partners and employees, as well as the support of local booksellers. It was no wonder, I thought, that she had the ears of the town's governor.

\* \* \*

Once the main courses had been served and the mood had begun to lighten somewhat, thanks in large part to the good quality French wine Cotton had plied us with, I realised that the time was rapidly approaching when I would need to instigate the plan of action that Wilbraham and I had agreed would be necessary, if we were not to return to Nantwich empty-handed.

"You will need to search Crewe's room," Wilbraham had said, pointedly, when we had returned to our chambers earlier that evening.

"And why is that my responsibility?" I had countered, knowing full well that Wilbraham was right. "We should draw lots for it."

"Don't be so dung-witted, Cheswis," the young

gentleman had replied. "You are the skilled investigator, and I am the one used to conducting small talk with the gentry. It is best I keep the guests occupied, whilst you conduct a search."

I had emitted a long and weary sigh of resignation, for there was no countering Wilbraham's argument.

"And how am I supposed to find out which room is Crewe's?" I had asked.

"You forget. I have been here before. Crewe's room is in the servants' block on the ground floor on the opposite side of the house. Third door on the right after the kitchens."

And so it was that, as soon as the nuts, cheese, and bread had been placed on the table, Wilbraham had aimed a conspiratorial grin in my direction and launched himself into a rambling account of King James's visit to Townsend House in 1618, a series of anecdotes no doubt passed onto him by his father, for Wilbraham had not even been born at the time of the old King's visit.

Once I was sure the guests were all fully engrossed in Wilbraham's story, I excused myself on the pretext of needing to go in search of the privy and left the library by the main door next to the central staircase.

Following Wilbraham's instructions, I descended the main stairs and, grateful for the fact that no-one was around who might question my movements, went straight through a doorway on the other side of the hall and passed the entrance to the kitchen, where, as I had correctly guessed, the household staff were too busy consuming the remains of our food to be concerned about house guests roaming the corridors of the servants' quarters.

The area of the house I now found myself in was very different from the opulence of the library – a plain corridor with walls of cold, grey, monastic stone. I realised I was in the remains of Abbot Massey's original residence. I walked across the stone-flagged floor, taking care to make as little noise as possible, until I reached the solid oak door to what I presumed to be Crewe's bedchamber. Tentatively, I turned the handle, pushed the door ajar, and entered the room.

The chamber was sparsely furnished, with a plain truckle bed, a rough-hewn table, and a rickety-looking stool pushed underneath it. On the floor by the window was a large wooden chest, which had been opened and its contents strewn across the floor; mainly clothes, but also a bible and some papers.

Most significantly, though, standing behind the door, wearing a malevolent grin and brandishing a pistol, was the unmistakeable figure of Jem Bressy.

I recoiled with shock at seeing my enemy at such close quarters, and gave a high-pitched gasp of astonishment, but Bressy merely waved the pistol at me and gestured towards the truckle bed.

"For God's sake, do not squeal like a girl, Mr

Cheswis," he said, simply. "Sit down, if you please. We need to talk."

I must confess, it is not every day that I face the barrel of a gun held by a trained killer such as Bressy, and many would call what I was about to do inexplicable, but at that precise moment I saw with perfect clarity what I needed to do to ascertain for certain whether Bressy had any involvement in Amy's disappearance.

"Talk?" I hissed, jabbing my forefinger in his direction. "Certainly we need to talk. You can begin by telling me what you have done with my daughter, you murdering whoreson bastard."

My unexpected aggression seemed to confuse Bressy, for instead of shooting me between the eyes, which I would have had every right to expect, he lowered the pistol and gave me an inquisitive look.

"Your daughter?" he said. "Has your brain become addled? I know not of what you speak. We need to discuss the matter of a certain set of engravings, but of your daughter I know nothing. I was not even aware you had a daughter."

"I am talking about Amy, the granddaughter of my housekeeper," I persisted. "She is a daughter to me. I am not stupid, Bressy. Confess it. You came to Nantwich, murdered Henry Hassall, assaulted Gilbert Kinshaw, and then kidnapped Amy whilst she was playing in Ridley Field."

Bressy stared at me and shook his head in

201

bewilderment. "Sweet Jesus," he said. "Are you mad? I did none of those things. I confess I gave Hassall's head a good rinsing in his ship, but I was not responsible for his murder. I also admit I ransacked your house trying to find your wife's engraving, but I have been nowhere near Gilbert Kinshaw. What the devil has he got to do with any of this? And as for your daughter, I never saw nor heard from her."

"And you expect me to believe this?"

Bressy shrugged. "Believe what you want," he said, "but I suggest we wait here a few moments, and I will give you good reason why you should not discount what I say."

I had no idea to what Bressy was alluding, but it did not take long to find out, for almost as soon as I had finished speaking, I heard the sound of a woman's footsteps approaching along the corridor outside the room. They stopped momentarily by the door, which was then flung open, and in stepped Alice, looking hot and flustered.

"I am sorry, Bressy," she said. "It was not so easy to escape the dinner table without attracting overdue attention. And your friend Wilbraham can certainly talk," she added, addressing me. "He is trying his level best to keep everyone's attention from the fact that you had obviously left the room for more than just the privy."

"He is no particular friend of mine," I said, "simply a

travelling companion with a shared interest, one which I appear to share with both of you. Firstly, Geffery Crewe is murdered in a manner which is made to look like an accident, then I find Bressy skulking in his bedchamber, and finally you follow me from the dinner table. Tell me, Alice, what on earth is going on?"

"All will become clear, I assure you," replied Alice, "but first there is the matter of Geffery Crewe's engraving. Has it been found?"

Bressy shook his head. "Gone," he said. "See for yourself. We were not quick enough. Whoever killed Crewe got here before me and found what he wanted. Probably escaped that same way I got in, through the window."

My head was beginning to spin. If Bressy was not responsible for Crewe's murder, then who was? I glanced at the wooden frame of the window and saw that it had been forced. Alice, meanwhile, stepped over to the wooden chest on the floor and searched quickly through the pile of garments with irritation.

"Daniel," she said, eventually. "Our absence from the dinner table will be noticed, so I will be brief. There are reasons why Bressy and I are interested in Abbot Massey's engravings."

"This I know," I replied. "You wish to find the treasure he secreted away and transport it to Shrewsbury, where it can be used to help finance the King's war effort."

Alice stared at me with raised eyebrows, whilst

Bressy sat down on the corner of the bed and began to chuckle.

"So you know of our design," he said. "I suppose I should not be surprised. You are an intelligencer after all."

Alice, however, was not smiling. "If he knows what we are about, it can only be because you have been too loose with your tongue," she snapped. "A little less whoring and drinking on your part would have served our purpose well." Alice aimed a withering glare at Bressy, who responded by glowering sullenly and looking out of the window.

"What is it you want of me?" I demanded. "We do not have all night."

"That is true," said Alice. "You will have deduced, no doubt, that we are not the only people searching for Massey's treasure. We do not know the identity of the other party, but what is clear is that he, she, or they are prepared to kill to achieve their aims. Henry Hassall and Geffery Crewe have already lost their lives, and others may be in danger. We believe that if we pool our resources with Mr Wilbraham and yourself, we will have a much better chance of beating our adversary to the hoard."

I looked at Alice in astonishment. "And why the devil would I do that?" I asked.

"I would have thought that was self-evident. Because it is the only way to find out what has happened to Mrs

Padgett's granddaughter."

Bressy looked up in surprise. "You knew about this?" he demanded.

"Of course," said Alice. "You forget, I still have relatives in Nantwich. Amy's disappearance is common knowledge. I confess," she added, turning to me, "I do not hold your housekeeper in any great regard, and I fear the feeling is mutual, but I would never wish to see the suffering of a child. Help us recover this treasure for the King, Daniel, and we will help you find Amy."

I looked at Alice with resignation and noted the look of triumph etched on her face. She knew that she had me and that I had no alternative but to co-operate with her.

"What do you propose?" I asked. "We do not have time to discuss this here."

Alice concurred with a nod. "Of that there is no doubt. Return to Nantwich tomorrow, and Bressy will make contact with you in due course."

"Are you going to tell me where and when?" I asked.

"Of course not," cut in Bressy. "Do you take me for a complete fool? If I show up in Nantwich at a pre-arranged time and place, I will be arrested by Colonel Booth and strung up in a trice. I will come when the time is right, and when I do, Cheswis, you will know of that, I assure you."

"Then it is decided," said Alice. "Bressy, you would be advised to be on your way before it occurs to someone to come looking here." With that she strode over towards the window and held it open for Bressy, who manoeuvred himself expertly through the gap and onto the gravel pathway, barely making a sound as he did so. With a brief smile of acknowledgement to Alice, he then sprinted over towards the walled garden and clambered athletically over the brick wall, where he would have been invisible to anyone other than observers from the top storey of the servant block.

"You know, it is a strange thing," said Alice, touching me lightly on the arm, "but I always knew we would meet again. It is as though God has decreed that our fates are inextricably entwined, you and I."

I recoiled slightly at the unexpected touch – just slightly, but it was enough for Alice to notice. She brushed her ringlets from her face, and as she did so, I thought I noticed an element of sadness in her eyes.

"Come, Daniel," she said, removing her hand. "It is time to return. I will go first. You would do well to leave it a few minutes before following, but I fear you will need a suitable excuse to explain your prolonged absence. I suggest you blame it on the herring pie."

With that she stepped noiselessly through the door and was gone.

\* \* \*

I took Alice's advice and returned to the library holding my stomach and feigning illness. I was in no mood for further socialising, so despite Wilbraham's inquisitive looks, I excused myself on the pretext of needing some fresh air and took a stroll down to the lakeside with a view to gathering my thoughts on the latest developments.

It was a calm, clear night, and the surface of the lake seemed like a mirror, disturbed only by a pair of ducks paddling their way towards a clump of reeds beyond the boathouse. Meanwhile, a fox slunk silently round the side of the washhouse and disappeared amongst the trees beyond. The workmen lining the water tank, I noticed, had long since stopped work, and silence reigned supreme. I sat down on the edge of the jetty next to the washhouse and began to contemplate the fomenting cauldron of intrigue in which I now found myself.

My most immediate concern was the fact that I was still no closer to finding out what had happened to Amy. I was acutely aware of the fact that the longer she remained missing, the less chance I had of finding her alive. Her disappearance, it seemed, was linked in some way to Elizabeth's engraving, the search for Massey's gold, and the murders of Hassall and Crewe. But how? As time went on, things were becoming less and less clear. Where I thought I had answers, there now seemed to be only questions.

The fact that Bressy was actively searching for the abbot's treasure was already known, and, although it had come as a shock, I suppose I should not have been surprised that Alice was involved too. But I had assumed that Bressy was the murderer and that it was he who had kidnapped Amy.

Bressy and Alice had insisted that an independent third party was responsible. Were they to be believed or was the murderer associated with them in some way? I hesitated to trust them, but could see no reason why they would try to solicit my help if they were not telling the truth; they could simply have extorted my help from me if they had Amy. Indeed, Bressy had possessed the ideal opportunity to shoot me dead in Crewe's bedchamber. The fact that he had not done so suggested that he had good reason to let me live.

Then there was the question of what Alice was doing at Combermere with Sir Fulke Hunckes and Lord Herbert and whether her official attendance as a guest of Thomas Cotton had anything to do with Bressy's activities. Herbert's presence amongst this group was somewhat puzzling, for the ageing lord had made it clear that he had no wish to nail his colours to the mast of either King or Parliament.

Thomas Cotton and Hunckes certainly had the air of people who might be involved in a pact with Alice and Bressy, but it was hard to see how they would have become embroiled in the murder of Crewe. Both were in the presence of Alice and Herbert at the time of Crewe's death, and consequently, if Alice and Bressy were telling the truth about not being involved in the murders, that would remove Cotton and all his house guests from suspicion. And as for George Cotton, he was with me at the time of the killing.

That left Gorste, who had been in the bakehouse at the time, and the two grooms, Beckett and Martland, who, as Gorste had pointed out, were the only people other than Crewe himself who could have deliberately lamed Demeter. Could I have been wrong about the two young grooms? Was one of them responsible after all for the killing of Crewe? And finally, what was behind the ill-feeling between himself and Eldrid Cripps?

I couldn't help feeling I was missing one vital piece of information, and perhaps this had been overlooked among the witness statements relating to the murder of Roger Crockett seventy years ago. I made a mental note to make another visit to Ezekiel Green once Wilbraham and I returned to Nantwich.

In the meantime, I also had to face the difficulty of what to tell Croxton. He had engaged me to find Bressy and prevent him from finding the treasure, arresting him if possible. Quite apart from the fact that I had been working with a known royalist sympathiser in Roger Wilbraham, I would now be forced to collude directly with Bressy himself. What was worse, I could do nothing about finding out who was responsible for the murders until Bressy himself deigned to show up in Nantwich.

I held my head in my hands and groaned. As things stood, I would be lucky to avoid being strung up as a traitor myself.

But everything revolved around Amy. How could I ever look Mrs Padgett in the eye again if I did not do the utmost to find out what had happened to her granddaughter? And what about Elizabeth and Ralph? Were they still at risk?

I considered that possibility for a moment and realised that this depended entirely on the location of the various engravings. I tried to take stock of the situation. Wilbraham and I were in possession of two of them, a third was unaccounted for, and the remaining three, those belonging to Elizabeth and the two murdered men, were in the hands of the killer. Suddenly, a light flickered in my brain. Why, I wondered, was Amy still being held prisoner if the murderer had taken Elizabeth's engraving from Kinshaw? Indeed, why had Amy been taken at all, for her disappearance had taken place after the attack on Kinshaw?

I then jumped to my feet as realisation dawned on me. I had to get back to Nantwich. Elizabeth and Ralph were still in mortal danger, Kinshaw too, if I didn't get to the fat merchant first. The lying swine had not given up the engraving at all. He still had it!

# Chapter 15

*Nantwich – Thursday, August 1st, 1644*

*T*<sub></sub>*oday was a very special day for Adolphus Palyn, the occasion on which he was to be fitted for a new suit of clothes, a suit fit to see his daughter married in.*

*Adolphus had not thought it possible. For what seemed like months, his daughter Bridgett had been consumed by a fog of despair following the tragic death of her best friend, Margery Davenport, killed during Lord Byron's bombardment of Townsend House in January, and so, when the young soldier David Rutter had arrived on the scene, he had seemed like a rescuing angel, a saviour in uniform.*

*Palyn had not been fooled. Like many of his type, Rutter had a wandering eye for a pretty maid, but he seemed to make his daughter happy, and he was a good catch too – a farmer's son from Bunbury – a second son, admittedly, but the lad's eldest brother had been killed fighting for Sir William Brereton at Middlewich, and so David now stood to inherit his father's farm. A* farmer's wife, after all, was far preferable to being the spinster daughter of a jobbing briner.

Today, therefore, was a cause for celebration. Adolphus had made an appointment to attend Gilbert Kinshaw at his newly established workshop behind Kinshaw's house in Hospital Street. Kinshaw had told him his master tailor would arrive at nine, but Adolphus was impatient. It would not matter, surely, if he was there half an hour early. He could always wait if the tailor had not yet arrived.

And so, a little after eight, Adolphus had kissed his wife goodbye and strolled off in good spirits from his modest worker's cottage at the far end of Little Wood Street. It was a fine morning, so he had taken the long way round – along the side of the brine-filled Great Cistern and through Strawberry Hill onto Welsh Row. From there he had crossed the bridge and passed through the Beast Market onto Beam Street, where he had stopped and bought a loaf of bread from a baker's shop.

From there he turned right up Pepper Street and into the square, where he had bid 'Good Morrow' to Clowes the bellman, who was calling anyone who would listen to the funeral of some poor soul who had died the previous day.

Adolphus would normally have stopped to pass the time of day with Clowes, for he found the bellman to be a genial sort. Today, however, he walked on, past the grammar school, round the church, and into Tinkers Croft. From there he passed the row of white tents, still occupied by those soldiers who could not find a billet in somebody's house, through a small alleyway between two tenements, and into Hospital Street.

Adolphus smiled in anticipation as he approached Kinshaw's workshop, for a light flickered invitingly in one of the windows. Despite the fact that it was summertime and the sun shone outside, the master tailor would always need a plentiful supply of candles to illuminate his workshop, in order to protect his eyesight. He noted from the lack of smell that Kinshaw had been using the best beeswax candles – no cheap tallow alternatives for him. The portly merchant must have been doing well since buying the business from that poor widow, Elizabeth Brett.

Adolphus noticed that the wooden door to the workshop was slightly ajar, so he pushed at it and called out Kinshaw's name. As he did so, a cat slunk out from under a table and shot between his legs as though in a desperate bid for freedom. At the same time, a chair placed behind the door tipped over and clattered to the floor.

Strange, he thought, why would Kinshaw deliberately place a chair behind a door?

He stepped inside and became aware of a low groaning sound to his right. Taking a couple of further steps towards the source of the noise, his eyes focused on the workshop table, and what he saw made his blood freeze.

Lying flat on his back on the table, his shirt shredded, exposing his ample abdomen, was the huge bulk of Gilbert Kinshaw.

The merchant was almost unrecognisable. His face was a mass of welts and bruises, and his torso a patchwork of red lines, dripping blood. Adolphus noted with horror that the lines were thin knife cuts. Kinshaw, he realised, had been tortured. The merchant was clearly very weak, but he summoned up enough strength to spit out a kerchief that had been rammed into his mouth and whisper two words.

"Get help."

It was then that Adolphus saw him, standing in the shadows in the far corner of the workshop. A tall, athletically built figure, dressed in dark clothing, but with piercing eyes of the deepest blue. The man, clutching a knife, fixed Adolphus with an intense stare and took one step towards him, but the briner was not waiting any longer. Nearly tripping over the upturned chair, he ran out of the workshop and out into Hospital Street.

'Get out into the crowds where you can be seen,' he thought, 'and shout for help.' Once in the street, however, all he could think of was putting as much distance between himself and the vision of horror he had just borne witness to. He looked over his shoulder with trepidation, but realised with relief that the man was not following him. Nevertheless, he quickened his pace and walked back towards the square. He would hasten his way back home, tell his wife what he had seen, and then go in search of Arthur Sawyer. The constable would know what to do.

As he walked back down the High Street towards the bridge, Adolphus started to breathe a little easier. He began to consider what he had borne witness to, and he realised that he had seen Kinshaw's attacker before. Was he not the lodger who had recently moved into the disused cottage halfway up Little Wood Street? Inherited the place, so he'd heard. The man was seldom there, so it seemed, but Adolphus had seen the man's striking figure in the street more often of late.

Adolphus crossed the bridge into Welsh Row and then left the busy main street to head back along the pathway that led behind the wich houses alongside the Great Cistern.

It was quiet alongside the brine-filled reservoir. The footpath was not used as often as Great or Little Wood Street. Briners usually only ventured around the back of the line of wich houses when they needed to run a theet into the cistern. The track was therefore overgrown in places, nettles and thistles hugging the banks of the reservoir.

Adolphus reached the stile at the end of the pathway and began to sigh with relief. He was now only a few *yards from the safety of his home.*

*Suddenly, he heard a rushing sound from his left, and a figure shot out from between the last two wich houses, careering into him and knocking him sideways into the brine pool. He turned over and looked upwards, but all he could see was the pair of menacing blue eyes. The man must have rushed back through Tinkers Croft and beaten him to the bridge.*

*Adolphus felt himself being turned over, and a crushing weight fell onto his back, thrusting his face into the pool of brine. He could not move, and he realised with a burst of panic that he was going to die. Against all his instincts he inhaled and he felt a sharp pain course through his lungs.*

*Suddenly he saw an image of St Mary's Church, a memory from the distant past, and he realised he was looking at a view of his own wedding thirty years ago. The image floated before his eyes, and he realised with a pang of regret that he would not live to see his own Bridgett wed in that same church.*

*And then, finally, as a feeling of unutterable peace began to take over his body, the image slowly faded into white, and he was gone.*

# Chapter 16

*Nantwich – Thursday, August 1st, 1644*

Due to a number of unforeseen circumstances, and to my considerable frustration, it was the middle of the following afternoon before we were able to commence our ride back to Nantwich. I should have known we were in for a difficult day when Wilbraham stumbled into my chamber at eight o'clock in the morning with a face as grey as the sky during a winter snowstorm.

"God's Blood, Cheswis," he moaned. "What the devil did we eat yesterday? I've been puking like a sick dog all night. I feel like someone has tied a rope around my innards and shaken them like a rag doll." He then leaned over the foot of my bed and filled my piss-pot with vomit.

"I take it that is not Cotton's French wine that is talking?" I remarked, in as sanguine a manner as I could muster. "You did drink rather a lot of it."

"No it bloody wasn't. And it's not just me either. I

just went downstairs for a walk in the hope of feeling a little better, and it seems half the house is sick."

To give Wilbraham some credit, this turned out to be not far from the truth. Of those who had sat down to table the previous evening, only George Cotton, Alice, and I seemed unaffected. The others had all remained in bed, seemingly too ill to move.

It was not until he was able to force down a bowl of pottage at lunchtime that Wilbraham was in any fit state to ride, and so for most of the morning I was left more or less to my own devices.

Once I had breakfasted, I took myself off to the stable block in search of news of how Demeter was faring. I found the young groom Martland there talking to a thin man in plain black garb, with greying hair and a long, prominent nose.

"Ah, good morning, Mr Cheswis. You come at an opportune moment," said Martland. "This is Mr Edwards, the coroner. I was just giving him my account of what happened to poor Mr Crewe. A tragic accident, I'm sure you will agree."

I greeted the coroner cordially, but thought I detected the kind of self-important posturing one often sees in petty officials of his kind.

"Good morrow," I said. "I had expected your work to have already been done, but I am pleased to have the opportunity to assist you."

"It was late when Mr Gorste called on me last night,"

explained Edwards. "I came this morning as soon as I could, but in truth, sir, I cannot see how this can be simply written off as a tragic accident. There appears to be more to Mr Crewe's death than initially meets the eye."

Martland flashed me a quick glance, and I smiled patiently at the coroner.

"Whatever gives you that impression?" I asked. Although Edwards appeared in most respects to be typical of his kind, I had not anticipated him choosing the difficult explanation when a simple one was readily available. I quietly breathed a sigh of relief that the stray musket ball had been removed from the vicinity of the farrier's workshop.

"I am the owner of a stables in Whitchurch," said Edwards. "I therefore know my way around a horse. Your mare does not seem the type to kick out unnecessarily, and she also has an injury on her hind quarters consistent with having been hit by a sharp object. I should like to know what that object was."

"I fear you are looking for a needle in a haystack, sir," I said, "even if she was injured in the manner such you suggest. However, no-one saw my mare sustain the wound you mention, and there are a hundred ways a horse could sustain such an injury." I laughed in order to make light of the situation, which was probably the wrong thing to do, for the official reddened, pulled himself to his full height, and began to bluster.

"I fail to see what is so amusing. I have many years' experience—"

"You are right, Mr Edwards," I said, realising I was making things more difficult than was necessary. "I spoke out of turn."

"Indeed. Then if there is nothing more, I will return to the farrier's workshop to conclude my investigations and arrange for the removal of the cadaver. Good day, sir."

"He is a pompous oaf," said Martland, once Edwards had gone. The young groom had been watching our exchange with interest, the corner of his mouth betraying a hint of a smile.

"That is true," I conceded, "but he is perhaps not quite so stupid as most officials of his kind. Until recently I was constable in Nantwich, and I know his type well, so let us hope that when he returns home he does what most of them do and chooses the easy option."

I was grateful to have Edwards out of the way, for if the coroner had been more persistent with his assessment of Crewe's death, I would have had to deal with the local constable, which would have had the potential to be even worse. As it was, at least I was free to pursue my own investigation unmolested.

"I see," said Martland, with interest. "Then that would explain your interest in matters of crime."

I smiled and decided to indulge the young groom.

"That is right," I said. "Tell me, what do you make of the situation?"

"From what I have seen, your mare seems a gentle creature," he replied. "I cannot imagine that she would have kicked out at Mr Crewe without reason."

I nodded slowly. "And how is Demeter?" I asked. "Does she fare better this morning?"

"Only slightly, I'm afraid," said the groom. "She is still lame. I do not think a ride back to Nantwich would do her much good today. She needs to rest. My belief is that we should keep her here for a week or two under our care. We can lend you one of our horses in the meantime, and you can return for Demeter when she has recovered. I will need to seek approval from Mr Gorste, though."

"He is not here?"

"He will return later. He left word that he would remain in Whitchurch this morning to carry out certain estate business on behalf of young Mr Cotton. It makes sense, as Mr Gorste is not in town every day. I would seek approval directly from Mr Cotton himself, except he is still abed. It seems several people were taken ill last night."

"So it appears," I replied. "Tell me, were any of the kitchen staff similarly affected? They ate our leftovers."

"Not to my knowledge, sir. They are all at work this morning."

I thanked Martland, and, after a brief visit to see Demeter, I walked back to the house and sought out Wilbraham with a view to dragging him out of his slough of self-pity.

"Come, a walk will do you good," I said. "The fresh air will help settle your stomach." The young merchant looked at me as though I had just proposed to extract one of his teeth, but nevertheless he forced himself to his feet and followed me gingerly down the stairs.

We walked in front of the walled garden, past the stable block, and through the jumble of workshops near the kitchens, before heading off through the orchards towards the fish pools. As we passed by the workshops, I noticed a narrow path, which led between the brewhouse and a carpenter's workshop, and into the jungle of trees behind the stable block. I realised this must have been how Demeter's assailant had made his escape.

Once I was certain we were out of earshot of the buildings, I recounted the events of the previous evening, and Wilbraham whistled with surprise.

"So let's get this straight," he said. "There are three different parties trying to locate Abbot Massey's treasure. The first party is ourselves, of course. Where do we stand?"

"Quite well, I think," I replied, "which is why Bressy is so keen on partnering with us. We know the names of five of the trustees – Hassall, Crewe, Ralph

Brett, Mr Maisterson, and yourself. We also know that Bressy is either the sixth trustee or the unique seventh trustee who has no engraving but knows the identities of all the other trustees."

"Bressy must be the sixth trustee, because otherwise he would know who the other trustee is and therefore also the identity of the person causing all this mayhem."

"A fair assumption," I agreed. "We also have three of the key words – yours, Maisterson's, and Crewe's, and, if I am correct, all we have to do is go back to Gilbert Kinshaw and we will be able to secure a fourth word."

"That sounds promising," said Wilbraham. "The second party interested in acquiring the engravings consists of Bressy and Alice Furnival. What of them?"

"They know Hassall's word and Bressy's own, which means between their party and ours, we should have access to all six. Bressy and Alice do not know much, but they have the whip hand because only Bressy knows his own key word."

Wilbraham nodded thoughtfully. We had just arrived at one of the fish ponds, which was teeming with trout being bred to stock the lake. Wilbraham sat down on a tree stump, still wearing a somewhat wan expression, and watched the young fish splashing around in the confined space of the pool.

"That leaves the third party," he said. "A person, or a group of people, quite prepared to commit murder to find the treasure. If it is the work of a single person, it is a man, for it was a man who kidnapped Amy, and only a man would have had the strength to drag Hassall to his death on Ridley Field."

Again, I had to agree with Wilbraham, but something was puzzling me.

"On the face of it, the murderer only knows two words, Crewe's and Hassall's – maybe Ralph Brett's too depending on whether he managed to extract the word from Kinshaw, but I doubt it. One thing does not make sense, though. Following Hassall's death, Ridley Field was covered in holes. Someone had been digging there, which suggests that whoever did that has had access to more of the engravings than we think, for how otherwise would he have known roughly where to dig? Remember, these engravings have been in circulation for seventy years. The question is, who dug the holes? Was it Bressy or the murderer?"

Wilbraham looked at me carefully and shrugged. "I have absolutely no idea," he said, "but we will not find out if we sit here all day. Come. The walk has made me feel a little better. Let us find a bite to eat, secure a horse for you to ride, and then we can be on our way."

* * *

The journey back to Nantwich was not a pleasant one, not least because the motion of his horse began to make Wilbraham feel ill again, and he spent most of the afternoon retching over his horse's shoulder.

For my part, I was more concerned about how I was going to face Mrs Padgett when we got home, for I was none the wiser as to Amy's whereabouts than when I had left for Combermere the day before.

Thomas Cotton had been full of apologies for the food poisoning. "It is not our wont to poison our guests," he had said when he had emerged from his chamber shortly after lunch, looking decidedly green around the gills. "This has never happened before, and I fervently pray such an experience does not befall us again. I cannot imagine how this has come about."

Cotton was more than happy to treat Demeter for me and lent me a good-natured chestnut gelding called Rupert.

"You might want to keep his name quiet in Nantwich," he said, with a wry smile. "In truth, though, he has little in common with his royal namesake. You cannot accuse Prince Rupert of lacking balls."

I smiled indulgently at Cotton's joke and thanked him for his hospitality. Whatever he was up to with Sir Fulke Hunckes and Alice, he had been a generous and courteous host, and he invited me to return two weeks later, once Demeter had recovered.

It was around six in the evening by the time our horses crossed the river at Shrewbridge and made their way towards the sconce at the end of Pillory Street. We rode past the gaol and into the square, which was full of people milling around in the evening sunshine.

I was just about to bid Wilbraham farewell when I noticed a familiar figure emerge from the Booth Hall. Marc Folineux had seen us coming and made a beeline straight for Wilbraham.

"You have been a somewhat elusive quarry, Mr Wilbraham," he said, reaching out to grab the reins of Wilbraham's mount.

"I have been away, as you can see, Mr Folineux. If you wish to see me, you need to make an appointment, as all others are expected to do."

"This I have tried to do on numerous occasions," said the sequestrator, "but your staff are somewhat obstructive. I would remind you that I am one of the chief sequestrators, and it is in your interest to co-operate."

"Oh, that I doubt, Mr Folineux. If you wouldn't mind, I suggest that it is in your interest to unhand my horse. I have been sick today, and at present you are in danger of having your smart black doublet covered by the remains of my lunch. Now, if you wouldn't mind..."

Folineux grimaced but let go of the reins. "Make sure you are at Townsend House tomorrow morning at nine of the clock," he said. "You need to be assessed to determine your delinquency payments. Avoiding the issue will just make things worse for you."

Wilbraham merely scowled at Folineux, but I could tell from his demeanour that this time there would be no avoiding the reach of the sequestrators. Folineux straightened his jacket and watched Wilbraham ride down the High Street. His face wore a barely suppressed look of self-satisfaction, but then he turned his attention to me and glared.

"And you be very careful, Mr Cheswis," he said. "The arm of the Sequestration Committee is long. You'll find we are capable of uncovering malignancy where it is least expected."

I would have said something in retaliation were it not for the fact that at that precise moment I caught sight of Alexander Clowes's substantial frame weaving his way through the crowds towards me. My friend immediately noticed Thomas Cotton's chestnut gelding and shot me a questioning glance.

"Demeter is lame," I said, "but it is a long story."

"Then it can wait," he said. "I have news to impart. Nantwich has been an eventful place since you left."

I sensed Alexander's urgency, and so, bidding Folineux a polite but cool 'Good day', I dismounted and followed my friend to a quiet corner of the square near the church.

"We have a missing person and an attempted murder," said Alexander, "and both involve Gilbert Kinshaw. This time, Sawyer and Cripps are at a loss to explain it. Their capacity for dealing with such matters seems to have been overreached."

"Kinshaw?" I exclaimed, a pang of foreboding

gripping my chest. "What of him?"

"He has been beaten within an inch of his life, early this morning. The bastard who did it knew what he was doing, and Kinshaw will be lucky to pull through, but he still refuses to speak to anyone other than you about it. We should go there now while you still have the chance."

I gave a groan of despair. If Kinshaw still had Elizabeth's engraving, I could guess what had happened to him.

"And the missing person?" I enquired.

"Adolphus Palyn, father to Bridgett Palyn and friend of the Davenports."

"The briner?" I said, somewhat nonplussed. "What was he doing at Kinshaw's?"

"He was being fitted out for a suit of new clothes. Had an appointment there this morning about the time Kinshaw was attacked but never returned home."

It only took a few minutes to walk up Hospital Street to Kinshaw's house. Sawyer and Cripps, I noticed, were nowhere to be seen, but Colonel Booth had placed a couple of guards on the front door. When they realised who I was, one of them went inside and fetched a footman, who took me upstairs to a dimly-lit room at the back of the house, where Kinshaw lay in a large four-poster bed. The only other person in the room was a slightly built, balding man with spectacles, who I recognised as Christopher Thomasson, Kinshaw's physician.

"He is very weak," said the doctor, "so you will need to have patience. He has taken a terrible beating, but he was adamant you should be brought here as soon as you returned.

I conveyed my gratitude to Thomasson and surveyed the mound of wobbling flesh swathed in bandages that lay in front of me.

"Is that you, Cheswis?" grunted Kinshaw. "What took you so bloody long?" The merchant's face was horribly swollen and bruised, which made him difficult to understand, but he still managed the belligerent tone to which I was accustomed.

"You have a nerve, Mr Kinshaw," I barked. "I have been searching high and low for Amy Padgett, who, as you know, was kidnapped by the same madman who did this to you. If you hadn't lied to me about the engraving, you might have saved us considerable trouble and saved yourself a beating."

Kinshaw emitted a strange rasping noise, which seemed to come from the back of his throat, and he turned to face me.

"Lied, Mr Cheswis?"

"Don't play the innocent with me, sirrah," I snarled.

Kinshaw flinched as I took a step closer to the bed. A look of panic began to spread over the doctor's features, and he began to struggle to his feet.

"Mr Cheswis, I-."

"Please, doctor," I said. "There is little I can do to him that has not already been done, and I do not intend to hang on account of so worthless a specimen as him."

I heard a spluttering noise coming from the bed as Kinshaw took umbrage at my words, but I was in no mood to be stopped.

"And you can cease your complaining, Mr Kinshaw," I said. "You have brought this upon yourself. You told me that you had surrendered my wife's engraving to your attacker the first time he was here, but that was a lie, was it not?"

Kinshaw gave me a snort of disdain. "What do you expect?" he demanded. "I am no fool. I could see the damned thing was of value, although the Lord knows why. It is an ugly-looking trinket at best."

"So you still have it?"

"Of course not, you imbecile. What do you take me for, exactly? I have an eye for an opportunity, Cheswis, that I cannot deny, but I am not going to get myself killed on account of a miserable piece of metal. My attacker took it with him this morning."

I sighed with exasperation. Not only did the murderer have access to one of the key words, one which Wilbraham, Maisterson, and I had little chance of getting, he now no longer had any reason to keep Amy as ransom.

"You are an ignorant fool, Mr Kinshaw," I said. "Your selfishness has placed Amy Padgett's life at risk. If anything should happen to her, I will see to it that you are held to account. And there is one more thing: you had an appointment with Adolphus Palyn this morning."

"Aye, he was to have been measured for a new suit. I thought I saw him standing in the doorway, but he took off like a frightened rabbit when he saw what was happening. Why do you ask?"

"Palyn has not returned home today," I said, grimly, "so you may yet have to account for your actions to his family as well as my own."

At this point Kinshaw's throat rasped again, and he began to cough uncontrollably. Dr Thomasson gave me a warning look and held a kerchief to Kinshaw's mouth. When he pulled it away, I saw that it was spotted with blood.

"I think you have talked enough, Master Cheswis," said Thomasson. "Mr Kinshaw is exhausted and needs to rest."

I turned towards the door to leave, but Kinshaw lifted his arm, and I caught the movement out of the corner of my eye.

"Just one thing, Cheswis," he said. "Are you going to tell me what is so important about this engraving?"

* * *

231

I sat in a dark corner of the bar at the Red Cow, cradling a tankard of ale in my hands to stop them from shaking. Alexander had moved quickly to bundle me out of Kinshaw's house before I had the chance to place my hands around his throat. As I was propelled into the street I could just hear the sound of Thomasson's voice telling the portly merchant that he had provoked me just a little too far.

I had since spent twenty minutes explaining to my friend what had happened at Combermere: the untimely demise of Geffery Crewe, the attack on Demeter, the unexpected appearance of Alice, the strange accord I had been forced to make with Jem Bressy, and the unexplained poisoning of Thomas Cotton and his guests.

Alexander listened to my account between gulps of ale, making occasional exclamations of surprise, particularly when I mentioned the reappearance of Alice Furnival.

"That is indeed curious," he said. "You and Wilbraham appear to have had a most eventful day. I cannot say I know how to find Amy, though, nor can I identify who has taken her, but I have managed to gather some interesting information, which may be relevant."

I slapped my palm against my forehead, chiding myself at my forgetfulness, and smiled gratefully at Alexander.

"Of course," I exclaimed, "Fletcher and Cripps. I had almost forgotten the surveillance work I had entrusted you with. What have you discovered?"

Alexander waved his tankard at a passing serving wench, who smiled provocatively at him as she placed a fresh beer on the table in front of him, making sure he got a good look at her cleavage. As she did so I placed a coin in the girl's hand and waved her away, impatient for my friend's response.

"Precious little at first," he said. "Fletcher has spent the last six days working at consecutive kindlings up on Snow Hill, so he's been busy for the whole week. I spent the first couple of days sat outside a bloody wich house wasting my time, before I decided to change my approach and follow Eldrid Cripps instead. That's when things started to get more interesting. When he's not fulfilling his duty as a constable, he spends most of his time either sleeping or in his workshop at the back of his cottage, making shoes."

"He won't have time for much else," I cut in. "I know from experience the demands being a constable places on one's time."

"Quite," said Alexander, with a touch more irritability than I thought was warranted. "Do you want to hear this or not, Daniel?"

I nodded sheepishly at Alexander and bade him continue.

"So I took the liberty of tracking down Sawyer and

233

finding out when Cripps was on duty. I then began waiting for him between two of the wich houses opposite his cottage on Little Wood Street. Truly, the man is a dozy lummox, Daniel, for I followed him everywhere for three days, and I swear he didn't realise he was being followed once."

"And what did you find?"

"On the face of it, little out of the ordinary: removing drunkards from the taverns, moving on vagrants and beggars, breaking up disturbances, and sorting out petty disputes between neighbours – you know the sort of thing you had to deal with. But one thing I did find unusual was that on each of the three days that I followed him, Cripps paid a visit to the Comberbachs' Tanners yard to seek out Roger Comberbach.

"I couldn't get too close for fear of being seen, but on the first two days he and Comberbach seemed to be engaged in heated argument, and on each occasion Cripps left looking worried. On his third visit yesterday afternoon, Cripps appeared to hand over a leather pouch to Comberbach, who seemed much pacified by this."

"So what did you do?"

Alexander grinned wickedly. I could see that despite his complaints about the amount of waiting around involved with surveillance work, he had been enjoying himself.

"At first I thought to approach Comberbach directly,"

he said, "but just as Cripps was leaving, I noticed young Edmund Wright appear from the workshop with a hide slung over his shoulders.

"You mean the young lad who's being walking out with Rose Bailey?"

"The very same," confirmed Alexander. "I had quite forgotten he worked for the Comberbachs, so I waited until Roger had gone back indoors and beckoned the young lad over. At first he didn't want to talk, for he is aware of my friendship with you and thought I was about to accost him for stealing your brother's betrothed."

"Simon has no-one but himself to blame for that," I said. "I have no quarrel with Wright."

"That's what I told him. So, eventually he opened up. Cripps, it appears, is seriously in debt to Comberbach for the leather he has supplied. He is several months in arrears and has been told he must pay Comberbach daily instalments until his debt is more or less under control. The small pouch he handed over must have been one of these instalments."

"I see," I said. "I am sorry for Cripps, for it cannot be easy trying to keep a struggling business above water whilst coping with the onerous duties of being a constable, but I fail to see what this has to do with Fletcher."

"I am not sure myself," came the reply, "but a constable in debt is often a poor constable. There has to be some connection with why Cripps is so adamant about Fletcher's guilt with regards to the murder of Henry Hassall. One thing I have not yet mentioned is that during his shifts, Cripps has seemed to spend an inordinately large amount of time patrolling the area of Wall Lane around where Fletcher lives, talking to his friends and neighbours. I have no idea why.

"Fletcher finishes his kindling tonight, so perhaps, if we keep an eye on Cripps' movements, we might learn something that could cast some light on this puzzle."

I thought about this for a few moments, and had to agree that there was a lot to be said for Alexander's suggestion. "Then let us go and search out my successor," I said.

Alexander drained his tankard and belched loudly. "Not so fast, my friend," he said. "Your enthusiasm is admirable, but there is time enough for that this evening. Cripps will be hard at work in his workshop at the moment. We will merely be sat on our arses all afternoon if we mount a watch now. In the meantime there are several other people who need your attention more."

I felt a pang of guilt course through my veins, and I realised how right Alexander was. How could I possibly forget? In my haste to solve the mystery of the murders of Henry Hassall and Geffery Crewe I had neglected to think of the people who meant most to me. Thoroughly chastened, I picked up my hat, followed Alexander out of the tavern, and headed up Beam Street in search of my wife, my adopted son, and Mrs Padgett.

# Chapter 17

They were waiting for me, all three of them. Ralph, one hand on his mother's skirts but trying nonetheless to look grown-up, Elizabeth, tight-lipped and fearful, and Mrs Padgett, wringing her hands in anguish and looking five years older than she had the week before. Believe me, there are few things worse in this world than seeing the faces of those you love disintegrate when they have been relying on you and you have let them down.

They could see it in my eyes, of course, as soon as I walked through the door.

"I am sorry," I said. "I did not find her. I do not know where to look next."

Mrs Padgett, who, judging by the dirty streaks on her cheeks, had already been crying, heaved a great sob, and Ralph looked quizzically at me.

"Amy is not coming back today?" he asked, his lower lip trembling slightly as he tried to suppress the tears he felt, as the man of the house, he should not shed. Ralph had accepted me unequivocally as a replacement parent, but even at such a young age he still felt keenly the loss of his real father, and he seemed to feel a protective responsibility towards his mother.

Elizabeth tousled his hair gently and tried to give me a reassuring smile.

"Not today, poppet," she said, "but I'm sure Daniel will bring Amy back to us soon."

I wished I could have been so sure, but there was one ray of hope amidst all the gloom.

"You should know," I said to my wife, "that the kidnapper's position with regards to the engraving we gave to Kinshaw is not as we thought – or at least that was true up until this morning."

I could see that Elizabeth did not have the slightest idea what I was talking about, so I explained the deception carried out by Kinshaw in order to keep hold of the engraving and watched as my wife's eyes narrowed and her face began to contort with anger.

"The evil, conniving ratsbane," she hissed, using language I had not heard from her before. "He would put at risk the life of a child for personal gain? It is as well he lies wounded and in fear of his life, for otherwise that knife given to Ralph by the Duke of Hamilton might have been put to good use."

"Then that means–" began Mrs Padgett, hesitantly.

"Exactly," I interjected. "At least until this morning

the kidnapper would have had every reason to keep Amy alive."

"But now he has the engraving," she said, bringing me back down to earth. "So where does that leave us?"

This, of course, was a very good question, and one to which I had no immediate answer. I was just about to say as much to Mrs Padgett, when my eyes caught sight of an envelope lying unopened on the hall table.

"What is that, Elizabeth?" I asked. "A letter for me?"

"Yes, I had almost forgotten." My wife picked up the letter and handed it to me. "It was delivered this lunchtime by one of Thomas Maisterson's servants."

I inspected the envelope, which was made of cheap paper, and frowned. "But this is not from Mr Maisterson," I said.

"No. The servant said it was delivered to Maisterson this morning by a street boy together with two other letters, one for Mr Maisterson himself and the other for Mr Roger Wilbraham. The servant said he thought the letter was important and that Mr Maisterson would like to see you as soon as possible. I did not like to open the letter, but I told the servant you would attend Maisterson tomorrow morning."

I thanked Elizabeth and tore open the letter, my hands shaking. If letters had been delivered for Maisterson and Wilbraham as well as myself, it would mean only one thing.

Inside the envelope was a single sheet of white paper.

I unfolded the letter and read it aloud.

> *Mr Cheswis*
>
> *You may consider yourself fortunate that I am not as gullible as your friend, Mr Kinshaw, appears to believe, and that I did not hold you responsible for this wicked deception. Fortunately, Mr Kinshaw was more forthcoming today, and he kindly surrendered to me what I came for. He paid for his deception well.*
>
> *Now I require the same from Mr Thomas Maisterson and Mr Roger Wilbraham. If you are to see your daughter again, you have until Wednesday 14th August to procure that which I need. When you have done so, I will know, and you will receive further instructions.*

Mrs Padgett gave a gasp of despair and started rocking to and fro on her chair, but Elizabeth sat down beside her and placed her arm around her shoulders.

"Do not distress yourself so, Cecilia," she said, with a grim smile. "This is good news, surely?"

"Good news?" wailed Mrs Padgett. "How can that be so? Amy has been gone a week now, taken by a callous murderer, and you have seen what he has done to Kinshaw."

"Elizabeth is right, Mrs Padgett," I said, in as calm

a voice as I could muster. "This means the kidnapper, wherever he may be, still has a motive to keep Amy alive, and it gives us two weeks of additional time to solve this mystery and find her. Let us pray that she is not being maltreated in her captivity."

Mrs Padgett sniffed slowly and nodded, wiping her tear-stained face with the back of her sleeve. Elizabeth, though, frowned and wrinkled her nose in irritation, as though something was bothering her.

"There is one thing which does not add up," she said. "Why give you two whole weeks to get the remaining engravings from Wilbraham and Maisterson? What is the point of that? It means the kidnapper will have to keep Amy secure for two whole weeks, thereby increasing the risk of discovery. Why not just give you a deadline of just a couple of days? It is not as though you do not know where to find Wilbraham and Maisterson. It just doesn't make sense."

I had to concede Elizabeth had a point. "Wednesday, August the fourteenth," I said, looking at the letter in my hand. "What significance could that date possibly have? Why would the kidnapper wait until then?"

Elizabeth shrugged. "I cannot say. August the fifteenth is Assumption Day. Make of that what you will."

I stared at my wife for a few seconds, but then I sat up straight as a thought occurred to me. A smile began to spread across my face, and all of a sudden I began to see things more clearly. It was like having a bucket of ice spilled down your back.

"Whatever is the matter?" asked Elizabeth, noticing the change in my features. "You look as though you have been slapped across the face with a fish."

"Of course," I said, cupping my wife's face in my hands and kissing her full on the lips. "You have answered my question." I leapt to my feet and started to gather my things together.

"Wait a minute," began Elizabeth. "Aren't you going to tell me what's going on?"

I looked my wife in the eyes and kissed her again. "I think it is safer, at this point, that you do not know any more than you already do," I said. "You will have to trust me."

"Then at least stay for dinner. You have been away for two days. Spend some time with us."

I hesitated, but forced myself to focus. "I will," I said, "I promise, but right now I need to see Alexander. Amy's safety may depend upon it."

With that I gave my wife, Ralph, and Mrs Padgett a hug, gathered up my purse and hat, and strode out once again into the street.

* * *

"Assumption," said Alexander, as we marched across the bridge towards Eldrid Cripps' cottage and workshop on Little Wood Street. "Wasn't 'Assumption' the word on Wilbraham's engraving?"

"Precisely," I said. "What conclusion can we draw from that, do you suppose?"

"Well, presumably Abbot Massey was referring to something that takes place on Assumption Day."

"Quite possibly," I agreed. "That's the way I read it, but whatever could he be referring to?"

"I don't know? Evensong, perhaps? That is Maisterson's word, after all. Perhaps we are talking about something that occurs during Evensong on Assumption Day."

He turned into Little Wood Street, and I lowered my voice as two briners passed us coming in the other direction, heading for the Black Lion on the other side of Welsh Row.

"You may be right," I agreed. "It would certainly make sense for Massey to use a religious feast day as a clue for where he would hide his treasure."

Once the briners were out of sight, Alexander and I slid through a gap between two wich houses and onto the path that led behind the houses along the banks of the Great Cistern. It was a quiet, windless evening down by the brine reservoir. Dusk was turning into night, and moths flitted through the nettles and long grass that lined the edge of the water. A half-moon shone over the long row of wich houses on the other side of the cistern, casting an eerie, shimmering light onto the surface of the briny water.

I stopped in the shadows, at a point in between two buildings from where we could view Cripps' cottage on the other side of Little Wood Street without being seen ourselves, and whispered to Alexander.

"There is one thing that bothers me," I said. "If the murderer is aware of the significance of Assumption Day to Massey, that means he already knows Wilbraham's word. If that is the case, where did he get it from, and why is he demanding to see both Wilbraham and Maisterson's words?"

"That I cannot say," said Alexander. "Perhaps he wishes to conceal the fact that he knows Wilbraham's word for some reason. Or maybe he knows Bressy and Alice are after Wilbraham's word too and wants to prevent them from getting hold of it. In any case, one thing it does suggest is that the kidnapper does not know what Maisterson's word is.

This, I considered, was probably true, but the whole thing was undoubtedly becoming more complicated. I was gathering a plethora of information, but the one thing that was missing was the vital clue I needed to identify who the kidnapper was and where Amy was being held.

At that moment, my attention was drawn by a movement from across the street, and Alexander nudged me gently.

"Here we go," he whispered. "Now we shall see

what Cripps is up to."

The shadows cast by the moon fell across Cripps' porch, so, at first, it was difficult to make out the identity of the dark figure fumbling with the front door. But then I heard Alexander give a sharp intake of breath as he realised the same thing as I had, for the person who stepped out into the moonlight, carrying a wicker basket, was not Eldrid Cripps at all, nor was it a man of any description. For the female figure scurrying down the street towards Welsh Row, glancing nervously from side to side, was unmistakeably none other than Sarah Fletcher.

# Chapter 18

*Nantwich – Friday, August 2nd, 1644*

'What had I learned?' I asked myself the following morning.

That Eldrid Cripps was having an affair with Sarah Fletcher? Probably – but what business was that of mine?

That Cripps had a motive for wanting to see Fletcher framed for the murder of Henry Hassall? Maybe – but in his position as constable, Cripps could have made sure Jacob Fletcher was arrested for any crime he chose, within reason.

Why then had Cripps been so adamant on pressing his claim that Fletcher was the perpetrator of this particular crime, even when it had become clear that he was not? That plainly did not make sense.

And what relevance did Cripps' money troubles have on the whole affair, if indeed they were connected at all?

I sat propped up in bed with my pillow jammed

behind my head against the wall, trying to shake off a fitful night's sleep and wondering if I was ever going to make sense of the conflicting jumble of messages that were bouncing about inside my head. With my mind spinning, I forced myself out of bed in good time and readied myself for my appointment with Thomas Maisterson.

Mrs Padgett, being in no fit state to be left on her own, had remained at our house in Beam Street overnight and had spent the night being comforted by Elizabeth, while I had been banished to a spare bed chamber. I could tell by the expression on Elizabeth's face that neither she nor Mrs Padgett had managed much in the way of sleep.

Around 8 o'clock, an exceedingly grumpy Jack Wade knocked on the door, wanting to know why nobody had been available to make his breakfast, but he soon calmed down when he saw how exhausted and careworn we all were. I gave him a hunk of bread and some small beer before packing him off to collect cheese from the nearby farms that had indicated they had produce to sell. It was beginning to irk me that once again I would not be able to help Wade in his preparation for market day and that I could not call personally on the network of farmers I had worked so hard to develop.

I watched as Wade manoeuvred my horse and cart down Beam Street towards the bridge that would take him along Welsh Row and out towards the villages to the east of Nantwich. Today Wade was due to visit farmers in Acton, Barbridge, Bunbury, and Faddiley, communities which were glad to find an outlet for their produce, now that Byron's royalist forces had been chased back to Chester. I had to admit that, with all the upheaval in my life since January's battle, if it had not been for my apprentice's diligent work my salt and cheese businesses would by now have been in a sorry state indeed.

As the wheels of the cart clattered over the cobbles at the start of the Beast Market, a youthful figure careered at speed out of Pepper Street, slipped on some of the detritus that lay discarded on the street, and nearly became entangled with the horse's legs. The horse shied slightly, but Wade controlled the animal expertly. Nevertheless, my apprentice shouted angrily at the youth, who raised his hands in apology and picked himself up gingerly, before continuing to jog in my direction.

It was then that I realised I was looking at none other than Ezekiel Green. The young clerk stopped breathlessly at my gate with a look of anticipation on his face.

"Have a care, young man," I warned. "I have lost one carthorse already these past few months. I do not want to lose another."

Ezekiel looked suitably contrite but could not hide

his excitement. "I am sorry, Master Cheswis," he said, "but I believe I have found some information that will interest you, relating to the murder of Mr Hassall."

"Indeed?" I said. "Where from?"

"From the archives, sir. I have re-read some of the witness statements from Roger Crockett's inquest and some papers from later court records, which I believe you might want to see. They cast an interesting light on the events of the past twenty-four hours."

I looked at Ezekiel with interest. "You mean the renewed attack on Gilbert Kinshaw and the disappearance of Adolphus Palyn?"

"I do, sir. Do you have the time to accompany me to the Booth Hall? I would show you my findings."

I glanced over the wall that ran to the rear of Lady Norton's house on the other side of Beam Street and focussed on the clock tower of St Mary's. It was already nearly nine o'clock.

"I am expected at Thomas Maisterson's shortly," I explained, "and I must attend him. However, if you would return to your archive, I will be with you as soon as I can."

Once Ezekiel had departed, I left Elizabeth and Mrs Padgett to their domestic business and walked over to Thomas Maisterson's residence, a fine half-timbered town house a few yards from the sconce at the end of Pillory Street. When I arrived, I was surprised to find a footman waiting for me by the front door. He ushered me inside with minimum ceremony.

The servant led me into a small reception room furnished with a low table and several ornately carved wooden chairs. On two of the walls hung expensive-looking tapestries, whilst above the fireplace a portrait of a distinguished-looking gentleman dressed in the fashion of Queen Elizabeth's time stared back at me. This I took to be one of Maisterson's ancestors.

I had barely been waiting two minutes when Maisterson himself strode purposefully into the room, followed by Roger Wilbraham, who was looking a lot healthier than he had done the day before. Both men wore worried expressions, but Maisterson's countenance lightened somewhat when he saw me looking at the painting.

"That," he said, "is my great-great-uncle, John Maisterson. This town owes him much, for he was at the forefront of the effort to rebuild Nantwich after it burned down in fifteen eighty-three."

"He looks like a man of some status," I agreed.

"Yes, unfortunately. However, it seems he may have been up to his ears in the intrigue that has ultimately led to the predicament we currently find ourselves in."

"Perhaps," I said, "but I find it hard to believe that any of the trustees appointed by Abbot Massey have been entirely blameless in all of this. It appears the honour of being appointed one of Massey's chosen trustees was something of a poisoned chalice. One of them, Roger Crockett, was most violently murdered, whilst the rest of them, at least those who we can identify, appear at the very least to have conspired to cover up the true nature of the murder and help the main perpetrator to escape, but may also have been guilty of conspiring to murder Crockett themselves. It is a veritable nest of intrigue.

"Massey must be turning in his grave to think that his plan, to put aside monies for the re-establishment of the monastery, a noble and godly aspiration, would end up creating the motive for bloody murder."

The two gentlemen shuffled their feet in embarrassment.

"It is indeed a bitter irony," agreed Wilbraham, "but we cannot dwell too much on that. Our task is now to make sure we do not become victims ourselves. What do you make of the messages that were delivered here yesterday?"

"I have not seen the messages that were delivered to you," I reminded Wilbraham, patiently.

Maisterson acknowledged this with a grim smile and extracted an envelope from inside his doublet. He then took out the single sheet of paper, laid it out on the table, and smoothed it flat for me to read.

*If you wish to avoid responsibility for the death of the hostage I hold, please submit your engraving into the possession of Master Daniel Cheswis by Wednesday,*

*August 14th.*

"The letter sent to me was identical," said Wilbraham, placing his own sheet of paper on the table.

I picked it up and examined it carefully. Both Wilbraham and Maisterson's letters were written in the same hand and on the same poor quality paper as the letter that was delivered to me.

"What I think is that the murderer is interested in Mr Maisterson's engraving, and not yours, Mr Wilbraham," I said, handing my own letter to Maisterson for both gentlemen to read. "I believe the murderer already knows Mr Wilbraham's word, although exactly how that has come to be, I cannot say."

I then went on to explain Alexander's theory about the significance of Assumption Day. Wilbraham, to his credit, looked a little surprised but not in the least flustered.

"I can only assume that this information was passed on unknowingly by one of my ancestors, either my father, my grandfather, or my great-grandfather, to one of the ancestors of the unknown trustee," he said.

"That is probably true," I agreed. "The problem is that your ancestor probably had no idea who the final trustee was, although the ancestor of the murderer of Henry Hassall and Geffery Crewe would have known the identity of all of the trustees. What is odd, though, is that your ancestor appears to have given the information over willingly."

"Or maybe he had no idea the information was being surrendered at all," ventured Wilbraham.

"But when could this have occurred?" asked Maisterson. "These engravings were entrusted to us as a secret. They are not the kind of thing you would show to a stranger."

Maisterson had a point. It seemed to me that there were relatively few occasions when it would have been possible for one trustee to gain knowledge of another's word without him being either aware of it or specifically wishing to divulge it.

"You are no doubt correct," I said to Maisterson. "It is seventy years since Massey's treasure has been an issue. In the interim, the importance of the treasure has been largely forgotten and has rarely been discussed. Most of the trustees, in fact, were not aware of each other's identities. Indeed, the Crewe family was not even in the area until recently.

"My guess is that the Wilbraham family's word was divulged around the time of the murder of Roger Crockett, but finding out how and by whom may require the skills of an archivist, someone who can distinguish the wheat from the chaff in seventy-year-old documents. I believe I know one such person."

* * *

254

As expected, I found Ezekiel Green in his dimly lit office at the back of the Booth Hall, leafing diligently through his reports and ledgers. I coughed lightly as I entered, causing the young clerk to blink nervously and look around himself in an owl-like manner. It was as though I had flooded the room with daylight, but then, as he recognised me, Green smiled and gestured towards a chair.

On Ezekiel's desk, I noticed, still lay the court documents he had shown me the last time I was there, but next to them were several other documents, which were bookmarked at specific pages.

"You have been busy, Ezekiel," I stated. "What have you found that you think will interest me so?"

Green placed his pen back in his inkwell and closed the ledger he had been working on, before swinging his chair round to face me.

"I have been carrying out considerable research since we last spoke," he said. "Just as you asked me to. Until yesterday, I was beginning to lose hope of finding any further information that might prove useful to you, but then I heard about the unfortunate attack on Mr Kinshaw and the disappearance of Adolphus Palyn. I didn't realise why at the time, but a bell rang in my head, as though this were important."

"Why would it do that?" I asked.

"Master Cheswis, it is well known that your wife sold her first husband's business to Gilbert Kinshaw, and that Kinshaw was attacked shortly before your housekeeper's granddaughter disappeared. The rumours are that this might be connected with your absence from Nantwich yesterday, and therefore also with the death of Mr Hassall. Rumours spread quickly round here, Mr Cheswis, as you know. Everyone is aware of your interest in solving Mr Hassall's murder."

I gave Ezekiel a sharp look. I was not sure I wanted to be seen as undermining Sawyer and Cripps' official investigation, but I guessed that the two constables would not hesitate to spread word that their work was being affected by a meddling ex-constable, especially if they were unable to solve the murder themselves.

"So what conclusion did you draw?" I asked.

"It took me a while to remember exactly what it was that was troubling me about Adolphus Palyn's disappearance," said Ezekiel, "but I knew it was something that I had read in the reports from Roger Crockett's inquest and the subsequent sessions trial. So I recovered the archives from the repository below and set about re-reading the statements from the inquest.

"It was then that I noticed a very interesting thing. Roger Crockett's main servant at The Crown was a man called Thomas Palyn, who was a significant witness on the side of Bridgett Crockett, both at the inquest and during Mrs Crockett's subsequent attempt to bring Richard Wilbraham and others to trial over her husband's murder."

"But Palyn is a common enough name."

"Quite, so I sought out Bridgett Palyn, who is of an age with me. She confirmed that this Thomas Palyn had been her great-great uncle, and that she herself had been named after the widow of Thomas's employer, who, of course, was Bridgett Crockett. She then went on to tell me an incredible tale of perjury and subterfuge, which almost resulted in Thomas Palyn ending up on the gallows. All hearsay, of course, and naturally I had no idea whether any of this could possibly have any relevance to Adolphus Palyn's disappearance, so I spent last night digging out more documents from our archives and was able to piece together a most fascinating story."

"Then I am all ears," I said, sitting down on a spare chair. "What can you tell me about Thomas Palyn, and why was he so important?"

"You will remember that at the coroner's inquest, which took place on the Saturday following Crockett's death, Bridgett Crockett argued that her husband had died as the result of multiple blows inflicted by a crowd of attackers, amongst whom, she swore, was Richard Wilbraham."

I nodded the affirmative.

"Well, the inquest, of course, found that Edmund Crewe, who had been conveniently spirited out of the vicinity, was solely responsible for the murder. This you already know. From the start, though, Bridgett

Crockett argued that the whole of the process presided over by Maisterson the coroner was corrupt.

"She accused him of intimidating John Hunter, the painter she had engaged to paint the corpse, of loading the jury with his own friends, and, most seriously, she accused him of hiding the wounds on her husband's body, of locking the church doors during the inquest so that the general public could not get in to see the state of the corpse, and of attempting to trivialise the fatal blow struck by Crewe – all, she said, in order to protect his own friends and kinsmen accused of the murder. One of the key witnesses who spoke out on Bridgett's behalf at the inquest was Thomas Palyn.

"That would, perhaps, have been the end of the matter if it were not for the fact that Bridgett refused to accept the coroner's verdict and initiated an 'appeal of murder' against Richard Wilbraham, the Hassalls, and others. This was the circumstance in which most of the witness statements we have been looking at were collated. Initial hearings related to the case were held over a twelve day period in Chester, Nantwich, and Wybunbury in the presence of the chief justice of Chester and other commissioners.

"One thing which emerged from these hearings was that there appears to have been several attempts to bribe Palyn by Maisterson's faction offering the servant money, pasture, subsidised rent, and other benefits if he were to testify to Maisterson's single blow theory. Indeed, Palyn made bribery claims at the inquest itself. However, this seems to have been followed by an apparent promise by Bridgett Crockett that Palyn would be well-rewarded if he testified to her version of events. In the event, he did exactly that, incriminating not only Wilbraham and Hassall, but Maisterson too."

"Are you saying that Palyn was not to be trusted?" I asked.

"Not necessarily," replied Ezekiel. "I cannot say. After all, these events happened seventy years ago. Although it is true that comments made about Palyn at the time were not particularly complimentary. At various times he was described as 'a naughty lewd fellow' and 'a venomous spider' amongst other names. What is certain is that the chief justice's investigation was by no means the end of the matter.

"In July fifteen seventy-three, over twenty people were bound to appear at the assizes in Chester, at which Edmund Crewe was indicted for murder in his absence. Then, in February fifteen seventy-four, most of these twenty-odd people appeared again before the chief justice to answer Bridgett Crockett's appeal of murder.

"As a result of this, six individuals, named as Richard, Anne and William Hassall, Richard Wilbraham, Thomas Wilson, and Robert Grisedale, were bailed to make a further appearance. However, at the Michaelmas assizes, all six were discharged by proclamation."

"So that was the end of it, and Bridgett Crockett had failed?"

"Well, as far as Bridgett was concerned, yes, although it was by no means the end of the matter for Palyn, and he may well have lived to regret testifying against such powerful families as the Wilbrahams, the Hassalls, and the Maistersons."

"Why do you say that?"

Ezekiel grinned, and he opened one of the dusty volumes that had been bookmarked.

"This is where it gets really interesting," he said. "In fifteen seventy-five, Palyn was arrested for allegedly stealing goods belonging to a traveller who was lodging at The Crown. He was indicted by a well-known thief called Roger Brook, who claimed Palyn was his partner in crime. Both Brook and Palyn were sentenced to hang."

"All seems very straightforward," I said. "Palyn, after all, was hardly a pillar of virtue, or so it seems."

"Quite. However, according to what Bridgett Palyn has told me, what happened on the day of the proposed execution was most illuminating. Apparently Brook was led to the gallows laughing and joking, confessed to the robbery, and was then immediately pardoned. Very strange behaviour indeed. Palyn, however, believing himself about to die, merely claimed he had been condemned as a result of a truth he had told regarding the death of his master, Roger Crockett."

"So Palyn believed he had been framed in revenge for the testimony he had given?"

"Clearly so, a belief which did not change when John Maisterson suddenly appeared on horseback and offered him a reprieve, if he would confess that he had been bribed by Bridgett Crockett to give false evidence to support her appeal of murder."

I gasped with disbelief. "So the whole case was cooked up by John Maisterson. Brook was in Maisterson's pay all along."

"Such is the inference. These are Bridgett's words, of course, and she has her own axe to grind. However, she says that, on the gallows, Thomas Palyn said he did not actually see Crockett being murdered, and as a result was pardoned. However, she also says he was later sued for perjury by Wilbraham and Hassall in the Star Chamber. Of course, I am not able to gain access to the documents of that case, but I presume that what Bridgett says could be verified by cross-checking against the records of the Star Chamber trial."

"You have done well, Ezekiel," I said, with genuine admiration. "You have been most thorough. This is a fascinating story, but what is the relevance of this information today, do you suppose?"

Ezekiel raised his eyebrows and looked at me disbelievingly.

"Why, don't you see it, Master Cheswis? Could it not be that Bridgett Crockett was so grateful to Thomas Palyn for his continual support of her case, right up to the point where he would have died for her, that she entrusted the Palyn family with continuing the fight for her cause. Crockett herself, I have found, eventually remarried and left the country."

I sat and considered Ezekiel's words for a moment, then slowly started to chuckle to myself.

"Something is funny, sir?" asked the young clerk with surprise.

"No," I said. "I mean yes, in a way. I was just considering how I would break the news to Thomas Maisterson and Roger Wilbraham that their ancestors were up to their necks in a quagmire of corruption. I can do little but laugh, for if I did not laugh at this state of affairs, I would surely cry."

# Chapter 19

*Nantwich – Sunday, August 4th, 1644*

"You are pushing at the very boundaries of where you will be permitted to tread," warned Alexander, ominously. "Maisterson and Wilbraham will not allow you to malign the memory of their ancestors by repeating what you have just told me. I advise you to keep it under your hat."

Alexander was leaning against the wall of his house, waiting for Marjery and his children to ready themselves for church. It was another bright, sunny morning, and Ralph had skipped onwards into the square with Elizabeth hot on his heels, trying to calm him into the sort of behaviour commensurate with our weekly visit to God's house.

Mrs Padgett, although still in no mood to venture too far from her front door, had expressed the desire to pray for the safe return of Amy, and Jack Wade, as gallant as you like, had led her down the street on his arm, his wooden leg clomping loudly on the cobbles.

Although I generally found the shared family activity of attending Joshua Welch's sermon to be an uplifting experience, even taking into account the Puritan minister's fire and brimstone approach to Sunday worship, on this occasion I was too preoccupied to make the most of the walk up Pepper Street, and so I had hung back to discuss Ezekiel's findings with Alexander.

"I do not see the relevance," my friend had said. "Whatever feud existed three generations ago, between the Maisterson, Wilbraham, and Hassall families on the one hand and the Crocketts and their employees on the other, does not exist today. The Crocketts have long since left Nantwich, and Adolphus Palyn is not your murderer, for Palyn was in Nantwich when Geffery Crewe was killed."

"Perhaps Palyn knew something about Massey's treasure that we are not aware of," I suggested. "Something passed down by Bridgett Crockett."

Alexander snorted loudly. "Now you're just speculating," he said. "There is nothing to link Adolphus Palyn to this business other than his surname and the fact that he has gone missing at a time when he had an appointment with Gilbert Kinshaw, who held one of Massey's engravings. You are clutching at straws, Daniel."

In truth, I had to confess that Alexander was probably right. After the market had finished the previous day,

I had taken the trouble to seek out Bridgett Palyn at her parents' home, and she was able to tell me very little, other than to confirm what she and Ezekiel had discussed.

The story of the injustice that Thomas Palyn had suffered had been passed down three generations of Palyns with remarkable clarity, but Bridgett could tell me little about her father's disappearance. He had left home on Thursday morning to be measured for a suit of clothes, but, apart from being seen by Alexander on his way to Kinshaw's workshop, there were no other witnesses who could recall seeing him at all. Adolphus Palyn had simply vanished into thin air.

The most obvious explanation was that he had simply left home and deserted his family for reasons unknown, perhaps due to some unspoken marital disagreement, or that he had become ill and fallen in the river. It would not have been the first time that such an event had happened. Even if the solution was a more sinister one, the most likely scenario was that he had simply seen something at Kinshaw's that he should not have. Nonetheless, there remained a nagging doubt in my mind that I had missed the one tiny piece of information that would bring the whole conundrum into focus.

After I had finished talking to Bridgett, I had joined her and a select group of neighbours, including the Davenports, in conducting another search of virtually everywhere within the earthen walls of the town where Palyn might have gone, although the crowd of helpers was much smaller than it had been on the previous two days. Palyn's wife, I noticed, could not face the task either.

We searched along the banks of the Great Cistern, along the Water Lode and down amongst the reeds by the river bank, down by the Beete Bridge at the bottom of Pillory Street, and in every back yard we could without causing a disturbance, but nothing was to be found.

We had returned downcast, swearing that Palyn would reveal himself when God permitted and not before.

St Mary's was busy with worshippers when Alexander and I finally arrived, and I took my place on my pew next to Elizabeth. She gave me a reproving look, but I merely shrugged apologetically and surveyed the scene around me.

There were, it seemed, plenty of churchgoers whose minds were preoccupied with matters other than Welch's sermon. Wilbraham fidgeted nervously in his pew at the front of the church, looking around at the rest of the congregation. He caught my eye and gave me a curt nod.

Maisterson, on the other hand, sat stock still in his pew, next to his wife, staring straight ahead at the empty pulpit, waiting for Welch's arrival. Colonel Booth was also present, as was Thomas Croxton, brimming with the confidence that power can give you. Next to him, stony-faced, sat Marc Folineux. Gilbert Kinshaw, I noticed, was not present, still too ill to attend.

I barely listened to Welch's sermon, although I do remember prayers were offered for the safe return of Adolphus Palyn and the swift recovery of Gilbert Kinshaw. As soon as the service was finished, I saw Elizabeth and Ralph safely out of the church and asked them to wait for me by the gate to the grammar school. I then sought out the one person I particularly wanted to see.

\* \* \*

Roger Comberbach was leaving the church with his two brothers, Thomas and John, his partners in Nantwich's largest tannery. All three had their wives with them as well as an assortment of children of varying ages, so I was not expecting it to be easy to attract Comberbach's attention, but to my surprise, as soon as he saw me, he raised his hand in acknowledgement, and, after a brief word with his wife, he weaved his way through the crowd in my direction.

Comberbach was in his early forties, but, despite his slightly greying hair, he cut the clean athletic figure of a much younger man.

"Well met, Daniel," he exclaimed. "I hear you may

want a word with me." Comberbach's familiarity came as a result of our shared experience fighting shoulder to shoulder in front of Acton Church against Byron and his army of Irish malignants. Before January, I had simply been Master Cheswis to him.

"Word travels fast," I replied. "I presume young Edmund Wright is the source of this information."

"Indeed. He fears you may wish to exact revenge on him for his choice of female company."

"Tush. He is a nervous young fellow," I said. "He needn't worry. That is my brother's business, and he is in Yorkshire somewhere. No, the person I am more interested in is Eldrid Cripps. You have some dealings with him, I believe."

"Cripps?" said Comberbach, frowning. "What do you want to know about him for, and on whose behalf?"

"I act on behalf of Colonel Croxton. There are some aspects of Cripps' recent behaviour that I am interested in. In particular I should like to know more about the money he owes you."

Comberbach opened his eyes wide with astonishment. "By the saints, Daniel," he said, looking from side to side. "Keep your voice down. How on earth do you know about that?"

I stared at him expectantly for a moment, but deliberately said nothing, waiting for an answer.

"Oh, very well," said the tanner, throwing his hands in the air in exasperation, "but he doesn't owe me a farthing anymore. He settled his whole debt, all fifteen pounds of it, yesterday. All in one go. Lord knows where he got the money from."

"Fifteen pounds," I said, "that's a significant amount of money for a man like him, the equivalent of several months' pay at least, I'd wager."

"Aye, that's true, but he'd built up his debt over six months or so, buying leather for his business. Last month his payments dried up altogether, so I lost patience."

"And so you threatened to expose him and have him thrown into gaol as a debtor? That would have ruined his standing within this town. He would never have been able to live that down or pay the money back."

"I know," admitted Comberbach. "I'm not proud of that, but what was I to do? It was the only option open to me – and," he added, with a self-satisfied grin, "it worked, did it not?"

"So it seems. Tell me," I persisted, "if you dealt with Cripps regularly, you must know something of the man. What else can you tell me about him?"

"Not much, really. Lived on his own. A fairly secretive fellow, to be honest, but I never thought badly of him until he stopped paying us. Rents his cottage and workshop directly from the person who owns the whole building."

"And who might he be?"

"I've no idea. The place has been rented out for as

long as I can remember, at least since I was a child."

"And the other half of the house?"

"Empty for about a year, I believe, at least until recently, although I understand someone new moved in there a couple of months ago. A travelling pedlar type, so I'm told. He's not there most of the time – and before you ask, no, I don't know his name."

I would have delved more into what Comberbach knew about my successor had I not been disturbed by the sudden appearance of a grinning Colonel Thomas Croxton and the contrasting sombre-faced figure of the sequestrator, Marc Folineux. Comberbach gratefully took the opportunity to make his excuses and fled into the crowds, aiming squarely for Barker Street and the safety of his tannery.

"Not something we have done, I hope?" commented the colonel, looking down his nose at the rapidly retreating tanner.

"I think not, sir," I replied. "What can I do for you?"

"An update on your progress with regards to the investigations I tasked you and Clowes with, if you please. What can you tell us?"

"Rather less than I might have been able to if you had not just allowed Roger Comberbach to escape," I said, flatly, "but rather more than I should be discussing in front of Mr Folineux."

I noticed a smile hover around the corner of the sequestrator's mouth, but Croxton's broad grin disappeared instantly.

"Very well," he said, stiffly. "You have a point, even though Mr Folineux is a trusted member of Sir William's inner circle, and his loyalty is not in question. You may report to my office tomorrow at nine o'clock sharp. In particular, I should like to know what you were doing gallivanting off to Combermere Abbey with the likes of Roger Wilbraham. You have until then to get your story straight."

For a moment, I thought Croxton was about to stalk off in anger, but Folineux gave a light cough and addressed me.

"Master Cheswis," he said, "as you have most recently enjoyed the hospitality of Mr Thomas Cotton, perhaps you may be of service to me. You will have seen much of the Combermere estate whilst you were there, I take it?"

"Some of it," I replied, guardedly.

"And the inside of the house itself?"

I groaned inwardly, for I knew exactly where Folineux was heading, and I had no particular desire to cause a problem for the Cottons, who had been gracious hosts during my stay.

"You wish to sequester the Cottons?" I asked. "I did not realise Nantwich had a claim on their estate."

"The Cottons own much property hereabouts," replied Folineux, evenly, "and the arms of the sequestration committee are long."

"You did not think to ask Roger Wilbraham about this when you visited him on our return to Nantwich?"

"Oh, indeed, but Mr Wilbraham was less than forthcoming, which is no surprise. I thought that, as a loyal servant of Parliament, you might be more inclined to help."

Folineux smiled meaningfully, and I glanced sideways at Croxton, but the colonel's face was undecipherable.

"Very well," I sighed. "What do you need to know?"

"I will require you to go through everything you saw when you were there, in order to compile a mental picture of the Cotton family's assets – what you saw in the house, the stables, the workshops – everywhere. As you will imagine, when I turn up somewhere, much tends to go missing. We can do this tomorrow, after you have completed your business with the colonel."

"Certainly," I replied, trying hard to hide my reluctance. "It will be my pleasure to help in any way that I can."

"And your duty," added Folineux.

"Indeed."

"And there is one more thing," added the sequestrator. "In my experience, the master of the house is, by sheer coincidence, I'm sure, very often absent when I come to call. Who is in charge of the household there?"

272

"The chief steward was absent when I was there," I replied, "but you may wish to make yourself known to his deputy. His name is Gorste, Abraham Gorste."

# Chapter 20

*Combermere – Thursday, August 8th, 1644*

"*A*hem."

Abraham Gorste looked up from his accounts book and assessed the soberly dressed figure who had appeared, as if out of nowhere, in the farm manager's office. The man had possessed the temerity to cough at him instead of addressing him in the manner to which he was accustomed, and Gorste did not like it. He did not appreciate being disturbed from his work at the best of times, but since the chief steward's return from his ailing sister's bedside, he had been more disinclined than usual to tolerate interruptions.

With the Grange being constantly short-handed and the farm manager himself busy in Whitchurch, he had been lumbered with the task of settling the bills of numerous individuals who had not been paid since the beginning of the steward's period of absence. Amongst other liabilities, there was a whole army of labourers who had to be paid for threshing and winnowing *the corn, as well as a bill from the local pinder for rounding up several cattle that had strayed off the farm onto neighbouring land. He had work to do, so the last thing he wanted was to be interrupted by a stranger who had not even bothered to knock.*

*"And who might you be, sir?" he asked, unable to completely keep the irritation from his voice.*

*The stranger flashed a smile at him and extracted some paperwork from inside his doublet.*

*"My name is Marc Folineux. I am a collector and apprisor for the Nantwich Hundred. It is Mr Abraham Gorste whom I seek."*

*"I am Gorste," said the deputy steward with surprise. "How is it that you know my name?"*

*The newcomer's smile grew a little wider, and Gorste immediately wished he hadn't asked.*

*"That, sir, is of little import. However, I am reliably advised that you are the one person with whom I should speak with regards to conducting an initial assessment of Mr Cotton's estate."*

*Gorste laughed out loud. "Me?" he said, feigning incredulity. "You think wrong, sir. You need to speak to Mr Frayne, the chief steward, and ultimately to Mr Thomas Cotton himself, but unfortunately neither is here."*

*He lied. Both, he knew, were somewhere in the main house, but Gorste knew he had to prevent the sequestrator from going anywhere beyond the Grange.*

"I'm afraid you have wasted your journey," he added.

"Oh, I doubt that," said Folineux, unmoved. "The master of the house is rarely present when I first attend. However, this document is a formal demand from the chief sequestrator for Nantwich Hundred to assess the value of this estate in order that Mr Cotton may atone for his delinquency."

"Delinquency? I don't suppose Mr Cotton will deny he is a supporter of His Majesty King Charles, but you won't find much of value here these days. Most of Mr Cotton's plate and other possessions of value have already been donated to the King's cause, and, as you can see, a good proportion of the estate was damaged by the presence of His Majesty's army here a few months ago."

"That is not what I heard," said Folineux, evenly. "I understand that your master's library is full of fine furniture and paintings. But no matter, we will assess that in due course."

Gorste looked sharply at the sequestrator. How on earth did Folineux know about the contents of the interior of the house? But then he smiled ruefully to himself. In truth it was not so difficult to guess. That confounded cheese merchant from Nantwich who had been here the previous week with Roger Wilbraham must be to blame. It was a pity for him that the rebel bastard had been beef-witted enough to leave his horse in the stables. He would return to Combermere for certain, and when he did, there would be a reckoning.

He turned his attention to Folineux, who did not seem to be showing any inclination to move from his place in front of Gorste's desk.

"You will need to return when my master is here," he repeated.

"Have no fear, sir, I will not embarrass you today by trying to insist on rifling through your farm records without Mr Cotton being present. However, I will return next Friday, when I will be accompanied by a fellow collector, and I assure you that on that occasion I will not be so easily deterred from doing my duty. I trust you will inform your master accordingly, and until then I bid you good day."

# Chapter 21

*Nantwich – Monday, August 5th – Wednesday, August 14th 1644*

My appointment with Thomas Croxton turned out to be less of a trial than I was expecting, especially when I remembered that the colonel's primary motive for engaging me was not specifically to arrest Jem Bressy, but to find and secure Massey's treasure before Bressy had the chance to carry it off to Shrewsbury. Although, make no mistake about it, Croxton would have taken as much pleasure as anyone in seeing the man strung up in the square in full view of the great and good of Nantwich, if for no other reason than that he had been responsible for the murder of Ralph Brett.

Croxton, though, was nothing if not practical, and when Alexander reminded me of that fact, it did not take me long to work out the best approach to keep the colonel at bay long enough for me to see through the plan of action that I had agreed with Wilbraham, Alice, and Bressy, assuming of course that Bressy presented himself for further discussions before Assumption Day.

So I told Croxton everything I knew about Massey's treasure, including the fact that Bressy was one of the trustees, but left out all references to Alice and the fact that I had seen Bressy, let alone been forced to make an accord with him. I told him about Ralph Brett being one of the trustees, about Wilbraham and Maisterson's involvement, about Kinshaw's deception, about the reason for Amy's kidnapping, and about the murder of Geffery Crewe in the farrier's workshop at Combermere. And finally I explained our belief in the significance of August 15th – Assumption Day.

The one thing I deliberately did not mention was the significance of Ridley Field, because I did not want Croxton to get the idea that the whole problem could be solved by having the men of the garrison dig up the field and make it look like a rabbit warren. After all, I had Amy to think about.

If dealing with Croxton was easier than expected, the very opposite was true of Folineux, whose meticulous approach to assessing the value of the assets of known malignants was something for which I was wholly unprepared.

It was common practice, he explained, to use third parties as informants to help assess the value of large estates, as it had become customary for wealthy royalists to secrete away as much of their valuables as they could, in order to minimise the amount to which they would be sequestered.

Folineux took me on a mental walk around the Combermere estate as far as I'd seen it, asking what produce the farm grew, what livestock I'd seen, both in the stables and elsewhere, and what furniture and valuables I had seen in the parts of the house where I had been. He seemed particularly interested in my description of the Cottons' fine library, which now doubled as a reception and dining room. He asked questions about the paintings and tapestries that hung on the walls in various parts of the house, the statues in the garden, the ornaments in the halls and on the staircases, the tableware we ate off at dinner, and even the quality of the linen in the bedchambers.

And then, when I thought I had finished, he made me describe it all again to make sure I had not missed anything, all the time furiously scribbling notes in a ledger.

Eventually, after about an hour, he removed the pair of spectacles he had been using to read with and gave a smile of satisfaction.

"Very good, Master Cheswis," he said. "That will do. You may go."

And that was it. No thanks, no explanation as to what he planned to do with the information I had given him or when he planned to use it. He simply gathered up his bundle of papers and marched out, leaving me alone in Croxton's office.

In truth, I was glad to get Croxton and Folineux off my back, as it gave me the opportunity to focus on more important things, but as the week wore on, I began to grow more impatient. There was no word from Wilbraham and Maisterson, no further communication from the kidnapper, and no sign at all of Jem Bressy. Meanwhile, Mrs Padgett was growing increasingly tetchy with my inactivity and started nagging me about whether there was anything else I should be doing to find out what had happened to Amy.

Alexander, meanwhile, had continued to monitor the movements of Eldrid Cripps, and also had little new to report.

"You know, it's strange, Daniel," he said to me one evening, as we enjoyed a tankard of ale in the Red Cow. "His behaviour seems to have changed completely over the last week. When he is not with Sawyer or carrying out the rest of his constabulary duties, he has spent the whole time in his workshop."

"And he has stayed clear of Comberbach's tannery?"

"No, not entirely. He went there yesterday to buy leather, but young Wright tells me he paid in cash. It is most puzzling."

"And Sarah Fletcher?" I asked.

"No sign of her since her appearance at Cripps' cottage the other night. What's more, since that day

Cripps appears to have given Wall Lane as wide a berth as possible. It's as though they have made a pact to avoid each other."

"There may be a good reason for that," I said. I had seen Sarah Fletcher at Mistress Johnson's earlier that day, and it had struck me how heavy with child she was.

"Aye, it must be nearly her time," agreed Alexander. "It would not do for Cripps to be sniffing around Fletcher's house at a time like this."

"Mmm," I said. I agreed with Alexander, but something had occurred to me. "Does it not strike you as odd," I asked, "that Sarah Fletcher should risk spending time at Cripps' house in her condition? And another thing. If they are having an affair, how long do you suppose it has been going on for?"

Alexander gave me a knowing grin. "You mean longer than nine months?"

"Precisely. Perhaps I should pay Sarah Fletcher a visit and find out."

And so I would have done, were it not for the fact that the very next day, with less than twenty-four hours to go before the kidnapper's deadline, Jem Bressy decided to put in an appearance, and my world once again descended into chaos.

\* \* \*

I was busy running a theet from the back of my wich house into the Great Cistern when the news came. We had a kindling scheduled for the following day, and so Jack Wade, Gilbert Robinson, and I were struggling with the long wooden pipes that would carry the brine from the cistern into the ship.

It was a hot day, and beads of sweat dripped from my forehead, as we clamped together the lengths of pipe and laid them out of the back door of the wich house and across the path towards the cistern. As I manhandled the theet into position, I was distracted by the sight of Thomas Maisterson walking purposefully along the footpath in my direction.

I stood up and stretched my back, grateful for the opportunity to have a brief rest, and motioned for Robinson and Wade to do likewise.

"Master Cheswis. Your wife said I would find you here. I should be grateful if you would accompany me to Townsend House," said Maisterson, through furrowed brows. "Roger Wilbraham awaits us there. He has an unexpected visitor."

I shepherded the merchant to a place behind a nearby wall, where we could not be overheard.

"Bressy?" I enquired.

"Naturally," replied Maisterson, "although how he has managed to find his way past Booth's sentries, the Lord only knows."

"Do I have time to change out of this sweat-soaked

shirt?" I enquired, wiping the perspiration from my forehead.

"I think not. Bressy is already pacing around Wilbraham's drawing room like an expectant father. If we are to keep him there long enough to conclude our business, you need to come now, without delay."

I own I was more than happy to leave Robinson and Wade to finish off the preparation for the kindling, so I made my excuses to them and walked with Maisterson up Welsh Row towards the impressive brick mansion and gardens owned by the Wilbraham family.

We found a sour-faced Wilbraham perched on the edge of a settle in his drawing room, examining his fingernails. Bressy, meanwhile, was stood with his back to us, staring anxiously out of the window towards the earthworks, which ran a few yards behind the wall marking the rear of Wilbraham's property. I noticed that both men were cradling cups of wine in their hands.

"Do not give me such a disapproving look, Master Cheswis," said the young merchant. "Mr Bressy may be a criminal in the eyes of Thomas Croxton, but right now he is a guest in my house, and I would not deny a man a drink when he sits under my roof."

Bressy swung around and looked me up and down with an amused expression on his face.

"My, Master Cheswis," he said, "you look as though you have just stepped out of a farmyard."

I scowled at the royalist spy. "Of course," I said, "what do you expect? I have a kindling to prepare for, and you have disturbed me. You certainly have a knack for picking the most inconvenient times."

"Gentlemen," cut in Maisterson, before Bressy could respond. "Enough of this nonsense. It will get us nowhere. I believe we have business to conduct."

"Indeed," said Wilbraham, suppressing a laugh. "Pray take a seat, Master Cheswis, although if you can avoid making a mess of my furniture in your work clothes, it would be appreciated."

I sat down on a chair opposite Wilbraham, and immediately a footman appeared with drinks for Maisterson and myself. The wine, I was glad to note, had been well-watered, for the weather was far too hot to drink it neat.

"So where do we begin?" I asked.

"I believe," said Bressy, "the arrangement was that we would share what we know about the key words on the engravings distributed by Abbot Massey, on the understanding I would recover whatever valuables he had secreted away for the rightful use of His Majesty the King. In return, I would help you in your quest to identify the murderer of Henry Hassall and Geffery Crewe, thereby removing the risk of Mr Maisterson and Mr Wilbraham being murdered themselves. I would also help you locate and bring to safety your housekeeper's granddaughter. A fair trade, I thought."

"Of course," I replied, "but forgive me for stating the obvious. You only have the word on your own engraving and that which you forced out of Henry Hassall. How do you propose to help us find this madman, when you actually know less than we do?"

Bressy took a sip of wine, and gave me a supercilious grin. "You mean you haven't worked it out yet?" he said, disbelievingly. "I confess, I did not have you down as such a dullard."

"Could you two please stop arguing?" snapped Wilbraham. "I am uncomfortable enough with a meeting such as this being held in Townsend House without it becoming more unpleasant than it needs to be. I would be most gratified if we could get this over and done with minimum fuss and maximum haste."

I grunted my approval, but I was not really listening, for the true horror of Bressy's meaning was suddenly beginning to dawn on me.

"Let me get this straight," I began. "Are you trying to tell me that the word you say is in your possession, which we thought had been entrusted to your family, is, in fact, that of the murderer?"

Bressy merely smiled, but Wilbraham jumped to his feet, spilling wine over the front of his shirt. "You mean Bressy is the murderer?" he spluttered.

Maisterson gave a low groan. "No he doesn't, Roger. Do sit down and try to keep up. He means that he is not the sixth, word-holding trustee as we assumed, but the seventh man."

Wilbraham glared at Maisterson and sat down sheepishly, wiping droplets of wine from his garments, but then sprang immediately back to his feet as he realised what Maisterson had just said.

"God's death, Bressy, you know who the murderer is, don't you?" he breathed.

"Of course, but he will not hurt anyone else so long as you co-operate with me."

The truth was worse than I had thought possible. I had always held Bressy for a cold-hearted individual, but I had not expected this from Alice, who must also have been privy to the information held by Bressy – and to think that I had once loved her.

"You are an evil bastard, Bressy," I said, trying to convey the full depth of the hatred I felt for him at that moment.

"Do not judge me, Cheswis. It is most unwise. We are engaged in a war and I will do what I need to do."

"But Amy is merely a child. Is she merely collateral damage to you?"

"Your housekeeper's granddaughter is perfectly safe. I know where she is being held, and she is not being mistreated. She is safe where she is for the time being. As for you, I freely confess I would have gladly shot you between the eyes in Crewe's bedchamber the other day, but Mistress Furnival appears to have a soft spot for you, although God knows why. And before you ask – no, she does not know where Amy is being held. I have kept that much to myself."

"And are you going to tell me where she is?"

"Of course – eventually, but not today. She is my guarantee that you will not pull any stupid stunts. You cannot seriously have thought that I would risk coming here on my own, into the lion's den, so to speak, without making sure I would be able to get back out again."

"I could always arrest you – here and now," I said.

Bressy laughed loudly. "Oh please, Cheswis," he said, his voice loaded with sarcasm. "Both you and I know that is not going to happen. Even if you were prepared to risk Amy's well-being, Mr Wilbraham and Mr Maisterson would not permit it, for such an action would put their lives at risk at the hands of the murderer. Now, can we please get on and stop playing games? I do not have all day."

Maisterson stepped over to where I was standing and placed a sympathetic hand on my shoulder.

"I fear Bressy is right," he said. "Come, let us see what we can make of this mess."

I downed my wine and got slowly to my feet with a sigh. From where I had been sitting I could see Booth's sentries patrolling the top of the earthen walls, and I thought how easy it would be to call some of them over. But then I considered the positions of Mrs Padgett, Ralph, and Elizabeth, and I knew I must act with their interests at the forefront of my mind.

"Very well," I said, reluctantly. "How do we proceed?"

Bressy smiled with satisfaction and gestured for me to return to my seat.

"I believe you have four of the six words. You can begin by telling me those."

I glanced quickly at both Maisterson and Wilbraham and received brief nods from both of them.

"Mr Wilbraham's word is 'Assumption' and Mr Maisterson's is 'Evensong'. We have taken this as an indication of some connection with Evensong on Assumption Day. This has been confirmed by the notes we have recently received from the murderer, which places a deadline of August fourteenth – the day before Assumption Day – for us to supply him with the remaining words. Geffery Crewe's word was Ridley, which obviously relates to Ridley Field."

"And your wife's word?"

"That," I admitted, "is where it becomes more problematical," and I explained Kinshaw's deception to Bressy, and the fact that the engraving was now in the hands of the murderer.

Bressy clicked his teeth in irritation. "Then we shall have to see what we can make of the five words we have – to see if they make sense."

"And what are the other two words?" I asked.

"Henry Hassall's word was 'Shadow'," said Bressy, "which means absolutely nothing to me. "The

289

murderer's word – and don't ask me to explain how I know it – is 'Bells', which is even less comprehensible."

"So we have 'Assumption', 'Evensong', 'Ridley', 'Shadow', and 'Bells'," said Maisterson. "What in God's name do you suppose it all means?"

"Just seems like a jumble of unconnected words to me," put in Wilbraham.

"I don't think so," I said, thoughtfully. "'Evensong' and 'Bells' will be connected, and we have already agreed on the significance of 'Assumption' and 'Ridley'. The only problematic word is 'Shadow', so I can only presume we are talking about a shadow cast by the sun in Ridley Field during Evensong on Assumption Day, and there is something very obvious in Ridley Field that would cast such a shadow."

"Of course," exclaimed Maisterson. "The stone pillar in the middle of the field."

"It was also where Henry Hassall's body was found," added Wilbraham.

"Yes," I agreed, "but that's not all. When Hassall's body was discovered, the whole of the area around the pillar was pock-marked with holes, as though someone has already been searching there, presumably the murderer, which raises some questions of its own."

"Does it?" asked Wilbraham. "I have to say, Cheswis, all it suggests to me is that the murderer only knows half the necessary information and went mad with a spade in an attempt to find the treasure. He has clearly made several attempts to dig up the hoard and failed miserably."

"Yes, but the question is how did he know approximately where to look? Remember, 'Ridley' was Crewe's word, and the murderer acquired that word only recently. His own word was 'Bells' and he also has 'Shadow', which is not enough for him to go on. More interestingly, he also knows the significance of Assumption Day, which suggests he has also found out Mr Wilbraham's word at some point. It seems there may be more to this murderer than meets the eye."

During this exchange, Bressy had remained silent, but now he coughed to attract our attention.

"The connection will eventually become clear," he said, "but you are straying from the point. You have established that the place where the treasure is buried can be found by measuring the shadow cast by the pillar in Ridley Field in two days' time at approximately the hour when St Mary's celebrates Evensong. All we have to do is come back here on Thursday and dig the treasure up."

"Assuming, of course, that the missing word isn't critical," I said.

"Let us hope it is not," said Bressy, "for all our sakes. In the meantime, it would appear our business is concluded here. I will see you all with your spades in Ridley Field at six o'clock sharp in two days' time. Cheswis, you may bring your friend the bellman along with you. He knows what this is about and will be useful for digging. Apart from that, come alone. If I get the slightest hint that Booth or Croxton know what is going on, then I will be off like a hare, and Amy Padgett, as likely as not, will not be seen again. Are we clear?"

The three of us nodded glumly as Bressy finished his wine and opened the door to the terrace that led to the back of Townsend House, and then disappeared across the grass and over the wall in the direction of the earthworks.

I watched as a man on the walls helped Bressy onto the top of the earthworks before waving to him as he disappeared over the other side. I strained my eyes to see if I could identify the traitor in our midst, but he was too far away and had been wise enough to march quickly along the walls to a point where he could no longer be seen. But then, I reasoned, what did it matter? There was always going to be some poor fool who would allow someone like Bressy into town when tempted by a few shillings, especially if he had not been paid for weeks.

"You seem pensive, Master Cheswis," said Wilbraham, who had been watching my expression.

"You are right," I said, smiling. "It seems there is always a compromise to be made in this war. I wonder if Mrs Padgett will see it that way, though, when I tell her she must wait another two days to discover her granddaughter's fate?"

# Chapter 22

*Nantwich – Wednesday, August 14th 1644*

It was Gilbert Robinson who found Adolphus Palyn's body in the Great Cistern. The squat, square-jawed head waller had been clambering about in the brine, trying to mend our theet, which had split lengthways, when he tripped over Palyn's corpse and fell head first into the salt-saturated water. The body was barely recognisable, grotesquely bloated; he had been identified by the colour of his breeches, which, like his shirt, had been stuffed with stones to keep the body submerged for as long as possible.

I had been busying myself amongst the salt pans when I heard the first frantic shout from outside, and a soaking wet and decidedly queasy-looking Robinson appeared in the doorway.

"You had better come outside, Master Cheswis," he said, before depositing the contents of his stomach on the wich house floor.

Of course, as I expected, it had not taken long for

Sawyer and Cripps to show their faces. Sawyer was his usual lackadaisical self, but Cripps was like a whirlwind, organising people, closing off the area around the body, asking questions, and making sure the coroner was sent for. It was as though he had been waiting for this moment for days and was not going to let it slip by without giving it his full attention.

"He's pissing me right off, Daniel," grumbled Sawyer. "Like an old mother hen, he is. And won't fucking shut up about that Fletcher lad, who he swears is guilty of all this. Says he'll have his balls in a vice before the week is up. He's like a bloody moth in torchlight he is. All over the bloody place."

"Aye, there's something not quite right about that one," I agreed, "but I have my eye on him. I think I know where the problem lies, and when I can prove it, you'll be among the first to know."

"Aye, well you'd better hurry up about it, mind, because the lad's dead set on picking a quarrel, if you ask me. Eh up, here comes trouble now, in fact."

I looked round to see Jacob Fletcher sticking his head around the door of my wich house. Thinking that with his and Sarah's child nearly due and that Jacob could do with the work, I had asked him to help with the kindling, an offer he had gratefully accepted, but the moment I saw his and Cripps' eyes meet, I began to regret the decision.

"Here, Arthur," I said. "There is going to be trouble.

You need to get involved. If Cripps wants to arrest Fletcher again, by all means let him, but make sure that's all he does, and try to keep him out of the way for an hour or two. There's someone I need to see. I need to get to the bottom of what Cripps' problem is."

Sawyer nodded his assent and set about his task with uncharacteristic gusto, and so whilst my erstwhile colleague, helped by Wade, Robinson, and several others, tried to calm Cripps and Fletcher down, a task not made easier by the fact that Bridgett Palyn and her mother had come out of their house, wailing with grief and anger, I took myself off to Wall Lane in search of Sarah Fletcher.

* * *

An enticing aroma of mutton stew was emanating from the Fletchers' kitchen when I knocked on Sarah's front door. She had been up to her ears in pots and pans, singing merrily to herself, and I felt guilty for being the one who would have to break her good mood.

"Something smells good," I said, as she opened the door to me.

"It is not often that we have been able to put meat on our table of late," she acknowledged. "It is thanks to people like you, who have given Jacob work, that we have been able to do so. But do you not have a kindling yourself today?" she asked, frowning suddenly. "What brings you here?"

And so I told her about what was going on outside my wich house. "But do not worry yourself, Sarah, I will have Jacob home in time to eat your stew. However, there are a few things I need to ask you about Eldrid Cripps."

I saw Sarah freeze momentarily, but then she pulled out a wooden stool from under her workshop, sat on it with her elbows on the table, and, with her head in her hands, she burst into tears.

"I wish that man would leave us alone," she sobbed. "He is ruining our lives; it was the biggest mistake I ever made."

"You had an affair with him?"

Sarah gave me a desperate glance and let out a huge sob.

"It only happened the once," she said. "It was last December. Jacob and I were going through a difficult time. There was little work, and Jacob was drinking too much. Everyone was worried about what would happen when Lord Byron's men came. Jacob had ordered some new boots from him, for his old ones were falling apart, and Eldrid brought them here one day. He was so kind, and he made me laugh, you know. We did it in his horrible little cottage, but I knew I had made a mistake straight away. I tried to finish it, but he wouldn't leave me alone, especially when he found out I was with child."

"And is the child his?"

"I don't know for sure. I don't think so, though. That would mean the babe would be early. But it doesn't feel that way. I'm almost certain the child is Jacob's. The problem, though, is that Eldrid thinks it's his, and he has been pestering me ever since, hanging around our house and causing trouble for Jacob."

"And does Jacob suspect, do you think? The way he is behaving in Cripps' presence suggests that he might."

"He didn't. He just thought Eldrid was infatuated with me, but he probably does now, especially after Eldrid had him locked up for the murder of Mr Hassall. He has been very moody since then, despite being busy with work."

"Then tell me," I said, "if your liaison with Cripps is over, what were you doing coming out of his cottage a week last Thursday while Jacob was at work?"

Sarah stared at me, a look of wild desperation on her face. "You saw that?" she said. "You were following me?"

"No, we were watching his home, and you happened to come out of it. What were you doing there?"

Sarah sat for a moment in quiet contemplation, but then she wiped her eyes, and a look of determination spread across her face.

"Very well," she said. "If it means you will be able to get him to leave us in peace, here it is. I'd heard Eldrid had been short of money since he took over your role as constable. His business was struggling, so I went round to his cottage, and I offered him money to leave us alone. We had a little extra in our pockets, you see, and I thought it would make him go away. But he said he wasn't interested, that no amount of money would deter him from proving that he was the right man for me, and, in any case, he had managed to borrow the money he needed from elsewhere."

"I see." I got up from my stool and paced around Sarah's kitchen. There was something nagging at my mind – a feeling that I had missed something important, and I couldn't quite put my finger on what it was.

"You won't tell Jacob, will you?" she pleaded. "I couldn't bear that. I love him despite everything. I would do anything to make things right."

"It is not for me to tell tales, Sarah," I said. "What goes on in your household is between you and Jacob."

Sarah smiled at me gratefully, but then her face contorted in pain and she clutched her belly.

"Are you all right?" I asked, concerned.

"I think so," she replied, grimacing, "but I think you'd better go and find my mother. I can't be sure, but I think the baby is on the way."

# Chapter 23

The next morning, Sarah gave birth to a healthy baby boy, which she and Jacob called Jeremiah. With a strong pair of lungs and a shock of black hair, he was every bit his father's son. Even now, many years later, whenever I see my godson, I wonder whether my discussion with his mother that day might just possibly have expedited his arrival into this world by a day or two.

Jacob, thankfully, had made it back home in time to see the new addition to his family, which he was allowed to do once the midwife had finished with Sarah. On the evening before the birth he had even managed to eat a plateful of his wife's mutton stew.

Arthur Sawyer, meanwhile, for once in his life, had excelled himself in dealing with Cripps. When his colleague had tried to arrest Fletcher outside my wich house, Sawyer had permitted Jacob to be led as far as the gaol house, but just as Fletcher was about to be locked in one of the cells, Sawyer had grabbed Cripps by the scruff of the neck and thrown him into the cell himself, telling him he could bloody well sit there until Master Cheswis had got to the bottom of whatever stupid game he was playing at.

Cripps had called him a two-faced, pock-nosed bastard, which had only caused Sawyer to laugh at him. The bailiff, Andrew Hopwood, later told me that Cripps' furious protests could be heard well into the night and from as far away as The Lamb.

Despite the temptation to interrogate Cripps straight away, I decided he could wait until later, as I was more pre-occupied with what lay before me in Ridley Field later in the day. Of particular concern was the fact that the fine weather of the previous few days had broken, and a thick layer of grey cloud had settled over Nantwich. By five in the afternoon it had brightened up considerably, but the sun had still not put in an appearance.

As Alexander and I made our way past Townsend House towards the sconce at Welsh Row End, we wondered how we were supposed to measure the shadow cast by the stone pillar. We must have looked somewhat conspicuous walking up the length of the street with spades slung over our shoulders, so we figured it was safer to go through the checkpoint at the sconce and double back through the fields, rather than clamber over the earthworks close to the stone pillar and attract the attention of the sentries.

When we arrived at the pillar, we found Wilbraham and Maisterson waiting for us, their shovels leaning against one of the water troughs.

"There is no sun. How are we supposed to measure the pillar's shadow?" I said.

"You do not think far enough ahead, Cheswis," replied Wilbraham, smugly. "It was a pleasant evening yesterday, so I left nothing to chance. There cannot be that much difference in the length and angle of the shadow from one day to the next, so I took the liberty of pinpointing the end of the shadow at six o'clock last night."

I looked at the ground about ten yards from the pillar, where a small, wooden stake had been driven into the earth.

"The sun may yet appear in time," continued Wilbraham, "but even if it doesn't, we cannot be far from the correct spot. If we dig here and work our way out in a radius, it should not take long before we hit the right spot."

I acknowledged Wilbraham's efforts with a smile. "That, Mr Wilbraham, was a good idea," I opined, "but I fear your thinking may be flawed. Evensong begins at six o'clock, but Massey's message refers to 'Evensong Bells', and the bell ringers begin their work a good twenty minutes before the start of the service. Did you not measure the shadow's position at twenty to six as well?"

As if to emphasise the point, just as I mentioned it, the church bells began to chime from across the river, and Wilbraham's smile began to fade.

"No," he admitted. "That did not occur to me."

"Gentlemen," interjected Maisterson. "This argument is pointless. Our measurements can at best be an approximation of where we think the treasure might be. After all, we don't even know for certain that Evensong was celebrated at exactly the same time when Massey set this riddle for us."

This was a good point, acknowledged as such by Wilbraham, so we all sat down on the steps of the stone pillar and waited for Bressy to arrive.

"We look like a bunch of bloody gravediggers," commented Alexander.

"Aye, that is correct," I agreed, "and we must take care to remember who it is we are dealing with here, lest it turns out to be our own graves we are digging."

And that thought was enough to reduce everyone to silence for the next few minutes. Eventually I caught sight of a movement behind the hedgerows at the far end of the field, and Bressy rode into view, a loaded carbine in one hand, the barrel lying menacingly across the neck of his mount.

"I see you are taking no chances," I said, as Bressy drew his black gelding up alongside us.

"Do you blame me?" he retorted. "We are out of

musket range, but I have no idea what you have told the sentries on the walls."

I looked over my shoulder at the red-coated soldiers patrolling the wooden walkway that ran along the inside of the earthen banks, a few feet from the top. One or two of them were showing an interest in what we were doing, but fortunately none of them had thought to come over and talk to us.

"I have taken a considerable risk coming here on my own," continued Bressy, "but you can be sure, if you have set a trap for me, things will not look good for you."

"Relax, Mr Bressy," said Maisterson, "the soldiers have no idea who you are. They are merely curious. It is not every day that a group of men with spades gathers here like this. We must be creating a rather odd impression."

"Then I suggest we make haste," said Bressy. "I see Mr Wilbraham has been busy and has already marked out the spot."

"You were watching me?"

"Of course. I realised there was no guarantee of sun today, and so I planned to mark out the spot myself yesterday, but then I saw you already had the same idea, so I left you to it."

Wilbraham scowled, but Bressy merely gestured towards the wooden stake.

"Gentlemen, I suggest you start digging," he said.

"Time is short."

And then, as if on cue, the clouds parted momentarily, and a brief shaft of sunlight illuminated the ground. The top of the shadow, I noticed, was pointing no more than a foot or so from where Wilbraham had placed his marker.

"It is six o'clock," I said. "Let us dig."

And so Wilbraham, Maisterson, Alexander, and I dug a hole around five feet in diameter and about three feet deep, throwing the spare earth to the side. Bressy, meanwhile, sat like an overseer on his horse, his carbine at the ready, in case anything unexpected should happen. As we dug, his face grew steadily darker, until after about half an hour he called on us to stop.

"We are wasting our time. There is nothing here," he said.

I wiped the sweat from my forehead with the arms of my sleeve and leaned on my spade.

"That, Mr Bressy, is self-evident," said Maisterson, with a grimace. "It would appear that we have either misunderstood Massey's message from the engravings, or that the missing word from Brett's engraving was crucial."

"I think we have understood the message correctly," I ventured, "but it would appear we are in need of my wife's engraving. Damn that man, Kinshaw."

Wilbraham flung his spade on the ground in disgust

and sat back down on the steps of the stone pillar.

"So what now, Bressy?" asked Alexander, climbing out of the hole we had just dug.

The royalist spy looked at my friend sardonically and raised an eyebrow. "I would have thought that would have been obvious, Mr Clowes," he replied. "I do not think you can be of any more help to me, but remember, I know who the murderer is and that he is in possession of the final engraving. I therefore have an alternative plan. I don't know about you."

And with that, Bressy put his carbine over his shoulder, swung his gelding round, and galloped off towards the edge of the field furthest from the earthworks.

"Wait," I shouted. "What about Amy?" But Bressy was already gone.

"Shit," said Alexander, kicking a huge clod of earth back into the hole whence it had come. "What now?"

Wilbraham and Maisterson said nothing. They merely looked on, horrified and speechless, but I slumped down on the mound of soil and clay and put my head in my hands. Tears started to fill my eyes as I began to realise the extent to which I had failed. I had failed everyone who had meant anything to me, failed to identify the murderer, failed to locate the treasure, and, above all, I had failed to identify the location where Amy was being held.

I had also let down Croxton, and by working

with two sequestered royalist sympathisers and co-operating with a royalist spy, I had run the risk of being accused of spying for the King myself. And what had I achieved? Precisely nothing.

Bressy now knew all the words except for the final one, and he knew the identity of the person who held both Amy and the final engraving, but, like a bumbling fool, I had let him escape.

But then, from the depths of my despair, it came to me. Seventy years on from Roger Crockett's death, there was, it occurred to me, one set of documents which had consistently pointed me in the right direction, but I had not taken the trouble to read them properly. Supposing there was an alternative scenario for what happened on that winter's day on Welsh Row, one that I had not considered, but one that was perfectly possible if you read between the lines.

All six of Massey's trustees who we were aware of – Richard Wilbraham, John Maisterson, Richard Hassall, John Brett, Thomas Bressy, and Crockett's replacement, Edmund Crewe, had been mentioned in the collection of witness statements originating from the investigations following the coroner's inquest presided over by John Maisterson.

If all six had managed to become involved heavily enough to feature in the murky proceedings that followed Crockett's murder, then surely there was a good chance that the seventh trustee would also be mentioned in these documents. All we had to do was re-read and understand exactly what had happened on that day in December over seventy years ago. There was, I realised, only one person who could now help me to get to the bottom of this mystery.

"Ezekiel Green," I said, to a startled Alexander. "I need to see Ezekiel Green."

* * *

Ezekiel still lived with his parents in a well-appointed cottage off Churchyardside, behind the grammar school, where his father was a schoolmaster. In front of the house was a small, well-kept garden, and it was here that we found Ezekiel, sat on a plain wooden bench holding a trencher of bread and cheese. The young archivist raised his eyebrows with curiosity and rose to his feet when he saw me coming.

"This is a surprise, Master Cheswis, Master Clowes," he said, wiping crumbs from his breeches onto the cobbles. "What brings you here?"

"I have a theory I would like to put to the test," I said, "but to do that I need your help."

"Of course. How can I be of service?"

"It has occurred to me that the answer to the riddle of who killed Henry Hassall and Geffery Crewe may lie in the court documents and witness statements that you showed me recently. Until now, we have always assumed that Roger Crockett was lured over the bridge to his death in revenge for his churlish behaviour relating to the lease on Ridley Field – that the attack was planned by a group of people, of which the Hassalls were the ringleaders, but which also included prominent members of Nantwich's other leading families. Our assumption was that the aim was simply to give him a good beating, but that things got out of hand, thanks to the blow delivered to Crockett's head by Edmund Crewe."

"Certainly," said Green. "That is the accepted view. The question was always whether it was Crewe alone who killed Crockett or Crewe in conjunction with several of the others, the degree to which the murder was pre-planned and, if such a plan existed, how deeply Wilbraham, Hassall, and the other accused were embroiled in it."

"Yes, but supposing the motive for dragging Crockett to the other side of the river was entirely different, that the argument over Ridley Field was just a smokescreen."

Ezekiel cocked his head to one side and looked at me thoughtfully. "You mean the plan all along was actually to get hold of Crockett's engraving?"

"Exactly. We know Edmund Crewe became one of the six trustees after Crockett's death. What we don't know is how Crewe came to be in possession of the engraving after Crockett's death. Bridgett Crockett would not have simply given it away. That is for sure."

"Then you are suggesting Crockett was somehow persuaded to bring the engraving with him the day he died? How would that have been achieved?"

"I don't know for certain," I admitted. "It is all conjecture, but let us say, for the sake of argument, that Maisterson, Wilbraham, and Hassall tried to cut him a deal. It would appear that the other trustees had long since come to the conclusion that Crockett was unsuitable as a trustee. Perhaps they decided to offer to let Crockett farm Ridley Field if he gave up his engraving and his position as a trustee."

"But why would they do that," asked Ezekiel, "if they were aware of the importance of Ridley Field?"

"At that stage they probably weren't," I said. "Remember, 'Ridley' was the word on Crockett's engraving. Only he knew the significance of the field in regards to the location of Massey's treasure, which is obviously why he was prepared to risk his standing in the town by resorting to underhand means to acquire the lease."

"I see, but if that was the case, Crockett obviously turned down the offer," said Ezekiel.

"Certainly, which is why everything came to a head on the day of his death. Having failed in their negotiations, Hassall and his mob decided to try and frighten Crockett into submission, so they beat up his friend Thomas Wettenhall. Crockett was so shocked that he changed his mind immediately, grabbed his engraving, and ran over the bridge to try and negotiate with those who had attacked his friend.

"Of course, the affray got completely out of hand, and Crockett was fatally wounded by Crewe, either acting alone or with the help of several others, depending on whose statement you believe. It is clear from several of the witnesses that the affray was co-ordinated, but what was not planned was the severity of the beating taken by Crockett.

"The original plan was not to kill him. This is shown by the actions of Richard Wilbraham, who came charging out of his house in his bed clothes to try and calm things down, and that of Anne Hassall, whose behaviour appeared to change from that of a raging mad woman to that of a caring nurse within the space of a few minutes."

"I see what you mean," said Ezekiel, "but how will any of this help you identify the murderer at large today?"

"A very good question," I conceded. "I believe the answer lies in the behaviour of Richard Wilbraham. It is clear that he was implicated up to his ears in the murky plot. It is no accident that Bridgett Crockett made especial mention of him in the days following her husband's death, and that he was the main focus of Thomas Palyn's subsequent perjury case. And why would John Maisterson go to such lengths as to frame

310

Palyn were it not vital that Palyn changed his story?"

"This is all by-the-by, of course, because of crucial importance is what Roger Wilbraham did when he tried to take control of the situation, when he saw Crockett dying in the street."

"He helped Crockett into a nearby house for a while, from where he was accompanied by a number of women back to The Crown," said Ezekiel.

"Correct. We have no record of what went on in that house, but I would hazard a guess that this was where the engraving changed hands. And where do you suppose this house is located?"

"On Little Wood Street, if I recall correctly," said Ezekiel, his eyes lighting up as he began to realise the significance of what I was saying. "Why, if I'm not mistaken, that is the very same house that Constable Cripps lives in."

"I knew it," I exclaimed in triumph. "In that case, all we need to do is to go back to your archive and dig out the list of witnesses. The name of the owner of that house is surely listed."

"Of course, but I can only gain access to the Booth Hall on the morrow. Colonel Croxton has the keys, and I dare say he will not be particularly enamoured if we disturb him on a Sunday evening."

"We cannot wait that long," I insisted. "Amy's life is at stake. Let us find the colonel and see whether you are right."

# Chapter 24

Croxton, as it happened, took a little while to locate. Rather surprisingly, given the tensions that had built in Nantwich between Sir William Brereton's network of deputy lieutenants and the moderate county elite typified by Colonel Booth, he was to be found in The Lamb, sharing a dinner table with the garrison commander, and, unluckily for us, having left instructions that he was not to be disturbed.

As we attempted to march through the gateway constructed between the mud walls which now surrounded the coaching inn, we were stopped abruptly by a determined-looking sergeant brandishing a halberd. He, in turn, was flanked by two foot soldiers, both of whom regarded us with suspicion, their hands on their swords, ready to draw them should it look like we were about to cause trouble.

"Where do you think you're going?" demanded the sergeant, eyeing Alexander warily.

"We would speak with Colonel Croxton," I said. "I understand he dines here this evening. It is a matter of the utmost importance."

The sergeant stared at me, stony-faced. "Not tonight, you won't," he said. "Come back tomorrow."

"Tell him Cheswis and Clowes are here," said Alexander. "He will see us if you tell him that. It is a matter of life and death."

The sergeant sneered, baring a set of crooked, yellow teeth.

"Oh aye? So says everyone. Well you're not getting in here, so you might as well piss off. We have strict instructions to leave the two colonels alone. They have important business to discuss."

Alexander took a step forward to plead with the sergeant, who immediately levelled his halberd at my friend's chest.

"Step back, bellman," he warned, "or you will soon resemble a stuck pig at a hog roast."

I was about to protest at the sergeant's overly aggressive manner when I heard a gentle cough behind me, and Ezekiel spoke up.

"Excuse me, Sergeant," he said, in a slow but insistent voice. "If you would be so kind as to tell the colonel that Ezekiel Green is here, and that I may have found the information he seeks, I am sure he will be happy to hear what I have to say."

I watched the sergeant's face closely, and for a

moment I could have sworn he was going to strike Ezekiel, but suddenly he stepped back, nodded curtly, and pointed towards a wooden bench against the wall next to the main entrance."

"Wait there," he instructed. "I will check whether the colonel is disposed to see you."

Alexander ran his hand through his hair in relief and gave Ezekiel a look of open-eyed wonderment.

"How in God's name did you manage that?" he asked.

Ezekiel shrugged and sat down on the bench, keeping his eyes on the two soldiers, who were still watching us keenly.

"Croxton's not stupid," he said. "He knows Master Cheswis has been delving into the archives to solve the mystery of where Massey's treasure is located. He asked me to keep him advised of any developments."

It was several minutes before Croxton appeared, but when he did, he strode purposefully through the doorway, slamming the door against the wall behind him. The colonel was clad in a fine slashed green doublet with red lining and matching breeches, but his face was like thunder.

"What in damnation is the meaning of this, Cheswis?" he growled. "What can be so important as to disturb me at this hour?"

"We need the key to the Booth Hall, Colonel," explained Ezekiel.

"The key? And you have dragged me from my table for that? I trust you have a good explanation for why it could not wait until tomorrow?"

* * *

Ten minutes later, Alexander, Ezekiel, and I were clattering across the cobbles of the square towards the Booth Hall. One or two soldiers loitering outside the taverns glanced across at us with curiosity, but most were too busy with their own business to notice three men in a hurry.

Ezekiel, to my considerable relief, had possessed the good sense to be economical with the amount of information he had given to Croxton. He had explained my theory as to how Roger Crockett's engraving had changed hands on the day of his death and how accessing the court archives would help us to identify Massey's sixth trustee, and, by process of elimination, the identity of the person who had killed Henry Hassall and Geffery Crewe.

Fortunately, he had refrained from mentioning anything about Jem Bressy. The last thing I needed was for Croxton to arrange for a regiment of troopers to chase the royalist spies across half of Cheshire. With my priority Amy's safety, the young clerk had been astute enough to realise that such an action could potentially put Amy in danger.

He had also correctly guessed that Croxton would not regard Amy's well-being as sufficiently important to second any of his men to search for her. The kidnap, after all, was essentially a civil crime. In addition, Ezekiel had persuaded Croxton that prioritising the identification of the sixth trustee would be the quickest way to recover Elizabeth's engraving, putting us in a prime position to recover Massey's treasure before Bressy. Ezekiel, I was pleased to admit, was proving himself to be a most able assistant.

With daylight beginning to fade and the interior of Booth Hall being as gloomy as ever, Ezekiel had sensibly thought to borrow a lantern from The Lamb, and from this he lit the candles in the sconces on the walls of his office.

"I shall return forthwith," he said. "The documents have been returned to their rightful place downstairs. I shall need to relocate them."

"So what is the significance of these witness statements?" asked Alexander, once Ezekiel had disappeared into the gloom of the archive room. "Why are they so crucial?"

"The documents give an indication of the furore Crockett's murder caused at the time, for they include the statements of dozens of working folk who just happened to be around Welsh Row on that day. All manner of people provided statements – bakers, briners, weavers, their goodwives – and it is the sheer volume of these documents which gives us a wider and more reliable view of what happened that day and helps give credence to the argument that the attack on Roger Crockett was deliberately orchestrated. Not only that, they help us come to the inevitable conclusion that events did not go as originally planned."

"How do you mean?"

"Well, there are numerous accounts of bystanders carrying tools such as dubbing hooks, fire shovels, and pikestaffs, items which could be used as weapons. A coincidence? I don't think so. There were also many statements to the effect that Crockett was struck not only by Crewe, but was set upon by many people.

"More importantly, as soon as it became clear that the plan had gone awry, the armed men vanished into thin air, and Crockett was helped by a number of women, several of whom had been haranguing him only minutes earlier."

"And that was when Richard Wilbraham appeared on the scene and led Crockett away."

"Correct – and now we shall see where he was taken."

Ezekiel was standing in the doorway, the relevant volume in hand. He laid out the manuscript on his table and flicked through the pages until he found what he was looking for.

"If I am correct," he said, "there are several witness accounts which describe Crockett being led away to a house on Little Wood Street, but the actual name of the owner of that house is mentioned only in the assimilated list of witnesses."

Ezekiel held a candle above the book so I could read the page properly, and I scanned the list of witnesses – two whole pages of them. As I did so, an icy chill began to creep up my spine, and I knew I had identified the name of my quarry, for there, amongst the Hassalls, Wilbrahams, and Maistersons was a name I was not expecting to see.

Alexander must have noticed the look of surprise on my face, for he looked at me quizzically. "What is it, Daniel?" he asked.

"Take a look at this," I replied, pointing to the words in the ledger, and I read out the entry.

John Gorste, to whose house Crockett was taken.

\* \* \*

Afterwards, I let Alexander and Ezekiel return to their respective homes and walked alone up Pillory Street. I would ride for Combermere on the morrow, but for now there was one thing I needed to do. I caught Hopwood the bailiff just before he was about to leave for the night. He gave me a curious look when I asked to see Cripps, but he opened up nevertheless.

"You'll be asking for your old job back next," he commented. "In fact, you can start now if you like.

Sawyer cannot cope on his own." He emitted a low chuckle as he registered my discomfort at the prospect.

I found Cripps slumped against the wall of his cell, his fleshy chin lolling limply against his chest. He stirred as the cell door creaked open, and regarded me warily.

"What do you want, Cheswis?" he demanded. "Are you not satisfied with having had me incarcerated in this hell hole?"

"Instead of the innocent man who you cuckolded?" I retorted.

Cripps sneered. "He does not deserve her. It is me who she loves. Fletcher bores her. Time will tell. You will see."

"You are deluded," I insisted, "but I am not here to discuss the rights and wrongs of your illicit relationship with a married woman. I should like to know more about Abraham Gorste."

"Who?"

"Do not even think of dissembling with me, Cripps," I snarled. "You are in enough trouble as it is. Gorste has killed three people already and kidnapped a fourth, Amy Padgett, the granddaughter of my housekeeper. If you value your neck, I suggest you start to co-operate."

Cripps paled and looked over my shoulder towards the door. "G-Gorste?" he stammered. "I know no-one of that name."

I was beginning to lose patience. I walked over

to where the corviser was chained to the wall and grabbed hold of his shirt, thrusting his back against the wall. My face was now right up against his, and I could smell his noxious breath.

"I talk of your landlord, as you well know," I hissed, "the man from whom you rent your cottage and workshop."

Cripps looked momentarily confused, but then he began to smirk. "I know not of what you speak," he said. "My landlord's name is Frayne."

"Frayne is the name of the chief steward at Combermere. Abraham Gorste is his deputy. You have met Mr Frayne before?"

"No, I pay my rent to his agent. Have done for years."

"And this agent, you know him?"

"Of course, his name is Baxter. In fact, he recently moved into the cottage next door."

I smiled with satisfaction. "I see. I take it you can describe this Baxter for me?"

"Naturally. Tall, about thirty years old, athletically built, unusual bright blue eyes. But I don't understand–"

"Mr Cripps, you have just described Abraham Gorste. I think it's about time you started talking."

I have to admit that I had been so consumed with the need to find Amy that the colour of Gorste's eyes had not registered with me, but, on reflection, I realised it was true, and both Kinshaw and Ralph had referred to the unusually penetrating nature of their assailant's eyes. I knew that I had my man.

"Gorste bribed you to frame Fletcher for Henry Hassall's murder, did he not?" I demanded.

"Bribery? No, of course not. What makes you think that?"

"Because you took money off Gorste to pay your debts to Roger Comberbach. In fact, you are fortunate he did, for if it were not for that, you may have been forced to accept the money offered to you by Sarah Fletcher to stay away from her."

Cripps stared at me as the shock of discovery began to spread across his face. He slumped back against the wall of the cell.

"That's not how it was," he said. "I had no idea at first that Baxter – I mean Gorste – was actually the perpetrator of this murder – and as far as Fletcher is concerned, he must have forced Sarah to offer me the money to get rid of me. He must have known the child was mine."

This, of course, was ridiculous. Cripps was so infatuated with Sarah Fletcher that he could not see the truth when it slapped him in the face. In truth, I felt sorry for him in some ways, for I knew from bitter experience the pain that unrequited love could cause.

"Fletcher does not have the slightest idea of what really happened between you and Sarah," I said. "He merely thinks you have a crazy infatuation for his wife, which is, in fact, largely true. The money was Sarah's idea. She feels guilty for what happened between you and her, and wishes to forget it ever happened."

"And Sarah told you this?"

"Of course."

"But what about the baby?"

"Again, you are deluded. Sarah gave birth this morning to a strapping baby boy. The timing is all wrong. If you were the father, the baby would have been premature and therefore much smaller."

Cripps looked defeated. He sat in silence for a few moments, and I watched as tears began to fill his eyes and roll down his cheeks. He tried to wipe them away with his shirt sleeve, but the chain which held his arms to the wall prevented him from doing so.

I took a kerchief from inside my doublet and offered it to him. Cripps accepted it gratefully with his free hand.

"I've been a fool, haven't I?" he said, eventually.

"You have," I agreed, "but there is still something you can do to minimise the damage and help me to find Amy."

Cripps nodded. "So what do you need to know?" he asked.

"Let's start by talking about when Gorste began to persuade you to frame Fletcher for Hassall's murder."

"At first I thought Fletcher truly was the culprit," explained the corviser. "I couldn't believe my luck. John Davenport saw Hassall being half-drowned in the ship in the wich house where Fletcher worked, and he gave a perfect description of him. Then I found out Fletcher had a row with Hassall over pay, so I figured it must be him, especially when Davenport identified Fletcher as the man he saw attacking Hassall."

"But then I came along and pointed out that Fletcher could not have been the attacker."

"Yes. At first I was in denial. I didn't believe you, which is why I continued to push for Fletcher's indictment."

"So when did Gorste become involved?"

"A day or so after the murder. I had been having trouble paying my bills, and Roger Comberbach was starting to lose patience with me. I realised I would need to pay my dues at the tannery or I would end up in gaol. Gorste had been staying in the cottage next door much more frequently, so I thought to ask him if he would defer one month's rent so I could pay Comberbach. He agreed to do this, but I knew it would not be enough to settle all my bills – just enough to keep Comberbach quiet for a month or two.

"But then things changed. A couple of days after I first approached Gorste, he came to me again and offered to pay off my whole debt if I was to continue to press for Fletcher's guilt."

"And you did not think this odd?"

"Of course, especially in sight of the fact that Gorste had clearly spoken to Comberbach to ascertain the exact amount I owed him. I began to suspect he might have had something to do with Hassall's demise, but I could not be sure."

"And you did nothing?"

"To my shame, no. He had me over a barrel, as I had already accepted his money, and in truth I could not afford to turn down his offer."

"And the idea of Fletcher being tried for murder was also attractive to you, no doubt?"

"Of course. That I cannot deny, but I swear I didn't realise the full extent of Gorste's guilt until much later."

"And when was that?"

"Not until Kinshaw was assaulted for the second time and Adolphus Palyn disappeared. I suspected as much after Amy was kidnapped, for your step-son gave a description of Gorste, but Gilbert Kinshaw also described an athletically built man with piercing blue eyes."

"But you still persisted in trying to have Fletcher arrested."

"Yes, of course. I was scared. Palyn had clearly disturbed Gorste in the act of attacking Kinshaw and paid for it with his life. It occurred to me that I was only a temporary solution, and that he would assume that I would eventually realise the true nature of his involvement in the murders. I realised that when that happened, I would be dead meat."

"So you tried to appease him by continuing to fight on his behalf, to give him a reason to let you live?"

"Do you blame me?" demanded Cripps. "I had no option. If I'd done nothing, I'd have been murdered myself or ended up in gaol."

"Which is exactly where you are," I reminded him.

"That is true," he conceded. "I should not have let this go so far. In truth I am relieved that this matter is out in the open and that I do not have to misrepresent my office any more. Tell me, Cheswis," he continued, "what do you suppose will happen to me now?"

"That I cannot say," I said, truthfully. "It depends on Croxton and ultimately on Sir William Brereton. I suspect you will lose your position as constable, but anything else depends on Croxton. I will ride to Combermere tomorrow, and let us hope for both our sakes that Amy is still alive."

# Chapter 25

*Nantwich – Friday, August 16th 1644*

*A*my looked with disinterest at the trencher of food
that had been placed in front of her. A slice of
boiled ham, a piece of cheese, a hunk of bread, and
an apple – pretty much the same fare as she had been
forced to eat for the past twenty-two days – or was it
twenty-three? She really had no idea anymore.

She turned over the piece of ham with her fingers
and gave a 'pah' of disgust. How she could have eaten
one of her grandmother's delicious pies.

"I'd eat that up if I were you," said the tall man who
had brought her here. He fixed her with those piercing
blue eyes that unnerved her so. "It's all you're going
to get."

Amy ignored the instruction and asked her captor a
question. "When are you going to let me out of here?
I'm bored, and I want to go home."

"That depends on how much Mr Cheswis wants you
out of here. Very soon, I hope, but you shouldn't be

bored. There are plenty of books to read."

This much at least was true, she reflected, as she watched the man leave the room and heard the key turn in the lock, shutting her inside her prison for yet another day.

The walls of the curious hexagonal space in which she had been incarcerated were lined with bookshelves, wall to wall. Half of the shelves were stacked with books on all manner of subjects, most of which were beyond Amy's twelve-year-old mind. The remaining shelves were empty, as though waiting for an impending delivery.

She had no idea where she was, for her captor had tied her up and blindfolded her as soon as he had managed to get her out of sight behind the wall at the corner of Ridley Field, and then, after a nervous fifteen minutes, during which she had been left entirely on her own, she had felt herself being hoisted onto the back of the man's horse, before they had ridden for what seemed like miles.

She knew she had spent part of her journey in a boat, for she had felt the gentle rocking of the craft she had been put into and the rhythmic splashing of the oars as he rowed. She also knew she was in some kind of cellar room, for she had remembered being led downstairs when she arrived, and she had heard her captor's footfall on the stone steps as he retreated each day to leave her in her enforced solitude.

*Apart from the rows of bookshelves, the room was furnished with a settle, an oak table, and several chairs, and her captor had laid a bed of rushes on the floor for her to sleep on. He had generally treated her well enough, except, of course, for the day she had tried to escape, but that had been her fault, or at least so the man had said.*

*On that particular occasion she had tried to spear his hand with the knife she had been given to cut up her cheese and make a bolt for the door. She had been neither accurate nor quick enough, however, and for her pains she had received a clout on the side of the head, which had left her ears ringing for hours. He had then taken away her food and all the candles in the little room, leaving her alone in pitch darkness for a whole day.*

*She was a fast learner and had not attempted the same trick again. Her captor had learned a lesson too, and henceforth she had been forced to eat her food with her fingers.*

*She had been taken out of the room just once since her arrival. A couple of days after her escape attempt, her captor had burst into the room in an agitated manner and told her she was to be temporarily moved. She had been tied up, blindfolded, and led up the stone steps, before being forced to sit once again in what she assumed must have been a rowing boat. This time she had tried to count the strokes, but she lost count half way through the crossing when the man realised what she was doing and threatened to tip her into the water if she didn't stop. She thought the journey had lasted about ten minutes, though.*

*She had then been marched along a wooden walkway, up some steps, and into a small room that echoed strangely. She had been fastened securely so she could not move, and gagged so she could not speak, before her blindfold had been removed and the man left her on her own.*

*She had found herself in a curious, circular container made of wood, perhaps fifteen feet in diameter, with two strange-looking pipes set into the wall, diametrically opposite each other.*

*She had been left there without food or water for what seemed like hours. At one point, she had heard voices outside the container, and she had kicked the side of the container with all the strength she could muster, but to no avail and, after a few minutes, the voices had disappeared into the distance.*

*Eventually, the man had come back for her, blindfolded her again, and rowed her back to her prison. But that was days ago, and the monotony of her existence had begun to blend one day into the next. She was beginning to wonder whether she would ever see the light of day again. How she missed the warmth of their house in Pepper Street, her grandmother's cooking, Jack Wade's jolly, joking demeanour, Master* and Mistress Cheswis, and, of course, her best friend, Ralph.

She let out a long, deep sigh and tore off a piece of bread. The food may have been boring, but she realised that if she wanted to see her family again, she needed to eat, and what was it the man had said about Master Cheswis? Was he on his way to rescue her, perhaps? Yes, that must be it.

She got up from her chair and went over to the bookshelves, scouring the rows of books for something to read. As she did so, she suddenly heard raised voices coming from the top of the stairs above where she was standing and then a heavy thud. A few seconds later, footsteps descended rapidly towards the door, and the man burst through the doorway, brandishing the blindfold and some rope.

"Quickly, girl," he said, "place your hands behind your back. We need to move."

# Chapter 26

*Nantwich and Combermere – Friday, August 16th 1644*

"If you think you are riding alone to Combermere to confront this madman, then you can think again," said Elizabeth, when I revealed my plan the following morning. "It is too dangerous. He has already killed at least three people. I have already lost one husband to murder, and I do not intend to lose a second." My wife wrinkled her nose and offered the kind of determined pout that I would normally not dare to contradict, but this was no normal occasion.

I had slept badly when I'd returned from gaol the previous evening. Elizabeth was already fast asleep by the time I crept into our bedchamber and settled down beside her beneath the sheets, and so I had no-one with whom to share the revelation of what Alexander, Ezekiel, and I had managed to unearth in the Booth Hall archives.

I had therefore tossed and turned all night, with

long periods of wakefulness punctuated by weird and unsettling dreams – the huge naked frame of Gilbert Kinshaw lying on a table in Nantwich's main square, being painted by a grinning Abraham Gorste. Alice, Jem Bressy, Roger Wilbraham, and Thomas Maisterson dancing round the pillar in Ridley Field as though it were a maypole, and Jacob Fletcher and Eldrid Cripps throwing a baby to and fro to each other with Sarah Fletcher trying to catch it, as though they were playing a bizarre game of piggy-in-the-middle.

Each time, I woke up sweating, realising that my dreams had the potential to be nothing compared to the nightmare that awaited me in Combermere.

Once I had breakfasted, I gathered Elizabeth, Alexander, Mrs Padgett, and Jack Wade together in my old house in Pepper Street to hear what I planned to do. I even invited Ezekiel Green around, as he had been instrumental in helping me identify who was holding Amy against her will.

I was not surprised to hear Elizabeth's objections to my plan to ride alone to Combermere, but I was unprepared for the reactions I received from the others.

"I fear Elizabeth is right," said Alexander, "you cannot risk going to Combermere on your own. The correct procedure would be to tell Croxton everything and let him deal with it. He would send a detachment of troopers down there to arrest Gorste and free Amy."

"Telling Croxton is the last thing we should do,"

I insisted. "Do you really think a dyed-in-the-wool royalist like Thomas Cotton will take kindly to having his estate invaded by a group of roundheads? Gorste will deny everything, and Cotton will insist the soldiers return to Nantwich empty-handed. Such an action carries a significant risk of failure, and if that happens, it will be enough to put Amy's life at greater risk than it already is. No, we need to be cleverer than that."

"Don't ask me to voice an opinion on this," said Ezekiel. "When Croxton comes into the Booth Hall this morning, the first thing he will want to know is what we found out last night, so I will have to tell him. If he ever finds out I am colluding with you to deceive him by discussing you riding out to Combermere alone without telling him first, then I am certain to lose my job."

"What about Wilbraham and Maisterson?" suggested Alexander, helping himself to one of the cakes that Mrs Padgett had brought out on a large platter. "Why aren't you involving them? After all, Wilbraham accompanied you last time you went to Combermere."

"Several reasons," I explained. "Firstly, I needed an introduction to visit Combermere last time. This time I don't, and Demeter is still there, remember. It would also look rather odd if Wilbraham and I turned up to see George Cotton a second time. Secondly, I have to bear in mind that we are under orders from Croxton to stop Bressy getting hold of Massey's treasure, and for that reason Croxton would not approve of me taking Wilbraham along again. Wilbraham is no friend of Bressy's, but he is a known royalist sympathiser.

"And, finally, there is the practical side of things. Wilbraham is no fighter. If it transpires that there is a problem with Bressy, then Wilbraham is more likely to get in my way than help me. I'm better off without him."

"Then remember what I have said to you these past weeks," interjected Jack Wade. "I may only have one leg, but I can still look after myself. Let me go with you. After all, I am your apprentice, and today is a cheese collection day. There is every reason for me to be seen out on the road with you."

Elizabeth and Alexander glanced at each other.

"Daniel, I do not think this idea is well-conceived," said my wife, but her words were only half-hearted, for she had already seen that I was not to be persuaded.

I felt a pang of guilt for having to put those who depended on me through such worry and pain once again, but what else could I do?

"Enough," I said. "It is on my account that Amy has been subjected to such danger, and it is I who must act now to save her."

And so it was. Wade went outside to prepare the horse and cart, whilst Mrs Padgett put together some mutton pies, cakes, apples, and two large leather bottles filled with ale to see us through the day. Ezekiel returned home with the strict instruction not to present himself at the Booth Hall until at least an hour after I had departed. The one concession I did make, however, was to send Alexander over to Roger Wilbraham's to tell him to keep watch over Cripps' house, in case Gorste decided to pay the corviser a visit, in which case Croxton was to be summoned immediately.

By ten o'clock we were ready to depart, so Wade drove the cart steadily up Barker Street, out through one of the sconces, and across the river at Shrewbridge. We were unarmed save for an old pistol that once belonged to Ralph Brett and which Elizabeth insisted that we take. This was kept hidden under a sheet at the back of the cart.

I was impatient to make our way directly to Combermere, but Wade correctly pointed out that our sudden appearance would seem less contrived if we were to show up with a load of cheese in our cart, ready for transportation back to Nantwich. That way, if we got back in time, at least we would have some produce to sell at market the following day.

We therefore called in at farms at the villages of Austerson and Aston on the way, and by the time we trundled up the approach road to Combermere, it was past lunchtime, and the cart was already half full.

As we drew up outside the gatehouse at the Grange, I noticed some activity inside the building where

Wilbraham and I had waited during my last visit, and, after a few moments' delay, a nervous-looking servant emerged and asked me who I was.

"We have no cheese delivery scheduled today, sir," he added.

"I am not here to sell cheese," I said. "My name is Cheswis, and I was a guest here two weeks ago. I have come to collect my mare, who turned lame during my visit, and who is still stabled here."

"I see. If you would both care to take a seat inside, I will see that someone attends you presently."

"I will stay here, if it's all the same to you," said Wade, who was sat with the reins across his knees, eyeing the servant with distrust.

The servant shrugged. "As you please, sir," and he turned on his heels to go back into the farm manager's lodge.

"Be careful, sir," hissed Wade. "Something is not right here."

I glanced quickly at Wade and nodded, before jumping down from the seat beside Wade and following the servant indoors. He then closed the door behind me and bid me sit down.

"It is Mr Gorste I would speak to in the first instance," I said. "Is he available?"

"No, sir. He is currently indisposed, but Mr Frayne is here. I will have him attend you personally."

I looked at the servant closely. Wade was right.

There was something about his demeanour that did not seem natural, and my suspicion was rewarded when his eyes flicked momentarily to the right. I followed his gaze through the window towards the boulevard that led through the orchards, and I thought I caught the sight of a figure weaving its way through the trees.

I turned to say something, but I was too slow. The servant had already reached inside a desk drawer and retrieved a pistol, which he now pointed firmly at my chest.

"Please do not make me use this, Mr Cheswis," he said, nervously. "I am not used to such weapons, but believe me, if I'm forced to use it, I shall."

I believed him. The man's hands were shaking like a leaf, but his eyes were focused firmly on mine.

"Have a care," I said. "I would not like to see that go off by accident, and relax – I am going nowhere."

My words seemed to reassure the servant somewhat, and he stepped backwards to sit down on a chair, but the gun remained pointed in my direction.

I quickly scanned the room for a means of escape. By the doorway to an adjoining room, there was a pile of hand implements – hoes, spades, and the like, but they were out of reach. If I tried to reach them, I would certainly be shot, and there was no point in calling for help from Wade. He could not see me through the closed door, and if I were to shout for assistance, I also risked being shot. There was no option but to wait until

Wade decided something was wrong and came to my aid of his own accord.

We sat there for no longer than ten minutes, but it seemed like an eternity. Eventually, though, I heard the sound of voices outside and watched as my captor's eyes moved towards the window.

I had to take my chance. I sprang from my seat and charged across the room towards the pile of tools. I heard the sharp report of the pistol and a crack as the wood splintered in the chair where I had been sat. The servant dropped the gun and made for the door, but he was too late.

I grabbed one of the spades and swung it in a wide arc, catching the servant on the forehead. He crumpled in a heap on the floor and remained still.

I opened the door just in time to see Wade dive over the back of the cart to grab the pistol and heard the dull clunk of his wooden leg against the inside of the cart. A split second later, his head appeared above the side of the cart, and he fired a pistol shot towards an unseen target behind the building to my right.

I stepped out of the building, only to see four men with muskets and fowling guns aimed at the cart. When they saw me, two of them pointed their pieces in my direction, and I immediately stopped and raised my hands. The other two, however, fired at the cart.

First I heard a dull thud as a bullet embedded itself in the side of the cart, behind which Wade was hiding, and then there was a piercing equine scream as a shower of shot scraped down the carthorse's flank. The horse reared, and the cart was thrown on its side, depositing Wade and our cheese onto the roadway. My apprentice, I noticed, although covered in cheese, was unhurt, but his pistol had spun away and had landed in bushes several feet away. Wade looked round like a startled rabbit, but as soon as he saw the two guns that were levelled at me, he groaned and placed his hands on top of his head.

At that moment, the well-dressed figure of Thomas Cotton emerged from behind the farm manager's lodge and glared at me malevolently.

"Take these two traitors and lock them up," he growled, addressing the four gamekeepers. "I will deal with them later. Then do something with all this bloody cheese, and for God's sake, put this horse out of its misery."

I then watched in horror as one of the gamekeepers produced a pistol and buried a bullet in my carthorse's head.

And finally, if that were not enough, as Wade and I were being marched at gunpoint past the front of the house, there, on the stairs, casting a questioning look in my direction, was the unmistakeable figure of Alice Furnival.

# Chapter 27

"What is the meaning of this?" I demanded. "You treat me first as a welcome guest, and then, two weeks later, when I come here openly and peaceably to retrieve my injured mare, you handle me as though I were a prisoner of war. Pray explain yourself."

Thomas Cotton stood facing us, with his hands on his hips in a display of overt belligerence. I had no idea how much time had elapsed since our arrest, for Cotton's men had thrown us into an empty cellar underneath the bakehouse, with no window and only a single candle for company. I guessed maybe a couple of hours had passed, but it could have been four.

"Prisoners of war?" exclaimed Cotton. "That, sir, is exactly what you are. Of course, if it had only been that you used your visit here to gather information about my estate for the sequestrator, Folineux, I would have been content with simply keeping your mare, using your cart for firewood, and eating your cheese, but that is not the whole of the story, is it, Mr Cheswis?"

"That's not how it was, Mr Cotton. Folineux got wind of the fact that Roger Wilbraham and I were here and interrogated us both."

"Perhaps so, but I would hazard a guess that the information he received came from your lips only. I cannot imagine that the Wilbrahams of Townsend House would openly collude with the Sequestration Committee."

"I am sorry for this," I said, honestly. "Folineux, I understand, has already made an assessment at Townsend House, and I was threatened with sequestration myself."

"You?" exclaimed Cotton, with incredulity. "This I might have believed if I hadn't taken the trouble to make some enquiries about you, as, I hasten to add, did Sir Fulke Hunckes, who also had his suspicions about your intentions here. Both of us unearthed more or less the same information.

"It appears both you and the accomplice you brought along today were arrested for spying at the time of January's battle in Nantwich and were imprisoned briefly at Dorfold Hall. You, I am told, escaped in mysterious circumstances, whilst your friend, who was badly injured, was freed the following day by Brereton's men."

"I am no spy," cut in Wade, suddenly. "I was a

trooper in the army of Parliament, and was dressed as such."

"Be quiet, churl," snarled Cotton. "You'll speak when you're spoken to." He then turned back to me and looked and me intently. "Your actions defending your home town I can understand, but I also have unconfirmed reports that you were active as an intelligencer during the recent siege at Lathom House, now thankfully lifted."

"I do not see–"

"Save your breath, Cheswis. I do not want to hear it. Keep it for His Majesty's interrogators. You will return to Shrewsbury with Sir Fulke Hunckes, where you will no doubt be hung as a spy. As for your mare, she will make a useful addition to our stables."

"You would steal my horse, Mr Cotton?"

"You will not need her where you are going. Have no fear, she will be well looked after. I believe Mr Gorste has taken a fancy to her."

In all the confusion I had almost forgotten about the deputy steward. I was sure now that the figure I had seen fleeing through the orchard was him. But where had he got to?

"That is another reason I came here," I ventured. "Abraham Gorste is wanted for the murder of two men in Nantwich as well as that of Geffery Crewe in your stables. He is also responsible for the kidnap of my housekeeper's daughter, Amy Padgett, who I believe may be being held somewhere on these premises."

Cotton gave me a wide-eyed look of stupefaction and scratched his forehead. Then I heard a strange gulping sound. It took me a moment to realise that Cotton was laughing. The gulping eventually gave way to a huge guffaw.

"God's Blood, Cheswis," he said, once the mirth had subsided. "You are indeed a strange one. Do you seriously expect me to believe such a story? Abraham Gorste is a trusted member of this household. I suggest you save your breath for when Sir Fulke arrives."

I looked up sharply. "He is not yet here?"

"He is on his way from Shrewsbury as we speak. He is expected here this evening."

This was interesting news. Firstly, it meant that Alice and Hunckes had travelled separately, which meant that Bressy, as likely as not, was not far away. Secondly, if Hunckes was on his way to Combermere, surely it had something to do with whatever he, Alice, and Lord Herbert had been discussing during my last visit. I suddenly had an idea. It was a long shot, but it was worth a try.

"As a matter of interest," I said, "what is the governor of Shrewsbury doing visiting this place on such a regular basis, and with Alice Furnival too?"

Cotton gave me a puzzled look. "That, sirrah, is none of your damned business."

I smiled patiently. "Of course not, but Alice Furnival

is a known royalist collaborator, whose husband was a known intelligencer. I'm sure Sir William Brereton would be more than interested to hear that you have been socialising with the likes of her, especially if I do not return today."

"Cheswis, you are hardly in a position to dictate terms."

"Perhaps, but if I am the dangerous intelligencer you think I am, do you seriously think I would have come here without telling someone where I was going and what I was doing, or that certain associates of mine don't already know that Mistress Furnival was here?"

"That is your word against mine," said Cotton, icily.

"Roger Wilbraham was a witness. His political sympathies may well lie with the King, but his primary interest is to protect his own estate. He will not deny it if pressed."

"And do not forget," added Wade, who had been listening to the whole of this conversation intently and with a hint of a smile on his face, "I am a witness to this whole conversation. You will never make the accusation stick that I have anything to do with Sir William Brereton's intelligence network, and if anything happens to Mr Cheswis, you can be sure I will testify against you."

Cotton said nothing, but I could tell that he was uncertain where he stood. A muscle in the side of his neck twitched involuntarily.

"I did not hear you answer, Mr Cotton," I persisted. "What were Alice Furnival, Lord Herbert, and Sir Fulke Hunckes doing here?

Cotton ran his hand over his neck and glared at me with contempt. "This is an entirely personal matter," he said. "I don't know why I am telling you this, but I suppose it is of no consequence. You will be safely locked up in a cell in Shrewsbury before long and will not have the opportunity to tell the sequestrators.

"Lord Herbert is an avid collector of books. He has a fine library in Montgomery, and he is concerned that it may be destroyed if the castle is occupied. We have a secure place for storing such valuables here at Combermere, and Lord Herbert is to send the most valuable part of his collection for storage until it is safe for his books to be returned. That is all."

And with that, Cotton stalked out of the room and slammed the door, leaving Wade and myself languishing in the semi-darkness.

* * *

After Cotton's departure, I sat in the gloom for a long time, deep in thought. Wade had fallen asleep and was snoring loudly, his wooden leg banging occasionally against the cellar wall.

What Cotton had said about Alice and Huncke's reasons for being in Combermere did not ring true.

Their motivation for talking to Cotton went way beyond personal considerations. Montgomery was clearly a strategically important location in the battle for the control of Wales and the Marches, especially so for Parliament, with the Red Castle having already declared for the King.

Lord Herbert, during his visit to Combermere, had expressed ambivalence about giving support to either side in the conflict, but a guarantee to keep his books safe from plunder would surely be a powerful persuasive tool to obtain his support. And once the books were safely under royalist control at Combermere, it would be very difficult for Herbert to change his mind.

And supposing some of Massey's treasure was to be used to pay Cotton to store Herbert's library, or, indeed, as a straightforward payment to Herbert to secure his loyalty? Was this why Alice was spending so much time at Combermere? Was she trying to kill two birds with one stone?

What interested me more, though, was the prospect of a secret store room. If Cotton was telling the truth and such a room existed, would its location not be known to Abraham Gorste? And would such a room not be the ideal place to keep a kidnapped child? It was logical to assume that Amy must be being held somewhere on the Combermere estate, but where could such a location possibly be?

It seemed unlikely to be in the main body of the

house, I reasoned, for this would make it easier to discover, unless, of course, the secret room had been built in the old part of the house which had existed in Massey's time. The room was also almost certainly not located in amongst the workshops and stables – that would be bizarre, as these areas were in constant use by servants and other estate employees. No, the best location would be somewhere relatively close to the house, but where few people ever went.

And then it came to me. It was obvious when you thought about it. On the day I first arrived at Combermere with Wilbraham, I had seen Cotton rowing with Alice, Herbert, and Hunckes from the summerhouse on the island on the other side of the lake. They must have been inspecting the secret room. Where better to hide Amy than there?

There was, however, one seemingly insurmountable problem. I needed to get out of this dark cell, and there seemed little prospect of that if I could not persuade Cotton to let me go.

But then, as if to answer my prayers, I heard angry voices outside. The cellar door flew open, and in burst Alexander and Roger Wilbraham, followed by George Cotton and a very sheepish-looking Thomas Cotton.

"You bloody fool, Thomas," swore the old man. "Harbouring a murderer, kidnapping one of Sir William Brereton's men. If you're not careful, you and your addle-brained schemes will have us sequestered for everything we own – and as for Hunckes, when he arrives you will send him back to Shrewsbury forthwith."

Thomas Cotton muttered something incomprehensible under his breath, which I took to be reluctant acquiescence.

"You are lucky Clowes had the good sense to come and find me, Cheswis," said Wilbraham. "You should have called for me in the first place."

Alexander said nothing, but his face carried an 'I told you so' expression, and I knew that this would not be the last time that this subject would be discussed.

"You are in the right of it," I said, "and I cannot be more thankful for your prompt response."

"All we need to do now is find Abraham Gorste," said George Cotton. "Has anyone seen him?"

"Vanished," said Thomas Cotton. "His room is empty, and he has not been seen since this afternoon. He will be long gone by now."

"Then I will ask for Frayne to arrange for a rider to be sent out to Whitchurch so that hue and cry can be raised. He will not get far. In the meantime, you are all invited to stay here tonight. It's the least I can do, and, Mr Cheswis, we will ready your mare so you can ride her home tomorrow. As for your cart, carthorse, and cheese, you can be sure that suitable recompense will be made, on my son's account, of course." The old man gave his son a sharp glance, which Thomas Cotton met with a sullen glare.

I murmured my thanks to George Cotton for his prompt and gentlemanly response to his son's actions, but in truth, compensation was the furthest thing from my mind at that particular moment.

"I will have one of my servants prepare rooms for you," continued the elder Cotton, "and in the meantime you are invited to join us in the library. I believe supper will be served shortly."

Alexander and Wade's eyes lit up at the prospect of enjoying some of Cotton's hospitality, but I had other ideas.

"I thank you for your offer, Mr Cotton," I said, "and I will be with you as soon as I can, but there is something I need to do first." With that, I pushed my way past Alexander and Wade, marched up the cellar steps into the open air, and headed directly for the boathouse.

* * *

I must have spent several hours imprisoned in the cellar of the bakehouse, for dusk was already falling as I passed by Geffery Crewe's window, from where Bressy had made his escape a few days earlier. The general impression of gloom was not helped by the fact that great billows of black cloud had gathered in the south-west, and a keen wind had begun to whip across the front of the house, whistling through the trees and bushes in the walled garden.

The boathouse was completely deserted when I reached it. It took a few moments for my eyes to get used to the dark, although an eerie light reflecting off the lake revealed several rowing boats bobbing on the water. Somewhere in the building, a door clapped intermittently in the wind.

I untied the furthest of the boats, jumped in, and fixed the oars into place. It was a little awkward manoeuvring the boat in the dark, but with a little effort I managed to push out into the lake and started to make a beeline for Cotton's summerhouse, its pink and white walls standing out against the dark backdrop of the trees.

The water was surprisingly choppy, and I kept missing my stroke, gusts of wind blowing cascades of water and spray into the side of my face. Within a couple of minutes I was drenched from head to foot, and I recalled Gorste's warning about the unpredictability of the weather on the lake. He had not been wrong. It was almost as though I were rowing in open sea.

About halfway across the lake, I glanced over my left shoulder and realised the summerhouse was no longer there – the wind was blowing me off course, and the island was now over my right shoulder. I lifted my left oar into the air and paddled furiously with my right, but in doing so I realised I was starting to fill the boat with water. I cursed and tried to moderate my stroke, but the wind was now blowing waves over the side of the boat, and the interior was filling up very quickly.

I looked over my shoulder and started to panic. The island was still a good fifty yards away, and I had nothing to bail out the rapidly filling craft with. I realised with a jolt of panic that I was going to sink, so I struck out towards land as fast as I could, trying to get as close as possible to the shore, but then the wind strengthened momentarily, and a large wave filled the boat. Like a fool, I over-compensated by moving my body too far to the left, and within seconds the boat was under water, leaving me clinging to one of the oars for safety. My hat flew off my head, sent spinning like a top across the surface of the water.

I started to paddle for the shore, gripping onto the oar for buoyancy, but then to my relief I felt the bottom of the lake beneath my feet. I was still twenty yards from the island, but by chance I had found an underwater spur. I pushed towards the land, the oar stretched out in front of me, and a few seconds later I collapsed, exhausted, onto the grass, which stretched right down to the island's shore.

I lay motionless for a few minutes, trying to get my breath back, and surveyed my surroundings. The island, perhaps seventy yards in diameter, was totally covered in trees, save for a small clearing on the island's high point, on which Cotton's summerhouse stood. Ten yards to my right was a small jetty, to which a little boat was tied. My heart jumped. That meant that somebody must actually still be on the island. I glanced upwards at the summerhouse and noticed with trepidation that a candle was flickering dimly through the arched windows.

I pulled myself to my feet and started to walk up the hill towards the wooden construction, my feet slipping on the damp undergrowth. The building, I realised, was made of clapboard painted pink, but carried a pointed slate roof with a gold-coloured weather vane at its apex.

After a few yards struggling through the undergrowth, I found a set of steps leading from the jetty, so I approached the building from the front. I tried the door, which opened.

Looking tentatively inside, I noticed that the room was furnished with a simple table, several chairs, and a large cabinet filled with fine porcelain and glasses, as well as more modest trenchers, mugs, and other eating implements. A barrel of wine sat propped up on a wooden frame in one corner of the room. The candle I had seen from outside stood on one of the window sills, its flame flickering in the wind.

My eyes scanned the floor, and I noticed that a roughly woven carpet had been pulled to one side to reveal a trapdoor, which had been set into the wooden floor. The trapdoor was firmly closed, but the fact that the carpet had not been replaced suggested the person present was either underneath me or had been forced to shut the trapdoor in a hurry. I smiled to myself. This must be the entrance to Cotton's secret room. I looked around the walls of the summerhouse to see if I could locate a key.

At that moment, however, I heard a faint sound coming from outside the building. I looked over my shoulder to see what it was, but I was too late. I saw a grey shadow fly across my peripheral vision and then felt a blinding pain in the side of my head. I shouted out as my hand flew to my temple, and I turned around, but all I was able to see before my world went black was a pair of piercing blue eyes staring at me through the gloom.

# Chapter 28

*Combermere – Friday, August 16th 1644*

*M*arc Folineux was not in the best of moods. He was used to being obstructed in his line of work, but Thomas Cotton and his household had gone too far. He would see that Cotton paid for his lack of respect where it hurt him most – in his pocket.

The sequestrator had arrived at Combermere just as dusk was falling, deliberately so, for he had figured that a late arrival would make it more difficult for the master of the house to feign absence, but from the moment he and his assistant had announced their presence at the farm manager's lodge, he had been met not only with obstruction and resistance, but downright avoidance.

He had been received at the lodge by one of the gamekeepers, who had looked at him oddly when he had asked to speak to Gorste.

"Mr Gorste is indisposed, sir," the gamekeeper had replied, in a tone that suggested something was being *left unsaid.*

*"Then let me speak to your chief steward, he should be expecting me."*

*"I am sorry, sir. Mr Frayne is currently also unavailable," the gamekeeper had insisted. "We have a minor crisis to deal with at the moment. If you would both care to wait here, I will see if I can get someone to see you."*

*The two sequestrators had then been left on their own in the farm manager's office, whilst the gamekeeper walked off, muttering, in the direction of the main house.*

*Twenty minutes passed by, during which time it got steadily darker, and the weather outside became stormier. A vicious wind had whipped up, rattling the glass in the window frames, whilst rain spattered against the panes. There was no sign of the gamekeeper, though, so Folineux got to his feet, brushed down his cloak, and announced to his colleague that he was going to find someone with better manners. Instructing his assistant to stay where he was, he marched out into the rain and made his way along the main pathway, between the rows of apple trees, towards the house.*

*A little way along the track he came upon a washhouse, next to which stood a wooden water tank and white picket fence. Standing by the fence and looking out across the lake was a woman in her thirties, who looked oddly familiar, talking to a slim, bearded man with dark hair. Folineux called out to them, but when they saw him, the two people appeared to take fright and scuttled off down a side path into the orchard.*

*"Ignorant snobs," he muttered to himself. "Another reason why people such as this should be sequestered."*

*But then he looked over towards the lake to see what had caught the two people's attention, and his eyes focused on a light bobbing its way across the water. As it grew closer, he saw that it was a man in a rowing boat, his face illuminated by a single lantern.*

*With a rush of adrenalin, he realised that he was looking at the very man he wanted to see – the deputy steward, Abraham Gorste – although what he was doing rowing a boat across the lake in the middle of a storm, God only knew.*

*An instinct told him that he should not call out to Gorste, that his interests would be better served by waiting and watching what the man was up to.*

*With an agility that belied his years, Folineux quickly vaulted the picket fence and then crept silently through the trees by the water's edge until he found a suitable vantage point. There he stopped, wiped the rain water from the brim of his hat, and waited.*

# Chapter 29

*Combermere – Friday, August 16th 1644*

I had no idea where I was when I woke up. Gorste had tied my hands round my back and bound my ankles together, but I was able to shuffle myself into an upright position so that I could survey my surroundings.

It was very dark, but when I looked up I was able to make out a circle of sky above my head. I appeared to be in some kind of circular, wooden container. There were pipes on the wall next to my left elbow and some kind of valve mechanism controlling what looked like an inlet sluice. Opposite to where I was sitting, I could just make out a ladder rising up the wall of the container. I realised with a start that I must be sitting inside the water tank next to the washhouse. In my unconscious state, Gorste must have rowed me back across the lake – but why, and where was he now?

I did not have time to consider this question, for suddenly I felt a movement and a muffled groan a few feet away from me, and realised I was not alone in the water tank. I strained my eyes and made out a small figure huddled against the foot of the ladder.

"Amy?"

There were some more muffled squeals, and the figure tried to wriggle towards me, but was only able to move a foot or two. I shuffled across the tank towards her and saw that Amy's wrists had been fastened with chains to the bottom rung of the ladder. She could not speak either, for her mouth had been gagged with a piece of cloth – a kerchief or some such item – and she had also been blindfolded.

"Stay still a moment," I whispered. "I will try and remove the cloth from your mouth."

I felt Amy relax her body, and I bent over her, trying to loosen the gag with my teeth. It took a bit of shaking, but eventually the cloth loosened just enough for Amy to be able to spit it out onto the floor of the tank. I then pulled the blindfold down over her nose with my teeth so she could see.

"Master Cheswis," she said, coughing and spluttering a little, "I thought you would never come. Where are we?"

"This is a water tank," I said. "It's used to pump water into a washhouse nearby. I will explain everything to you later, but right now we need to find a way out of here. My hands are tied behind my back with leather. If I shuffle up alongside you, do you think you might be able to untie me?"

"I don't know. I will try."

I pushed myself round so that my back was up against the ladder, and I felt Amy fumbling with the straps around my wrist. Unfortunately, though, the chains that had bound her wrists to the ladder were such that she could not grasp the leather behind my back with both hands at the same time.

"I can't do it, Master Cheswis," she cried. "I can't grip the knot."

At that moment, however, all thoughts of freeing myself became superfluous because a door opened in the side of the tank, and a beam of light flashed in my face.

"You are a persistent fellow," said Gorste. "Come, you can sit outside. I would like to talk to you."

Gorste hauled me to my feet and pushed me in the direction of the door to the tank. I hopped through the entrance, but then lost my balance and went sprawling onto the grass by the white picket fence. Gorste calmly closed the door, leaving Amy alone inside the tank, and walked over to me. Grabbing me by the collar, he propped me up against the outside of the tank so that I was comfortable.

"I must say, I am intrigued," he said. "How did you know it was me?"

"It is amazing what historical documents can reveal when you read between the lines," I said, breathlessly.

I began to explain to Gorste about the archives held

in the Booth Hall, and in particular the set of witness statements showed to me by Ezekiel Green. "I realised some time ago that the key to solving this crime was understanding exactly what went on in Nantwich in fifteen seventy-two, when Roger Crockett was murdered.

"Two things occurred to me. Firstly, the most likely way that Crockett's engraving ended up in the hands of Edmund Crewe was that it was taken from Crockett at some time between Crewe's attack on him and Crockett being returned to The Crown. Secondly, it was clear that this needed to have occurred somewhere out of public view, and where Crockett was in the presence of at least one of the other trustees. The only obvious location which falls into this category is the house where Crockett was taken by Richard Wilbraham immediately after the attack. I realised that there was a fair chance that the owner of this house was also one of the trustees and was most probably known as such by Wilbraham.

"This was confirmed by the fact that you have clearly known what Roger Wilbraham's word was from the start. Your ancestor will have found this out from the Wilbrahams in some way."

"Most perceptive," said Gorste. "My great-grandfather was a steward at Townsend House. There was a pact among those trustees who knew each other's identities not to reveal the key words to each other, but my great-grandfather knew where Wilbraham kept his engraving, so he gained access to his room one day, found the engraving, and memorised the key word."

"Yes, that is more or less what I thought. So all I needed to know was the name of the owner of the house on Little Wood Street. Once I found that in the archives, everything fell into place. The murderer, for example, seemingly knew where Edmund Crewe was. This pointed to someone who knew Combermere well. After all, Crewe disappeared off the face of the earth shortly after Roger Crockett's death, and his descendent, Geffery, did not show up at Combermere until relatively recently, so it is only since Crewe's employment as a farrier that it has been possible to gather all six words. Presumably it was Crewe's sudden appearance that prompted you to believe that you could resurrect the search for the treasure and gather all six words."

"Of course."

"But what I don't understand is the sudden urgency and the need to kill Henry Hassall."

Gorste shuffled uncomfortably and put his lantern on the ground. "That was unfortunate," he said. "I overheard Mr Thomas Cotton speaking one day to two new guests at the house. One was Mistress Furnival, whom you know, and the other was a man named Bressy. They were talking about treasure hidden by Abbot Massey, which they wanted to retrieve for the King. I realised that Bressy must be the seventh trustee, the one who knew the name of all the other six. Once I knew that, I realised I would have to act."

"And Hassall?"

"He recognised me. Hassall has been a visitor to Combermere before, but the plan was not to kill him at first."

"But everything went wrong when you realised Bressy had been there first."

"Exactly. When I turned up at Hassall's wich house, he was in a terrible state – half drowned he was. Told me that some madman had dunked his head in the ship repeatedly until he told him the word on his engraving."

"But Hassall didn't know you were also a trustee," I pointed out.

"No, but I told him that I was one, that I knew who Bressy was, and that the only way he could prevent him from stealing the treasure was if we shared each other's words and marched over to Ridley Field together. He fell for it. We took a couple of spades and walked up through the sconce at Welsh Row End and back across the fields, telling each other our respective words on the way. He wasn't really fit for the task, to be honest, and he threw up all down his shirt on the way. Nevertheless, when we got to the pillar we dug a few holes around it in the vain hope of finding the treasure ourselves, but of course we got nowhere. It then occurred to me that if I killed Hassall, it would most likely be blamed on Bressy, and I would be able to pursue the treasure on my own.

"There was no-one watching on the walls, so I hit Hassall on the back of the head with my spade. I must have caught him with a lucky shot, for he went down like a sack of potatoes. I then tied him up around the pillar, picked up the spades, and escaped across the fields."

"That," I said, "brings us neatly onto the subject of your tenant."

Gorste smirked knowingly. "You mean Eldrid Cripps? He is naught but an incompetent fool."

"I would not argue with that assessment," I agreed, "but he also happens to be a fool with money difficulties. He owed you rent, and when you tried to get him to pay you discovered the full extent of his debts to Roger Comberbach. You were helped inadvertently when John Davenport mistakenly identified the perpetrator as being Jacob Fletcher, whose wife you knew had enjoyed a brief illicit relationship with Cripps. You grabbed this piece of good fortune with both hands and persuaded Cripps to arrest Fletcher and actually pursue his indictment for the murder of Hassall. In return you gave Cripps the money to pay off his debts to the tannery."

"Correct again, Mr Cheswis," said Gorste, "and it would have worked if not for your involvement, although I concede that, in many respects, that was

363

unavoidable. I knew that Ralph Brett had been one of the trustees, and that his engraving was in your wife's possession."

I nodded. "But how did you know that, and how did you know the identities of the other trustees?"

"There is no great secret," said Gorste. "My family have known most of the names since the Crockett murder. Crewe and Wilbraham we have already discussed, Hassall was obvious, having been the instigator of the plot to attack Crockett, and Maisterson's identity also did not take much deducing, especially considering his close kinship to Wilbraham and the way he conducted the coroner's inquest.

"That leaves Brett and Bressy. The latter's identity I did not know until he turned up here with Mistress Furnival, but John Brett was one of the town constables in fifteen seventy-two. His testimony at the time of the inquest also led my great-grandfather to suspect he might be a trustee, so he asked him straight – simple as that."

I looked at Gorste in the light of the lantern and realised that the deputy steward was enjoying this conversation. If only I could keep him talking long enough for someone in the house to realise how long I had been absent and to come looking for me. I decided to change the subject.

"Let us talk about my first visit here and the death of Geffery Crewe," I suggested.

"Gladly," came the response. "You are doing very well so far, so why don't you tell me what happened?"

"Very well. After your first attack on Kinshaw, who you originally thought had my wife's engraving, you were no longer sure exactly where the engraving was, but suspected we might still have it, so you kidnapped Amy to use as a ransom, in the hope that we would exchange the engraving for her safe return. This was actually a mistake, because you intended to kidnap Ralph, my wife's son, but as you later realised, Amy is also very much part of my family.

"You were not expecting Roger Wilbraham and myself to turn up at Combermere with two of the engravings in our possession, but when we did, you decided this was too good an opportunity to miss. You also realised that our presence there was a result of your previous attack on Geffery Crewe. I now realise that at this point you already knew Crewe's word – your great-grandfather would have known it since the time it was taken from Roger Crockett – but you needed to stop Wilbraham and myself from finding it, so you took the decision there and then to kill Crewe.

"You deliberately lamed Demeter to keep me in Combermere as long as possible and then took the horse for Crewe to look at. You then left Crewe alone but doubled back behind the farrier's workshop, waited until Crewe had hold of Demeter's hoof, and then used a stone-bow or some other such contraption to shoot a metal bullet at her hind quarters.

"It was a very risky plan, because it had a high potential to go wrong. You only had one shot, so you might easily have missed, and Demeter might have missed Crewe, but again you were fortunate. It worked better than you could have imagined, and Crewe lay dead on the floor. You then went directly to Crewe's room and removed his engraving, before Wilbraham or I could get to it.

"As far as your plan to purloin the engravings held by Wilbraham and myself was concerned, this went badly awry. Your intention was to incapacitate the whole household by poisoning the bread."

"That is even more impressive," exclaimed Gorste, his eyes lighting up in the dark. "My stone-bow is normally used for shooting birds, squirrels and the like, but it was the ideal weapon in this particular instance, as it makes no sound and is not powerful enough to break a horse's skin. But tell me," he continued, "how did you deduce it was the bread that was poisoned?"

"Three people at the table were not affected by the poison – Mr George Cotton, Alice Furnival, and myself. The bread was served only with the cheese after the main courses, when Mistress Furnival and I had left the table. I don't know for sure, but I presume George Cotton did not have any bread. I also remembered that you had been in the bakehouse shortly before Geffery Crewe's death, which, I presume, is when you poisoned the bread. It would have been a simple task to make sure that just one loaf was poisoned and kept separate from the rest. This would explain why no members of the kitchen staff were poisoned.

"The fact that I failed to be affected by the poison rather scuppered your plans. I imagine that if both Wilbraham and I had been affected, we would both have been shipped off to see a physic, and our engravings would have vanished by the time we returned."

"That was indeed most irritating – and most unfortunate too," said Gorste, "for if I am correct, you were carrying Maisterson's engraving, the only engraving whose word I still do not know. Had I succeeded, today's unpleasantness could have been completely avoided. Indeed, once I had prised your wife's engraving from the possession of that stubborn fat oaf, Kinshaw, I could have returned your housekeeper's granddaughter to Nantwich without delay."

"That is a great consolation," I said, unable to keep the sarcasm from my voice, "but you are forgetting one thing. Jem Bressy. He knew the identity of all six trustees. He even knows the word on your engraving, so I presume he has managed to search your belongings at some point."

The grin on Gorste's face momentarily faded.

"You have been colluding with Bressy?"

"Of course; merely out of necessity, I hasten to add.

Bressy is a hard-nosed royalist spy who is bent on securing Massey's treasure for the King's cause. If you were to find it first, do you seriously believe you would get away with it?"

"He would have to find me first," said Gorste, scowling now. "Anyway, we have talked enough about this. It is time you told me the word on Maisterson's engraving, and we can all go our separate ways."

I confess, in retrospect, that what I said next was not the wisest of responses, for trussed up like a chicken, I was in no position to negotiate.

"What makes you think I will do that?" I said.

Gorste said nothing, but gave me a long, hard stare, and then got to his feet before stalking off in the direction of the washhouse. From where I sat I could not see him, but I heard the sound of a key being turned, the creak of a door, and the clank of machinery. There was then a gurgling sound and a shriek from inside the water tank.

"Sweet Jesus," I murmured.

Gorste had opened the sluice to the water tank. I wriggled again furiously to try to free myself from my bindings, but within seconds Gorste was upon me, grabbing me by the collar and breathing into my face.

"Now, I think you understand," he hissed. "The word on Maisterson's engraving, if you please."

It only took a second to decide what to do. The shrieking and crying from inside the tank was horrifying, and any will to resist Gorste vanished in an instant.

"Evensong," I screamed, "the word is Evensong."

Gorste let go of my collar, his face shining with triumph, but then an odd thing happened. The deputy steward suddenly pitched forward, his face landing with force in the middle of my chest. I wriggled to the side and was stunned to see Gorste's lifeless body flop onto the floor. In the dark, I could see a wet patch start to grow on the earth next to his temple.

I thought I was dreaming, but then I glanced upwards, for stood before me, dressed entirely in black, and looking every inch like the angel of death, was the figure of Marc Folineux, brandishing one of the oars from Gorste's rowing boat.

# Chapter 30

"I heard every word," said Folineux, as he untied the leather straps that bound my wrists together. "Miss Padgett is in the tank?"

I opened my mouth to answer, but Amy's increasingly panicked cries beat me to it.

"Master Cheswis. Help! The water," she shouted.

"We must get her out of there," I said, as I struggled with the ties around my ankles.

Folineux produced a knife from inside his doublet and cut neatly through the bindings. I nodded my thanks and ran straight to the door in the side of the water tank, pushing with all my strength, but it wouldn't budge. Folineux joined me and charged at it with his shoulder, but to no avail. The water inside the tank must already have been a couple of feet deep, and the pressure on the door was too much for it to be moved.

"The sluice," said Folineux. "Inside the washhouse.

370

We must close the sluice."

The sequestrator ran off to the nearby building, but a few seconds later I heard a rattling sound and an exasperated shout.

"He's locked the door. Is there a key in his pocket?" I turned Gorste's body over and fumbled with the inside of his doublet, but found nothing.

"I think he's hidden it somewhere," I shouted, "but we don't have time to search for it. The tank is filling fast."

"I will look for it," came the reply. "It can't be far."

I could not wait, however. I needed to be with Amy. So I clambered up the ladder on the outside of the tank, swung my legs over the top, and started climbing down the ladder on the inside.

"Hold on, Amy, I'm coming," I said.

I slid down the last few rungs and noticed that the water was already above my knees and up to Amy's neck. I only had a minute or so to free her. I fumbled for the chains around her wrists, but they were fastened tight. The only solution was to try and rip the wooden ladder off the wall of the tank. I pulled hard at the bottom rung, which creaked a little, but did not budge.

I then wrapped my legs around Amy so I could put my feet against the wall of the tank for leverage. Again, the ladder moved slightly, but it remained fastened to the wall. I looked round in desperation. The water was now lapping around Amy's chin.

I glanced over to the sluice on the opposite side of the tank. Perhaps if I took off my doublet and shirt and jammed them into the sluice, they might staunch the flow of water and buy me a few minutes. I waded over to the other side of the tank, ripping off my garments as I did so. I jammed my shirt and doublet into the sluice, which slowed the flow from the pipe, but not completely.

At that moment, however, I heard a coughing sound from behind me and realised that Amy's mouth was beginning to fill with water. I turned round in wild panic, waded back across the tank and tried to lift Amy's body. She moved a few inches and was able to cough out the water, taking a few deep, rasping breaths.

This was no solution, though. I could not hold her there forever. Tears began to stream down my face, and I began to wonder how I was going to break this news to Mrs Padgett, what she would say to me and whether she would blame me.

As I fought to keep Amy's chin above the water, I was vaguely aware of some shouting from outside the tank, and suddenly a face appeared above the top of the wall.

"Watch out, Cheswis," said an oddly calm voice, and suddenly the flying form of Jem Bressy landed beside me with a splash. A second later Alice's face also appeared over the edge of the tank.

"Here, you grab one leg and I'll grab the other,"

shouted Bressy, and he placed both his feet against the wall of the tank. For a split second, in my panic, I thought Bressy was asking me to grab hold of Amy's legs, but then I realised he was referring to the ladder.

I kissed Amy on the forehead. "Take a deep breath," I said. When she had done so, I let her gently into the water and watched her head submerge. I then grabbed the other leg of the ladder and placed both my feet against the wall like Bressy.

"One, two, three," yelled Bressy, and we both heaved with all our might. Nothing.

"It still won't move," I cried in desperation.

"Try again," said Bressy. "Harder this time." On the second pull I thought I heard a slight cracking sound, but the ladder still stayed stubbornly fixed to the wall.

"One more time," Bressy insisted.

"We need to lift Amy again," I said. "She needs another breath."

"There's no time, and the water's too deep. Come on, one more pull will do it."

So we pulled on the ladder once again, and this time there was an ear-splitting crack and a splintering sound as the ladder came away from the side of the tank. Bressy and I flew backwards into the water, and Amy, coughing and spluttering, came floating to the surface.

\* \* \*

Ten minutes later, Amy, Bressy, and I sat on the grass, recovering. All three of us were soaking wet. I wrung out my shirt and doublet, and put them back on, for a chill breeze was still whipping across the lake. Alice removed her cloak and wrapped it round Amy's shoulder. I curled my right arm around her too, for she was shivering with the shock, and her teeth were chattering.

Folineux eventually returned from the washhouse, having kicked down a side door to enter the building and open the tank's outlet sluice, so that it would empty. He then carried out a thorough search of Gorste's body and found a key to Amy's chains secreted inside the dead man's hose. The sequestrator unlocked the chains and threw the remains of the wooden ladder onto the grass.

Amazingly, given the noise we had made, nobody had come from the house to see what the commotion was about. I could only assume that the wind whistling along the length of the lake had carried all noise away from the main building.

Bressy and Alice acknowledged the sudden arrival of Folineux with looks of reserved suspicion, but the sequestrator did not stand on ceremony.

"Don't I know you from somewhere, mistress?" he asked, fixing Alice with a penetrating stare. "You seem strangely familiar. Were you not in Nantwich quite recently?"

Alice's eyes flicked instantly to Bressy, who gave her an almost imperceptible shake of the head.

"I think not, sir," replied Alice.

"My wife and I have never had the pleasure of visiting Nantwich," interjected Bressy, smiling broadly at Folineux. "We are from Shrewsbury. My name is Cotton," he added, extending his hand for the sequestrator to shake, "James Cotton. Thomas Cotton is my cousin."

"Marc Folineux. I am a senior collector and assessor for the Nantwich Hundred."

Bressy gave me a quick glance of surprise but quickly regained his composure.

"You wish to sequester my cousin?" he asked.

"He knows I am coming, sir," said Folineux. "I was to assess his estate on behalf of the Sequestration Committee, in order that he may atone for his delinquency, although seeing as I have just killed his deputy steward, I do not think that such an action will be considered appropriate on this particular occasion."

"Under the circumstances," said Alice, "perhaps it would be better if you were to accompany me to the house. I will introduce you to Mr Cotton, and you can explain what has happened here. My husband will stay here with Mr Cheswis and the young girl until help and some dry blankets arrive."

Folineux acquiesced with a nod and started to follow Alice towards the house. I breathed a sigh of relief.

"That was skilfully done," I said, gratefully. "It would not have done for Folineux to find out who you were."

"From your point of view, I imagine that must be something of an understatement. However, we now have a problem. We still don't know the word on your wife's engraving, and the only person who does is dead."

"You mean you didn't locate the engraving? I thought that was your plan."

"It was. I searched Gorste's room, but he was no fool. He had removed the engravings to a safe place, but I have no idea where to look, unless, of course, you are able to shed some light on the matter?"

It was hard not to laugh at the irony of it. Four people, including Gorste himself, had lost their lives as a result of Massey's treasure, and there would have been a fifth, had it not been for Bressy. But now, unless someone managed to dig in the right place quite by chance, the treasure had been lost forever.

But then Amy said something that changed everything once again.

"You are talking about the ugly little medallion we found in the trunk upstairs in your house in Beam Street?"

I nodded. Of course, Amy had been there when we found it. How could I have been so stupid as to forget.

"There is a single word that was cut into the metal on

the engraving," I said. "It is that word which we seek."

"Well, that is easy," said Amy, as Bressy looked on in astonishment. "I remember because I thought it so odd at the time. The word on the engraving is 'Thrice'."

I laughed out loud, and went to kiss Amy on the forehead, but Bressy was already looking at me earnestly. We were still enemies, and now both of us knew exactly where the treasure was buried. All that had to be done was to take a line from the stone pillar in Ridley Field to the most recently dug hole and measure the distance twice more in the same direction.

"I trust you will abide by the terms of our agreement," said Bressy. "We agreed I would help you locate your housekeeper's granddaughter in exchange for a free run at the treasure."

It had not happened exactly as either Bressy or I had intended, but it could not be denied that Amy would have drowned had it not been for the royalist spy's intervention. I owed him something, and it would have been churlish of me to pretend otherwise.

"You know I cannot agree to that, Bressy," I said. "I will have to report today's events to Colonel Croxton, and he will want to recover the treasure himself, but one thing I will say is that Amy is in no fit state to ride back to Nantwich tonight, and I need to recover my mare from the stables and negotiate with Cotton about what is to be done to recompense me for the carthorse he killed and for the loss of my cart and cheese. I can't see me getting back to Nantwich before tomorrow afternoon."

I did not need to say anything else. Bressy understood my meaning. He gave me a long, hard look in the eye, nodded curtly, and made off at a run through the fruit trees in the direction of the Grange, just as the sound of Alexander, Wilbraham, and Wade could be heard coming round the corner of the house.

# Chapter 31

*T*he soberly dressed young colonel paced up and down in his office in Nantwich's Booth Hall and sucked his teeth in irritation. He was not a happy man, for the cheese merchant and the chandler he had entrusted with the job of finding Abbot Massey's hoard of hidden treasure had failed in their task of keeping it from the hands of the King's agents.

The fledgling intelligencers had returned from Combermere two days earlier, with the kidnapped girl in tow, to inform him that they had not only solved the murders of Henry Hassall, Geffery Crewe, and Adolphus Palyn, but that they also knew the location of the missing treasure, and would go and dig it up at once. What they had failed to realise was that the royalist intelligencer, Bressy, had beaten them to it by a matter of several hours.

That morning, shortly after dawn, guards patrolling the walls had reported seeing a lone horseman digging *furiously a few yards from the stone pillar in Ridley Field, extracting a small, wooden chest from the hole he had dug, and then making off at speed across the fields in the direction of Whitchurch. Not one of the sentries had been able to explain why nobody had thought to apprehend the man and bring him in for questioning.*

*The colonel now faced the uncomfortable prospect of having to explain to Sir William Brereton why Prince Rupert's campaign in Shropshire and the Welsh Marches was likely to be boosted by this unexpected piece of additional funding. The royalist controlled mint in Shrewsbury was likely to be busy in the coming days, he reflected.*

*But no matter, they would have to make the best of it, and with Sir Thomas Myddelton already planning to move on Montgomery, there would be plenty of opportunity for Parliament to hit back. And when it did, he knew which two men he would place at the forefront of any covert operation that might be deemed necessary. Make no mistake about it, the cheese merchant and the chandler would have every opportunity to make amends for their failure, and they would find out about it sooner than they realised.*

*Meanwhile, in Shrewsbury, the young widow stood in the drawing room of her elegant town house and watched her three children playing in the garden outside. They were growing up quickly, she mused.*

*The two boys were chasing each other with wooden swords, the eldest, Hugh, defending an attack by his younger brother, Edward, whilst the youngest child, a girl, every inch a princess, was pretending to cower in a makeshift wooden shack constructed in the middle of the lawn.*

*How typical, she thought, that Hugh, the very image of his father, had chosen to play the kidnapper rather than the brave rescuing knight, and she wondered whether her eldest would grow up like her dead husband, more suited to operating in the shadows, unlike brave young Edward, who was an outgoing and straightforward child. How, she wondered, would her children have turned out had she chosen her childhood sweetheart for a husband all those years ago rather than the printer who had swept her off her feet?*

*The young widow was glad to be back in Shrewsbury, but she had been unable to settle since her return. Her trip had achieved its main objective, but she could not shake off a nagging sense of disquiet, as though something were not quite right.*

*She could not deny a sense of unease that her path had crossed again with the man who was such an integral part of her past. It was as though God were constantly trying to question the choices she had made. She could not deny the pang of pain she had felt at his rejection of her during the brief time they were alone in the murdered groom's bedchamber, and she now realised how much she had hurt him.*

*But this was not the end for them, she realised. She knew his paymasters would not allow him to let Bressy return to Shrewsbury unopposed with a chest full of plate and coin. He would be sent to Shrewsbury, she was sure of that, and when he arrived, she would be ready for him.*

*At the same time, in a country house several miles away, the middle-aged landowner who had taken over the day-to-day control of the Combermere estate sat by a window in his fine library and stared out to the right of the building and across the lake, reflecting on the disasters of the previous few days.*

*Not only had he enraged his father by arresting and imprisoning that confounded cheese merchant, he would now be forced to compensate the man by buying him a new horse and cart and paying him the value of half a cartload of best Cheshire cheese.*

*And then there was the issue of Abraham Gorste. The nature of the deputy steward's murderous deeds had come as a severe shock, but, although the man had doubtless come to a deserved end, it did not alter the fact that the estate was now short of a deputy steward and, despite everything, it could not be denied that Gorste had been a damned fine servant.*

*The only positive angle he could take from the whole debacle was the fact that the collector sent by Brereton had sheepishly agreed to postpone the assessment of the estate, which was the least he could do, considering he had been responsible for the death of one of his senior employees.*

*Cotton was under no illusions, though. The collector was no fool. He would be back, and next time assessment would be unavoidable. And as if that were not enough, his carefully negotiated deal to store Lord Herbert's valuable library had fallen through.*

*Sir Fulke Hunckes had arrived at Combermere on the previous Friday evening to find that the house was in chaos, and that the location of the secret room under the summerhouse had been compromised and was now known by several of Sir William Brereton's underlings. Hunckes had explained that it would now be impossible for Combermere to house Lord Herbert's property, and had left without ceremony the following morning in the company of Mistress Furnival.*

*Back in Nantwich, the briner's wife sang gently to her baby son, who gurgled contentedly in her arms, his belly full of milk. Things could not have turned out better, she thought. Her husband had thought it a bit odd that she had insisted that the wich house owner who had employed him when times were hard should be named as a godfather to the child, but she explained it away by pointing out that he had been present when she had gone into labour, and had been most helpful in ensuring that she had been placed in good hands for the birth. The real reason had remained mercifully* under wraps.

Eldrid Cripps, however, was free again, all charges against him having been dropped on the agreement that he would leave her alone. But this suited her just fine, as she had no wish to ruin the man, just so long as he kept his side of the bargain. He was even back in his job as constable, which she was not so sure about, but she suspected that this had something to do with the lack of available replacements and the desire of his predecessor to avoid being lumbered with the job for a second time.

The wich house owner himself was back where he liked it the best, in the arms of his family. He knew this would not last for long, and he understood the loss of the abbot's hoard would not be allowed to be forgotten, but for now he was content.

His housekeeper was a changed woman now that her granddaughter was once again safe at home, seemingly none the worse for her experience, other than a reluctance to sleep without a lit candle in the room.

His adopted son was delighted at having his best friend back again and was generally to be found running in and out of the house like a whirlwind, wielding his wooden sword with the kind of innocent exuberance that can only be found in childhood.

The wich house owner's apprentice was happy too, having been able to make an active contribution to the kidnapped girl's safe return, an act the like of which, despite his confident outward demeanour, he had never been wholly sure he would be able to perform again. But now he knew for certain that his missing leg would not stop him living his life to the full.

Only the wich house owner's wife seemed to have mixed feelings. The fact that her husband had been forced to co-operate with the man who had murdered her first husband weighed heavily on her mind. She had the strange feeling that this was not the last she was going to hear of Jem Bressy.

The wich house owner sat in his chair at his home in Beam Street, his legs resting on a footstool, watching the people he loved and who formed his household go about their daily business, all five of them. Yes, he was content, even more so because his wife had just told him that their unusually structured family was soon to become a family of six.

But that was not until next Spring. Plenty of time for things to change. He was just considering that thought when he saw Ezekiel Green walk past his window. He caught the young man's eye, but the look on the young archivist's face bore an apologetic expression, one that he had seen on more than one occasion before. The wich house owner sighed and waited for the inevitable knock on the door.

# Historical Notes

The murder of Roger Crockett, the landlord of The Crown, Nantwich's largest coaching inn, which took place on 19 December 1572, has been shown to be of considerable interest to historians, partly because the case is so well-documented, but also because of the remarkable aftermath to the killing. The legal battle between the victim's widow, Bridgett Crockett, and those she accused continued for several years and eventually ended up in the Star Chamber.

Roger Crockett was a self-made man, who derived the majority of his income from the success and the profitability of The Crown. However, despite his success and his desire to be upwardly mobile, it is likely that Crockett was looked down upon by the town's elite, which included a number of key families who had owned land in and around the town for generations. These included the Maistersons, the Wilbrahams, and the Hassalls.

The feud which culminated in Crockett's murder began when Crockett outbid the Hassall family for the lease on Ridley Field, a prime piece of pasture land adjacent to Welsh Row on the opposite side of the River Weaver to the town centre. Crockett and Hassall had clashed over legal issues before, and the town was split over its support for the two protagonists.

The feud between the two camps lasted for several months and got to the point where many of Crockett and Hassall's supporters were forced to sign declarations to keep the peace. The dispute finally came to a head on the day that Crockett was supposed to take possession of Ridley Field, when one of Crockett's friends, Thomas Wettenhall, was set upon by a group of Hassall's supporters and badly injured.

The questions which have never been definitively answered are whether this was a deliberately orchestrated attempt by Hassall's supporters to lure Crockett across the bridge to attack him, the degree to which Richard Wilbraham was involved in any such collusion, and whether the plan (if it existed) was to kill Crockett or just to frighten him into submission.

In any case, Crockett rose to the bait and crossed the bridge in Welsh Row, where he was viciously assaulted by a crowd of people, among whom was a cordwainer called Edmund Crewe, who dealt Crockett a blow on the head which eventually proved to be fatal.

At the height of the fracas, Richard Wilbraham emerged from his house still dressed in his bedclothes and calmed the situation down. Crockett, mortally wounded, was led first into a house on Little Wood Street and then back to The Crown, where he died later the same evening. At this point, the arguments of the two factions diverge.

Bridgett Crockett's claim was that the assault on her husband was deliberately planned by Hassall, Wilbraham, and several others, and that he was attacked and killed by multiple blows from a number of people. She even went to the lengths of displaying her husband's naked body in the street outside The Crown, so that the townsfolk could see the multiple wounds suffered by him. She also engaged a local artist, John Hunter, to paint the corpse as evidence.

The Hassall version of events was that the affray was unplanned, that one man, Edmund Crewe, was responsible for the killing, and, in a manner quite contrary to Bridgett Crockett's statements, that Richard Wilbraham tried his level best to save Crockett by intervening and stopping the disturbance. Conveniently, by this time, Edmund Crewe had been spirited away, having possibly been persuaded to take the blame for the killing, and he was never seen again.

Crockett's inquest, carried out three days after the affray, was presided over by John Maisterson, Richard Wilbraham's brother-in-law, and from the start there were disagreements about the procedure.

Bridgett Crockett tried to produce Hunter's painting as evidence, but this was pronounced inadmissible.

Crockett then tried to have the accused subjected to the so-called 'ordeal of the bier', in which they would be brought before the corpse to see if the dead man's body would start to bleed again. Maisterson, however, refused this too.

The inquest eventually found that Crockett was killed by Edmund Crewe alone, prompting Bridgett Crockett to accuse Maisterson of systematic corruption, of a deliberate attempt to hide the evidence by holding the inquest behind closed doors, and of intimidating key witnesses, in particular John Hunter, the artist.

Following her failure to influence the coroner's jury, Bridgett Crockett initiated an 'appeal of murder', and a commission was assembled to investigate whether the widow had a case. During this period, an extensive collection of witness statements was gathered from well over a hundred Nantwich residents who were present at the time of Crockett's death.

These were collated in a document called Examinations touching the death of Roger Croket, of Namptwiche, in the County of Chester, Gent. It is this document which my fictional town clerk, Ezekiel Green, uses to help Daniel Cheswis identify potential suspects for his case seventy-two years later.

It is worth pointing out that the document does indeed name John Gorste as the owner of the house into which the dying Roger Crockett was carried, identifies John Brett as one of the two town constables at the time, and lists Thomas Bressy as one of the additional witnesses.

Bridgett Crockett's 'appeal of murder' eventually resulted in proceedings held at Chester assizes in July 1573, at which Edmund Crewe was indicted for the murder of Crockett in his absence. The following February, 21 people were summoned by the chief justice, and six of them, including Wilbraham and three members of the Hassall family, were bailed pending a future appearance. However, at the following Michaelmas assizes, all six were discharged by proclamation. This, however, was not the end of it, and the case rumbled on in the Star Chamber for several years.

This brings us onto the strange case of Thomas Palin (or Palyn), who was a servant at The Crown under the Crocketts. Palin gave evidence in favour of his mistress at the Chester assizes in 1573. However, there are suggestions that both Crockett and the Hassall/Maisterson/Wilbraham faction attempted to bribe the servant to testify in their favour. This may have been a deliberate attempt to cast doubt on Palin's value as a witness.

In any case, Palin was subsequently accused of perjury, and the story relating to his gallows reprieve is absolutely true. Palin was indicted for theft from a guest at The Crown together with a notorious local thief and sentenced to hang. He was reprieved on the gallows, when John Maisterson showed up at the critical moment and offered to spare his life if he would admit to perjury. Not surprisingly, the servant chose to save his own skin. The question which remains unanswered is whether this whole event was a deliberate 'set-up' by Maisterson and his associates.

Although Thomas Palin was a real person, his fictional descendent, Bridgett Palyn, is not. Bridgett makes an appearance in The Winter Siege, and was actually conceived as a character before I started the research for The Crockett Legacy. It was a happy coincidence when I came to write about the Crockett affair that I already had a ready-made character with the same surname as Thomas Palin and a first name that suggested she may have been named after Palin's employer.

At this point, I should also add a few words about Ridley Field, the site of which sits immediately opposite Mill Island, where the modern day reconstruction of the Battle of Nantwich takes place every January.

At the time of the Civil War, Ridley Field would have been located just outside the earthworks that surrounded Nantwich, and therefore would have been in plain view of soldiers patrolling the walls. The stone pillar I describe, however, did not exist, and is a creation designed for the purpose of the fictional plot.

\* \* \*

Although I have attempted to give an accurate portrayal of the events surrounding the death of Roger Crockett, the plotlines relating to Abbot Massey's hidden treasure and the suggested connections between the Crockett murder and Combermere Abbey are entirely fictional.

Although John Massey was indeed the last abbot of the Cistercian Abbey at Combermere, and presided over the handover of the abbey to the Crown at the time of the Dissolution, there is no evidence to suggest he hid any of the abbey's assets, and he retired on a healthy pension, dying, as the book suggests, in the 1560s. The idea of a set of engravings with key words pointing to a hidden treasure, is, of course, a product of my own imagination.

By the time of the English Civil War, the Combermere Estate had been in the hands of the Cotton family for over a hundred years. The estate was awarded in 1539 to Sir George Cotton, who was an Esquire of the Body to King Henry VIII. The octogenarian George Cotton, who appears in The Combermere Legacy, was his grandson. By the 1640s, the original abbey had long since disappeared, and the abbot's original residence had been converted and expanded into a fine country mansion.

My descriptions of Combermere in the 1640s are largely based on a painting by the Dutch artist Peter Tillemans, which still hangs at Combermere today.

Although painted in the 1730s, the layout of the gardens and the rest of the estate are much as they would have been in the 1640s. The farm buildings at the Grange, the stable block, the walled garden, the boathouse, the washhouse with its attendant water tank, and the summerhouse on the island are all described as depicted by Tillemans.

Today, however, the two original lakes have been joined together to form a single stretch of water that extends around where the gardens, statues, and coach turning circle used to be. The wind, however, can still whip across the lake, and I have it on good authority that being out in a rowing boat on a bad day can indeed be akin to being caught out at sea.

As far as the interior of the house in concerned, the servants' quarters were on the right hand side of the house, with the guest rooms on the left so that they could overlook the lake. The fabulous library with the Tudor paintings on the wall has recently been lovingly restored by current owner Sarah Callander Beckett, and remains much as described in the book.

During the Civil War, the Cottons were staunch supporters of the King and allowed the estate to be used as a base for troops in the build up to the Battle of Nantwich. Both George Cotton and his son Thomas died in 1646, but it is not known whether either's demise was directly related to the Civil War.

By mid-1644, Sir William Brereton had increased his control of Cheshire, which he ran with a number of loyal deputies such as Thomas Croxton. By early summer, Brereton had started the process of sequestering the estate of a significant number of royalist supporters. Both Thomas Maisterson and Roger Wilbraham were sequestered during the course of 1644. The Sequestration Committee operated through a number of assessors and collectors, known for their loyalty to the parliamentary cause. The lawyer and diarist Thomas Malbon was one of these. Another was Marc Folineux, a particularly assiduous individual known simply as 'The Collector'. The attempts made by Folineux to sequester the Cottons in August 1644 are fictional. However, he did sequester the Combermere Estate in October 1644.

Looking further afield, Sir Thomas Myddelton, at the time, was looking to make further advances into Shropshire and the Welsh Marches. Oswestry had been captured, and the governor, Sir Fulke Hunckes, had been thwarted in his attempt to regain the town when one of his officers, Colonel Marrow, was defeated at Whittington. Momentum was very much in parliamentary hands, but much depended on the strategic location of Montgomery, the home of Edward, Lord Herbert of Cherbury, who despite being a royalist by inclination had already refused Prince Rupert access to Montgomery Castle to establish a garrison there. Herbert, in fact, showed little enthusiasm for supporting either side – of key importance to him was the safety of his valuable library.

There was, of course, never any plan to transport Herbert's library to Combermere. This is pure fiction, but the eccentric old aristocrat's collection was to play a further role in developments as Myddelton looked to increase his influence in the region.

Unfortunately, for some unexplained reason, history fails to record the role of a certain Nantwich cheese merchant and wich house owner in what happened next.

# Acknowledgements

Once again thanks to Matthew, Tom, and Vanessa at Electric Reads, whose editing and design services I have used for all three Daniel Cheswis novels. Once again they have made a significant difference to the quality of the final product..

I am also indebted to Colin Bissett of the Sealed Knot for checking the historical accuracy of my first draft, and to Dr Steve Hindle, Director of Research at the WM Keck Foundation in San Marino, California, for providing me with a copy of his fascinating paper on the murder of Roger Crockett.

A special thank you is due to Sarah Callander Beckett for allowing me inside her fabulous home at Combermere and to archivist Steven Myatt for showing me around and for his valuable input throughout.

Thanks also to Nantwich Bookshop, BookShrop, National Civil War Centre, Ed Abrams, Kate Lea-O'Mahoney, and Ian Dicker, all of whom have helped me in one way or another during the course of the year.

And, of course, thanks to Karen, Richard, and Louisa for their love and support.

# Bibliographical Notes

In researching the historical background for *The Combermere Legacy* I used a number of resources, which I have listed here.

Invaluable, as always, for information on Nantwich and the structure of local politics in the 1640s, were James Hall's *A History of the Town and Parish of Nantwich or Wich Malbank in the County Palatine of Chester* (1883) and JS Morrill's *Cheshire 1630-1660 – County Government and Society during the English Revolution* (1974).

For information on the Civil War in Wales I used John Roland Phillips' *Memoirs of the Civil War in Wales and the Marches 1642-49* (1874) and *Sir Thomas Myddelton's Attempted Conquest of Powys 1644-45*, which is an abstract from the Montgomery Collections Vol. 57, Part 2 (1962). I also referred to *The Autobiography of Edward, Lord Herbert of Cherbury,* edited by Sidney Lee (1886).

Vital for information on the Crockett murder was Steve Hindle's paper '*Bleedinge Afreshe*' – *The Affray and Murder at Nantwich, 19 December, 1572* and Foul Deeds around Crewe by Peter Ollerhead and Susan Chambers (2010).

For information on Combermere I used *The Book of the Abbot of Combermere 1289-1529* from *Miscellanies Relating to Lancashire and Cheshire Vol. 2* (1896) and an article I found on British History Online called *Houses of Cistercian Monks – The Abbey of Combermere*, which was taken from *A History of the County of Chester Vol. 3* (1980). I also used Combermere Abbey's own website, compiled by archivist Steven Myatt, as well as information provided by Steven himself.

# Glossary

| | |
|---|---|
| **Clotpole** | Idiot |
| **Corviser** | Shoemaker |
| **Kindling** | A fixed allocation of time allowed for salt making, equivalent to four days |
| **Lead (relating to wich houses)** | A salt pan |
| **Pinder** | An officer charged with impounding stray cattle |
| **Sconce** | A star-shaped fortification |
| **Ship (relating to salt making)** | A hollowed-out tree trunk used to store brine |

| | |
|---|---|
| **Theet** | A wooden pipe used to transport brine into a wich house |
| **Waller** | A brine worker |
| **Wich house** | A salt house |

Made in the USA
Charleston, SC
05 March 2016